Susan Holoubek was born in Melbo[urne?] [...] moved to Adelaide in 1976. She l[...] community development and health care. Her PhD in Creative Writing from the University of Adelaide was awarded the E.W. Benham Prize for English Literature in 2010. In 2011 she was shortlisted for the Wet Ink/CAL Short Story Prize. Susan is married to guitarist Charli Holoubek. They have three children, Martin, Eloise and Damian. *Traces of Absence* is her first novel.

Traces of Absence
SUSAN HOLOUBEK

Pan Macmillan Australia

First published 2013 in Macmillan by Pan Macmillan Australia Pty Limited
1 Market Street, Sydney

Copyright © Susan Holoubek 2013

The moral right of the author has been asserted.

All rights reserved. No part of this book may be reproduced or transmitted by any person or entity (including Google, Amazon or similar organisations), in any form or by any means, electronic or mechanical, including photocopying, recording, scanning or by any information storage and retrieval system, without prior permission in writing from the publisher.

National Library of Australia
Cataloguing-in-Publication data:

Holoubek, Susan, author.

Traces of Absence / Susan Holoubek.

9781742612171 (paperback)

Missing children—Fiction.

A823.4

Typeset in 13/16.5 pt Adobe Garamond by Post Prepress
Printed by McPherson's Printing Group

The characters in this book are fictitious and any resemblance to real persons, living or dead, is purely coincidental.

Papers used by Pan Macmillan Australia Pty Ltd are natural, recyclable products made from wood grown in sustainable forests. The manufacturing processes conform to the environmental regulations of the country of origin.

For Eloise

2005

Prologue

When the alarm stabbed her into consciousness, Dee couldn't for a moment remember where she was. She registered dread in the pit of her stomach – something to do with a bad dream – but any relief she felt at having escaped an imaginary terror sputtered out almost immediately when she remembered that she was in a hotel in Buenos Aires. The bedside clock read 8.22. The last time she had checked it was four am. She thrust aside the quilt and sat up with a giddy lurch. They were sending someone from the embassy at nine to take her to the police station so she could file a formal report about Corrie.

Dee got up, slid apart the heavy curtains, fumbled with the catch and pushed the window open. The streets were rain-glazed and the noise of traffic a welcome intrusion of normality. A faint flutter of hope rose within her. Everything was going to be OK. There would be a reassuring explanation for the sudden loss of communication with her backpacking daughter – some petty drama or exuberant youthful adventure – something that Corrie didn't want over-exposed to parental scrutiny. The police would know what to do. They would have systems and processes. They would deliver Dee's wayward daughter back to her with a whiff of annoyance at having their time wasted. Dee would turn the whole episode into an entertaining story for the future amusement of her friends at dinner parties . . .

No, she wouldn't.

'Dee, it's Marco Torres.'

When she'd received the call from her daughter's Argentinean friend a week ago, the tone of those four words had been like bouncing pebbles ahead of a sliding slagheap of fear.

'Marco? What's wrong?'

'I think maybe nothing. But my mother is a little worried. She wants to know if you have heard something from Corrie.'

Dee had hosted Marco as a Year-11 exchange student two years earlier. His family had been delighted to return the favour when Corrie decided to visit Buenos Aires.

'From Corrie? Not recently. Why?'

Dee had begun to calculate the weight of sudden anxiety even as she tried to dismiss it. 'Why is your mother worried?'

'Corrie went to Posadas to see the falls. She planned to return last week, but she hasn't come back.'

Words registering. Meaning at bay. Gut turning over.

'She might have decided to stay longer.'

'It's possible.'

'But you don't think so?'

'I tried to ring her, but she's not answering her *celular*.'

'Does it ring out or is it switched off? Maybe she lost it. Or the battery's flat. Did she take her charger with her?'

'I don't know. She left most of her things here, but I'm pretty sure she took her charger.'

'Knowing Corrie, she probably left her phone on a bus or dropped it down a toilet or something. She's forever losing her damned phone.' Dee knew even in that moment that the irritation she felt was the soft edge of anger: a way of drawing down strength to keep the fear at bay.

'It might not have been her fault. Maybe it was stolen.'

Stolen. Intimations of violence. Foul play. Headlines about missing backpackers in her own country had flashed through her mind . . .

'What do you think I should do, Marco?'

'I don't know. Probably, she's OK. But my mother thought I should call you.'

The Department of Foreign Affairs had been less dismissive than she anticipated. A young woman travelling alone in South America, without her luggage, who had not stuck to a pre-arranged plan and who was now uncontactable, seemed to tick the requisite number of boxes for action. Dee had been worried that they would fob her off but felt even worse when they agreed there were serious grounds for concern. In a sick flurry she negotiated compassionate leave with her school principal, made arrangements for her fourteen-year-old twins, Ben and Luke, to stay with her brother, and boarded the next available flight to Buenos Aires.

And so here she was. The opportunity, finally, to take practical action in response to Corrie's disappearance focused the sickening surges of adrenaline but also sharpened her fears. The surreal had become real. In the shower, her knees nearly gave way beneath her. She slid down the wall and sat on the floor of the cubicle, staring at needles of water bouncing off the bone-coloured tiles.

Pull yourself together.

She rose shakily, turned off the hot tap and stood shivering and gasping under a surge of cold water.

Come on. Get a grip. for God's sake. For Corrie's sake.

After towelling herself dry with determined vigour she padded back to the bedroom. The curtains billowed and her skin was prickled by a gust of cool air, scented with rain.

Her clothes, ironed the night before, hung in the open wardrobe. What does one wear to a police interview? It had been a distracting dilemma, seemingly trivial, but not something she wanted to risk getting wrong. She knew from experience that first impressions mattered. The appearance of wealth mattered. Especially in Latin countries, she thought, although she wasn't quite sure how she knew this. Something to do with power and influence and the exchange of favours. It was an aspect of public life that had assumed increasing importance in her own country in recent times, although she was old enough to remember when it was otherwise – when people deliberately dressed down to defy snobbery and demonstrate freedom from the need to conform. But that was a long time ago.

She recalled a passage from an Agatha Christie novel, in which Hercule Poirot had sniffed out the guilty party by observing the suspect's haggard appearance, the neglect of her toilette, her theatrical overplay of grief. *Real* grief in a woman, Poirot had argued, was always expressed in a dignified attempt to conceal the ravages of suffering, not the reverse. Dee must have read the story thirty years ago when she was still at high school, but it had left an impression. It resonated with a range of other influences that persuaded her to mistrust raw emotion, to defer instinctive reaction, to craft more considered responses to the vicissitudes of life. She wasn't quite sure why she needed to convince the police of her grief – of what she might otherwise be suspected – but she attended with great care to making up her pale face, pinning back her thick hair, carefully knotting a peacock-blue scarf over her charcoal suit jacket, wiping the street soil from her matching blue pumps.

She knew she should eat something, but by the time she made it to the hotel foyer it was nearly nine and the consular official was already waiting for her. She saw him standing by the reception desk as she emerged from the lift: compact, neat and unmistakably Anglo. He was younger than she expected. Well, everyone was these days. Children she had taught were beginning to appear in various professional guises and it made her uneasy. She was too intimate with their essential weaknesses to believe in their authority.

'Mrs Sutherland?'

'Yes.' She extended her hand.

He gripped it with a show of masculine assurance, his hand small and dry. There was a note of commiseration in his smile. 'Andrew Flint. The car's out the front.'

He made a sweeping gesture with his other arm and she turned obediently towards the gold-rimmed doors. It was grey and overcast outside and the air carried an indefinable smell of foreignness. She took in a fleeting impression of broken pavements, dripping trees and elegant, grey-stoned buildings before Andrew Flint stepped neatly around her to open the door of the Mercedes. He slid into the seat beside her and gave instructions to the driver.

'What time did you get in yesterday?' he asked.

'Around four.'

'How was the flight?'

'Long.'

He made a sympathetic noise as the car nosed forward into the traffic.

'How far is it to the—?'

'Police station? Not far, ten minutes or so.' He glanced down at her clasped hands, flexing compulsively in her lap.

'Richard – the ambassador – wanted me to assure you that we're here to provide full support.'

'I know. Thank you. I'm sorry. I'm a bit all over the place.'

'Understandable.'

He pulled a briefcase onto his lap, flipped open the lid and withdrew a folder that contained a copy of Corrie's passport, a slim compilation of papers and email printouts and the photographs of Corrie that Dee had emailed to the embassy several days earlier. She glanced over at the school photo on top of the pile. It was not really representative of Corrie's current style, but it was the most recent close-up shot that Dee had been able to find. Corrie was wearing that artless, dishabille look that Year 12s cultivated: her short, dark hair was chopped into thick slabs, streaked with blonde and caught at asymmetrical angles with a random collection of bobby pins; her blue eyes, languid and long-lashed like her father's, gazed obliquely over the concessionary flicker of a smile.

'How recently was this taken?'

'Last year. March.'

'It's a nice photo.'

'Yes.'

'Did she have any photos taken while she was here in Buenos Aires?'

'Her friend, Marco, has some.'

'His family is meeting us at the police station, aren't they?'

'Yes.' Dee stared out of the window at the stalled traffic.

'It's your worst fear – you know? From the moment they're born. The fear of losing them. And you *do* lose them. Again and again. They're late coming home from school and you're immediately out in the car looking for them. Or they wander off in a shopping centre or go missing at the Royal Show. And for the five, ten, twenty minutes that it takes you to find them you're just about dry-retching with terror. But then they turn up. Usually, they turn up. Don't they? In these sorts of situations? It's usually just some sort of misunderstanding. Isn't it?'

'Nine times out of ten,' he reassured her, but he didn't meet her eye as he slipped the folder back into his briefcase and closed the lid. The car turned out of the heavy stream of traffic into a narrow side street, then on to another main road, similarly jammed with cars. Flint glanced at his watch.

'Are we late?' Dee asked.

'Right on time.'

The driver eased into the kerb outside a three-storeyed building with grilles on every ground floor window and bars on those above. Flint got out of the car and opened the door for Dee. He held out a hand and she took it in a daze as she levered herself from her seat.

Marco was waiting for them in the reception area. She clung to him when he stepped forward to greet her.

'Dee, this is my mother, Alicia.'

The woman with him was slim and dark with long black hair pulled into a high ponytail. Marco moved aside to let his mother take both of Dee's hands. Her dark eyes, laden with concern, claimed a connection with Dee's before she embraced her tightly. The staff stepped in to direct them through a metal detector and accompany them down long corridors, into an elevator and up several floors where they were eventually shuffled into separate interview rooms. Flint pressed Dee's shoulder reassuringly as she took a seat opposite a portly detective with a thick moustache. The detective reached over and poured her a glass of water from a jug that was already on the table. Dee was relieved when he addressed her in English.

'Mrs Sutherland, this is very difficult for you, no?'

She reached for the glass with a trembling hand, sipped at the water, nodded her assent.

Flint's folder was open on the table. The detective picked up Corrie's photograph in his chubby hands and studied it.

'Let us be positive for a moment. We have no evidence that anything bad has occurred. No accidents, no hospital presentations – forgive me, Mrs Sutherland – no unidentified bodies.' He put down the photograph, interlaced his fingers and rested them on the table.

'In situations like this, it is necessary to explore many different possibilities. It is important to know as much as we can about the person who is missing. It helps us to build up a picture of who they are, to develop ideas about where they might have gone or what they might have been doing.'

He picked up the photo of Corrie again.

'We have the details about her appearance that you sent through.' He raised the photo a little and scanned the sheet beneath it. 'Height: 170 cm, build: slim, complexion: fair, hair colour: black, eye colour: blue.' He looked at Dee quizzically.

'Yes, that's correct.'

She wanted to tell him that those bald facts did not evoke her daughter at all.

'Anything else that might help us identify her?'

'She has three piercings in her left ear. And one in her right ear and one here.' She raised a hand to the crease of her right nostril. 'And she has a brown mole, here, on the side of her neck.'

The detective jotted down notes as she spoke. There were other memories jostling for attention in Dee's mind – the way

Corrie walked with her feet turned outwards like a duck, images of her dreamy countenance suddenly transformed by intense delight or surprise, the halting cadences of her speech, her long-fingered hands tracing patterns in the air, illustrating intensities that she could not put into words. But how does one capture those kinds of details in identikit form?

'She has a dimple in her right cheek when she smiles.'

The detective scribbled a few more comments, then put down his pen and read through what he had written. He looked up and stroked his chin with one hand, gazing thoughtfully at Dee.

'Why did your daughter come to Argentina, Mrs Sutherland?'

Dee tried to gather her scattered thoughts, sift them for the relevant facts. 'She wanted a break.'

The studiously blank expression on the detective's face made her wonder if he was receiving this information in the right way.

'She had started her university studies, but she was having problems—' She immediately regretted the use of the word, 'problems'. 'Her father — I'd lost my husband a few months earlier. She was very close to him. It was difficult for her to concentrate on her studies. She had a friend here in Argentina – Marco—'

He nodded his cognisance of this.

'I suggested that she might like to take the second semester off and go travelling. Lots of young people in Australia do that,' she added. 'Take some time off after school. It's not so unusual.'

'How would you describe her state of mind when she left home?' he asked. 'Can you tell us how your daughter was feeling when you last saw her?'

It wasn't an unreasonable question, but Dee felt a stirring of resistance to its implications.

'She was OK. She was looking forward to her trip. She was sad about her father. That's only normal. We were all sad. It was a very difficult time for our family.'

'Maybe you could tell me a little about what happened with your husband, Mrs Sutherland?'

Dee sighed heavily. 'He'd been having chest pains. I told him to go to the doctor, but he kept putting it off. He collapsed at home one evening. I wasn't there. Corrie called the ambulance. They had to use those shock pad things. They thought they'd stabilised him, but he had another heart attack on the way to the hospital. By the time he arrived there wasn't much they could do.'

'That must have been very traumatic for your daughter?'

'Yes.'

'To be the only one there with your husband.'

Dee stared at him dully.

'Sometimes, in such circumstances, people feel guilty that they were not able to save their loved one.'

Dee contemplated the man's jowls, his multiple chins, the folds of flesh cinched by his shirt collar. She wondered if he had noted his own risk factors. If he believed his family should pick up the onus of guilt if he went into sudden cardiac arrest.

'Of course Corrie was upset, but she has nothing to blame herself for. She rang the ambulance immediately. They were there within ten minutes.'

'Where were you, Mrs Sutherland, while your daughter was dealing with this very difficult situation?'

Why did it always come back to this? The fact of her own absence? The implications of neglect? Years of diligent servitude counted for nothing in the face of this one bald fact: You weren't there . . .

'I was having dinner with a friend.'

The detective cocked his head quizzically.

'The restaurant was very noisy. I didn't hear my phone ringing.'

'It happens, no? But perhaps your daughter felt a little angry that she couldn't get in touch with you?'

Dee closed her eyes wearily. 'Perhaps she did. But we're talking a year ago. I'm not sure that this is entirely relevant.'

'Mrs Sutherland, how would you describe your relationship with your daughter?'

She had been anticipating the question. It was what they always asked in these sorts of cases, wasn't it? What should she say? Normal? *Was* it normal? What is *normal*? She couldn't claim that they had one of those cloyingly intense mother–daughter relationships, but they got along all right. Mostly. There was a degree of healthy distance. Children don't want their parents spilling over into all the available space in their lives. Do they?

'Pretty normal. Up and down. We had the odd argument. Nothing serious.' She felt herself under steady scrutiny.

'What sort of things did you argue about?'

'Oh, the usual: not coming home at a reasonable hour, leaving mess all over the house, not helping out.'

Dee recalled Corrie packing the day before she left. She'd been out the previous night and was pale and sullen with lack of sleep. Her hair was flattened on one side and sticking up in spikes on the other. She was dressed in the black singlet top and track pants in which she'd slept, picking things at random from drawers and cupboards and tossing them distractedly into the open case. Dee had watched her from the doorway.

'Can I iron anything for you? You'll be able to fit more things in if they're ironed and folded up properly.'

'Just leave me alone, please.'

Corrie's tone had been sharp-edged. Dee put it down to tiredness and travel anxiety and had withdrawn without another word.

At the airport she embraced her daughter with what she hoped was reassuring warmth, but Corrie had quickly disentangled herself and turned to say goodbye to the small group of friends who had gathered to see her off. Dee had tried not to be offended. She knew how it was with young people. Their friends were everything.

She looked up at the detective and smiled sadly. 'She was looking forward to her adventure. I don't think she was thinking much about me when she left. She couldn't wait to experience a bit of adult independence.'

'She was excited about her trip?'

'Yes, she was.'

'And maybe a little thoughtless about her mother's feelings?'

Dee resented his sly tone and the imputation against Corrie, veiled as sympathy. 'That's normal, isn't it? And besides, I didn't want her to worry about me. That was the whole point of the holiday. To cheer her up – give her something to look forward to.'

'So she seemed happy to you? The trip was helping to distract her from the loss of her father? And she was not worrying about anything else?'

Dee hesitated, dropped her eyes and frowned slightly, gave the question due consideration before shaking her head. 'No, No. She wasn't worried about anything.'

The detective studied her face for some time, made a last brief note and closed the folder.

'What happens now?' Dee asked.

'We're going to send some officers back to the Torres' house to go through your daughter's things. It would be helpful if you could accompany them.'

'Yes, of course.'

'We will see if there is anything there that gives us some clues about her intentions. Then we'll check with the bus company she used and the hotels in Posadas. We'll circulate her picture, speak to everyone she knew here in Buenos Aires. The Torres family have prepared a list of names for us. We'll contact the airlines and border control and try to trace any phone calls and credit-card usage. We will do everything we can, Mrs Sutherland. But, you know, if someone doesn't want to be found, it is not so difficult to lose yourself in a country as large as ours.'

Dee looked at him sharply. 'Why are you making that assumption?'

'Calm yourself, Mrs Sutherland. We have no evidence to suggest anything else at this stage.'

'But a young girl on her own? Anything could have happened. People don't just disappear. She could have been taken somewhere. It's all jungle up there isn't it? She could have been left . . . anywhere . . .' She faltered.

'It's not the most likely scenario, Mrs Sutherland. Let us deal first with the more probable. Robbery, physical attack – it's always messy – there are usually witnesses, trails of evidence. That will come to light very quickly.'

'What about human trafficking?' The pitch of Dee's voice sounded shrill even to her own ears.

The detective blinked at her.

'There are stories on the internet. Hundreds of women have gone missing—'

'Poor women, Mrs Sutherland. Women whose disappearance will not draw attention. Women who can be manipulated into silence. Not foreign tourists.'

Dee closed her eyes, wanting to believe him but frightened that too easy an acquiescence would leave her daughter at greater risk. Who else would advocate for her? Who else would push the police into undertaking the things that needed to be done?

'I'm sorry. I know you think I'm being hysterical.'

The detective stood then, folder in hand, signalling the end of the interview. 'Please be assured that we are taking this matter very seriously, Mrs Sutherland. We will do everything possible to locate your daughter.'

Andrew Flint extended his hand to the detective. 'We're very grateful for your swift response. We'll keep in touch.'

Dee picked up her handbag in a daze, allowed herself to be steered out of the room, into the lift, down the long corridor and back to the reception area, where she found Marco and Alicia waiting for her.

The confusion she was feeling must have shown on her face because Alicia moved over to her swiftly, put an arm around her shoulders and spoke in rapid Spanish to her son.

'We live about an hour out of the city. My mother says that if you would rather stay with us than at the hotel tonight you are most welcome.'

Dee rubbed at her forehead with tense, probing fingers. 'Thank you. I don't know.' She looked to Andrew Flint for guidance.

He responded to Alicia directly in Spanish and Alicia nodded her understanding.

A male and female officer had joined them and began to discuss arrangements for the trip with Alicia and Marco. Flint rang his driver and instructed him to pick them up out the front. Dee allowed herself to be guided outside and into the car, sinking with some relief into the back seat. They drove for a long time down a series of freeways, flanked with sprawling shanty towns. When they left the freeway they were forced to negotiate roads pitted with potholes, passing dilapidated shops and high-walled housing estates until eventually they reached streets of well-maintained bungalows with pleasant gardens and shady trees. The driver slowed down, scanning house numbers, and pulled up outside a property with a tall hedge and wrought-iron gate.

'We're here.'

Dee was momentarily consoled by the affluent suburban comfort of the home to which her daughter had been welcomed and then remembered that it was no consolation at all anymore. She followed Flint along a winding, gravel path to the open front door. A housekeeper in a floral apron waved them into a sunken living area, all polished slate and tapestries, with floor-to-ceiling windows opening out onto an expanse of green lawn.

Alicia, Marco and the detectives had arrived ahead of them. They stood up from their seats when Flint and Dee entered the room.

Alicia addressed a question to Dee, which Flint translated. 'Would you like a drink of some kind? Water or coffee or Coca-Cola?'

Dee shook her head. 'Can I see Corrie's things, please?'

Alicia glanced at the detectives. They nodded. She took Dee's arm and led her down the corridor, ahead of the rest of the group.

They formed quite a crowd in the small, blue-walled room that had once been Marco's older sister's. It was still decorated with photographs of her school friends and items of teenage memorabilia. Dee recognised Corrie's suitcase immediately.

It was bright red and secured with a dark green strap, standing beside the dressing table.

The detectives lifted the case onto the bed and opened it. It was only three-quarters full. They removed the items one by one: coloured underwear and rolled-up socks, summer dresses and T-shirts, a pair of high-heeled shoes. Corrie's toiletry bag was gone, as was the brown leather jacket she loved. Her hiking boots were not there, nor were the black flats she always wore. There were a few pairs of tights, a couple of colourful loose-weave jumpers, some scarves, her hairdryer. In a zip-up pocket they found AA camera batteries, photocopies of her travel documents, insurance papers and a spare cash-card. The last item they removed was a photograph. They held it out to show Dee. It was Corrie with her father, taken down at Glenelg Beach several summers before. They were leaning against the jetty railing, eating ice-cream cones. Corrie was looking up at Ross and laughing. It was a photo that Corrie had framed and kept on her desk at home. And now, here it was, abandoned in a foreign house in a foreign country, a terrible reminder of irrevocable loss. Dee experienced a wave of nausea before her head slumped onto her chest and she collapsed.

2009

Chapter One

Ben hefted Dee's suitcase into the back of Luke's lovingly maintained second-hand Subaru Impreza.

'Got everything, Mum?'

'I think so.'

He closed the boot carefully, in deference to his brother's sensibilities about the car and waited, self-consciously, with his hands thrust deep in his pockets. 'Well, I hope it goes OK.'

Dee ached a little over their mutual awkwardness. Some barrier to spontaneity had evolved between them and she suspected it originated with her. She enacted normality with some effort. She held herself a little apart lest she infect her sons too deeply with her sadness.

Luke emerged from the back door of the house, talking on his mobile phone. He ruffled his brother's hair in a rough parody of affection. Ben ducked away from the assault with a grimace, smoothing his hair back into place.

'OK. Catch ya.' Luke finished his call and slid the phone into the back pocket of his jeans. 'Ready to go?'

'I'm ready. You two ready to fend for yourselves for a few months?'

Luke threw his arm round Ben's neck and grinned at her, as if to reassure her with a cheesy tableau of brotherly love.

When they were small the twins had been almost impossible to tell apart. They both had their father's shaggy hair, dimpled chin and lopsided smile, but Luke's hair was long now while Ben kept his cropped short. Ben was clean-shaven. Luke's square face gleamed with a bright dusting of copper-coloured stubble. They were both tall and strongly built, but where Luke was thick around the middle, Ben was gym trim.

'Get in the car, you clown.'

Luke let go of Ben's neck and threw a mock punch to his brother's stomach. Ben deflected him offhandedly. Years of practice. Dee reached up her arms towards Ben and he bent to hug her. It didn't feel right that he was taller and stronger than her. It made her feel shrunken and old. He drew back and smiled at her a little sadly. She held her open palm briefly against his cheek.

'Keep your brother out of trouble, OK?'

'That's not humanly possible, Mum.'

'Keep him out of hospital then.'

'Say hi to Marco for us.'

She patted his cheek and got into the car. Ben raised his hand in farewell as Luke reversed down the driveway, gave several blasts on the horn and roared off down the street.

'What are you looking for?'

Luke was steering with one hand while scrabbling around in the glove box with the other.

'Herbie Hancock.'

'Concentrate on the road. I'll look.'

Dee found it, tossed among the other uncased CDs, identified as 'Herb' in thick, black marker scrawled across its surface. 'Is this it?'

'Sweet.' He slid it into the player and turned up the volume.

She reached over and turned it down.

'Oh, come off it!' He turned it back up a couple of notches.

'I suppose I should be grateful that you display some vestiges of musical taste.'

'Damn straight.' He grinned, tapping out the snare drum rhythm on the steering wheel.

Neither he nor Ben asked many questions about her annual trips to Argentina. When Corrie had first disappeared Dee had gone back as often as she was able – taking advantage of every school holiday, running up a line of credit on the mortgage – determined to exhaust all possible lines of inquiry. Hope was raw and charged in those days. Even though the police investigation was scaled down after six months, the files were kept open and Dee prevailed upon the Australian Embassy to accompany her to police headquarters for regular updates on their 'progress'. After a while, the information was always the same, but she knew that if she didn't ask the questions, no one else would. The files would be relegated to a basement to gather dust, the original investigators would be posted elsewhere and no one would really care anymore. So she made a polite but persistent nuisance of herself with the authorities and she kept in touch with Alicia and Marco, who helped with her own amateur inquiries – placing advertisements in newspapers and on internet sites, handing out flyers in the places Marco said Corrie had frequented. But eventually there was nothing more to be done. Dee's visits had trailed off to an annual October holiday pilgrimage, marking the anniversary of her daughter's disappearance. This year, the fourth year, she had felt something shift in her. She hadn't given up hope, but she had given up the belief that her efforts could make any further difference. While she hadn't framed the intention formally to herself, she suspected this visit to Buenos Aires, which coincided with her long-service leave, would be her last.

'There's enough cash for food and bills in the savings account,' she told Luke, 'but it won't cover endless takeaways. You're going to have to do some shopping and cooking.'

'You don't mind if I swing by and pick up Belinda, do you? We're going to grab a bite to eat at the Bay after we drop you.'

Dee experienced a fine cascade of disappointment at the prospect of sharing the trip to the airport with Luke's girlfriend. After a brief silence, she supposed a comment was required.

'Of course not. How's she enjoying her new hairdressing job?'

'Yeah, all right. Her boss is giving her a hard time.' Luke had become adept at ignoring Dee's tone of stoic politeness. Or perhaps he didn't notice it.

'In what way is he giving her a hard time?'

'Oh, you know – picking on everything she does.'

'That's pretty stupid. You don't get the best out of your workers by eroding all their self-confidence.'

'You should have a word with him, Mum.'

'Yes, I imagine that would really improve things – sicking her boyfriend's mother on to him.'

'Note my defence of your girlfriend,' Dee thought. 'Note that I am bigger than my dislike of her.'

They wove through the narrow backstreets of Stepney before pulling up outside a semidetached bungalow with a narrow strip of front garden and one straggling banksia tree. Luke sounded the horn. They waited several minutes but Belinda failed to materialise. Luke got out of the car and went around the back of the house. Dee pinched the bridge of her nose and shut her eyes, exhaling deeply. She knew punctuality was anachronistic but it was difficult to resist the temptation to interpret Belinda's cavalier disregard of other people's schedules as anything other than lazy and undisciplined.

Belinda eventually came tripping around the side of her house, made up to within an inch of her life, ebullient with laughing, self-referential apologies.

'I'm soooo sorry. I've had the worst day. One of the girls in the salon put a new colour through my hair and it was foul and I've spent all afternoon stripping it out and now my hair's like straw. I'll get them to put a treatment through tomorrow, but I needed to find a scarf before I could show myself in public. Do I look disgusting?' she appealed coquettishly to Luke.

'Yep.'

She squealed and punched him.

Wisps of honey-coloured and white-blonde curls escaped from a saffron-coloured scarf wound around her head. Silver and amber jewellery drew attention to the delicate lines of her jaw and neck. Are we supposed to feel sorry for her? Dee wondered.

The growing resentment she harboured towards young women surprised her. She had always imagined that she would be more gracious in her middle years, consoled against diminishing physical resources by wisdom or greater self-assurance, but that had not been the case. She felt like a heavy, blunt instrument in the presence of the willowy, delicate creatures Luke brought home. There was something in their fragile, girlish style that made her want to shake them. Slap some sense into them. It was not only that they reminded her of Corrie's absence, their lighthearted nonchalance an affront to the cavity in Dee's life that Corrie's lighthearted nonchalance should have occupied. It was, she suspected, as trite as envy. This was not something she was prepared to admit very widely. She observed the reactions of other women her age and attempted to mimic their motherly indulgence of their younger counterparts, hoping that if she enacted kindness with enough vigour it might, eventually, become the truth.

Luke turned into Fullarton Road to bypass the city. The parklands were bleached yellow by the long drought.

'How long are you going away for?' Belinda called out from the back seat.

'A month or so. Maybe longer. Maybe less. It depends.'

'You might meet some hot Latin lover!'

Dee twisted around to look at Belinda but there was no mockery in her face, just wide-eyed delight at her own audacity. She gave the younger woman credit for her attempt to transcend Dee's gloomy reserve and make a little fun.

'You never know your luck in the big city, Belinda.'

As they approached the airport she turned down the music and spoke to Luke. 'You don't need to park. Just drop me at Passenger Loading.'

'Sure?'

'You know I can't bear all that standing around business. And I'm guessing you don't have any money for parking.'

He arched his back to slide his hand into the change pocket of his jeans.

'It wasn't a serious question. I really don't want you to park. I'd have to find things to talk to you about.'

Luke gave a grunt of laughter and swung into the passenger-loading lane. He left the engine idling while he took Dee's suitcase from the boot. She watched him, marvelling a little over the mannish ways of her young son.

'Well, good luck, Mum.'

'Thanks, love.'

He put his arms around her and gave her a wrestler's squeeze that forced the air out of her lungs. She thumped him on the back a few times.

'Don't spend all my money and for God's sake eat a few vegetables. Here—' she pulled a wad of bills from her purse. 'Toast your old mother at dinner tonight.'

He deposited the cash in his shirt pocket and hugged her again, awkwardly.

She turned away quickly and wheeled her case towards the sliding glass doors of the terminal.

*

Taxi drivers jostled for attention in the arrival hall at Buenos Aires airport, holding their licences aloft, obviously aware that tourists had been warned against uncertified drivers. Dee dodged their waving arms as she pushed her way through the crowd to the toilets. She splashed cold water on her face and critically surveyed her crumpled appearance in the mirror above the basin.

She was embarrassed by vanity, but perhaps that was only because she felt unqualified to indulge it. Her younger brother had always been regarded as the one with the 'looks' in her family. She couldn't remember how this had been communicated, but somewhere along the line it had become part of her family narrative: he was the one with the 'looks', she was the one with the 'brains'.

The mirror reflected back the pale, travel-creased face of a 44-year-old woman whose luxuriant mass of chestnut hair, once considered her best natural attribute, was now the product of artful hairdressing. The years had added the hint of a double chin to her square face. Large grey eyes stared back at her, rimmed by smudged kohl. She dabbed at the smudges with a tissue, smoothed down her dishevelled hair and applied a dash of lipstick. Ready to face the world again.

The crowd of drivers had thinned by the time she returned to the main hall. A middle-aged driver, more formally dressed than the others in black trousers and a white shirt, moved forward to take her case as she headed in his direction.

'The Hotel Gran Vía on Avenida de Mayo.'

He led her across the car park and deposited her case in the back of a small, battered car.

'You are here for a holiday?' he asked, his arm stretched along the back of the seat next to him, his head craned in her direction as he backed out of the parking spot.

'Yes.' She had learned to keep things simple.

'Your first visit?'

'No.' She hesitated. 'My seventh.'

'So many times. You like Argentina very much?'

'Yes.'

He waited for her to elaborate, but she had learned to resist the impulse to fill out such pauses with light social fictions.

'*Bueno*. The Hotel Gran Vía?'

'Yes, thank you.'

He pulled out onto the wide freeway, negotiating the traffic expertly but without the cowboy antics she had experienced with other drivers. Dee remembered the first time she had made this trip from the airport, disoriented and fearful but even more fearful about appearing so. She had allowed herself to be hustled into a decrepit-looking cab by a weedy driver sporting a bedraggled moustache and wearing a black vinyl jacket. Without language, or any clearly understood social clues about the type of man she was with, she had felt intensely vulnerable. Was she going to be driven to some remote barrio slum for the purposes of rape and robbery? Was that what had happened to Corrie? Her head had been full of ugly scenarios and the bleak landscape between the airport and the city had done nothing to relieve her fears.

The freeway was now flanked by revived construction projects and newly completed housing developments.

'The economy seems to be improving,' she observed. 'They're building again.'

'Yes, 2001 was a disaster but things are better now. More exports. More tourists,' her driver replied.

'So Cristina Kirchner is doing a good job?'

'Our lady president is too friendly with that madman Chavez. She needs to be careful she doesn't frighten off international business and investment.'

'Michelle Bachelet seems to have got the balance right in Chile.'

'Bachelet is capitalising on the economic infrastructure established by Pinochet. It is not understood how essential Pinochet was for Chile. Allende was a dupe of Castro. The United States had no choice but to get rid of him. We had terrorist insurgents in Argentina as well. We went to the military and we begged them to protect us.'

Dee remembered the arguments. In the late 1970s, in Adelaide, the university campuses had been abuzz with comfortable outrage about the CIA-backed military governments in

South America, about their predilection for torture, abduction and murder, their persecution of the underclasses. There were a lot of politically exiled folk groups floating about with a surfeit of ethnic instruments, giving concerts and teaching eager undergraduates to chant, '¡El pueblo, unido, jamás será vencido!' with the best of them. 'The people, united, will never be defeated.' Dee had felt so heroic in those days, standing in the crowd, taking up the cry, but she didn't feel very heroic anymore.

'They weren't all terrorists,' she said quietly.

Her driver shrugged. 'OK. Yes – sometimes people were arrested because they gave their telephone number to the wrong person, but you can't be too careful when you are dealing with extremists.'

She noted that he had borrowed George Bush's vocabulary of terrorism to reframe the tale of the 'dirty war'. Thirty thousand Argentineans had disappeared during the 1970s and 1980s, an embarrassing aberration from the European urbanity on which the country prided itself. Over the last few years she had learned that there were certain citizens who were so deeply offended by this stain on the national character that their hostility towards the victims knew no bounds.

She dropped the conversation and stared out of the window. It was overcast and drizzling – a novelty of sorts; there had been no rain in Adelaide for months. They passed extensive tracts of land crowded with slum dwellings. There were more and more every year, thousands upon thousands of refugees from the rural areas, from Paraguay and Bolivia, flooding into plots of vacant land and erecting little neighbourhoods of iron sheeting and salvaged brick in the red mud. During her last visit people had been laughing about the overnight appearance of a village of more than a thousand families on a polo field. The locals greeted these anarchic waves of human migration with shrugging pragmatism. Slums butted up against gated mansions with landscaped gardens and sunken swimming pools; horse-drawn vehicles appeared incongruously on suburban roads, which were deliberately kept in a run-down condition to deter the passage of potential thieves and kidnappers.

As they approached the city, they turned off the *autopista* onto the avenue that ran beside the wide brown waters of the Río de la Plata. Dee noted the now-familiar sequence of landmarks: the controversial biblical theme park, Tierra Santa – plaster rocks, plastic palm trees and mechanical biblical figures – and the Club de Pescadores, perched halfway down an old jetty and evoking sixteenth-century Europe with its half-timbered façade, mansard roofs and spire-topped tower. Turning towards the city they passed the Floralis Genérica – a huge aluminium floral sculpture with gleaming petals turned skywards. Beyond the famous Cementario de la Recoleta, the traffic slowed to a crawl. The fourteen lanes of Avenida 9 de Julio were jammed with cars.

'The traffic is bad today,' Dee observed.

Her driver shrugged. 'It's always like this now. Mothers, teenagers – everybody has a car. The amount of traffic has doubled in the last year. Too much for the roads.'

It took another twenty minutes to drive the final half-kilometre to the hotel. The cab driver double-parked and hurried to help Dee with her baggage. 'Don't leave your case on the footpath,' he warned. 'We are very close to the subway here.' He hauled her suitcase inside the heavy revolving doors of the hotel, solicitous suddenly as she waved away her change. 'Enjoy your stay in Buenos Aires, *señora*.'

Over the last four years, Dee had become very familiar with the Hotel Gran Vía. Notwithstanding its lavish art deco foyer and its boast as the former residence of the poet García Lorca, it was an old-fashioned, three-star hotel of small, shabbily furnished rooms, but it was reasonably clean, centrally located and within her means. She was greeted with something that passed for genuine warmth by the receptionist on duty. He arranged for a porter to bring up her luggage, a necessary service, she had discovered, in order to avoid the ancient lift that lurched and shuddered and got stuck between floors with alarming frequency. Dee took the stairs. Her room on the seventh floor contained two single beds, a small table and chair, a television set mounted on the wall and a white-tiled, grey-tinged bathroom. When her cases were delivered to the room, she pressed two pesos into the porter's hand, closed the door, peeled off her travel-soiled clothes and headed straight for the shower.

Afterwards, she sat naked on the bed, savouring the air on her skin. She was weary from the sixteen-hour journey but knew that she would be incapable of sleep until nightfall. Some time over the last twenty years, during Corrie's infant colicky patches and the twins' rotation through the usual catalogue of childhood complaints, she had willed her body too often to resist the imperative of sleep. Corrie's disappearance had ground the habit of eternal vigilance into the bedrock of her being. It was now a default position, even in the face of the most annihilating weariness. She relied on tablets, but her doctor would only write her a script every three months and she was obliged to ration her moments of luxurious oblivion. The tablets were saved for the long, black nights, for those four-am moments when she could sense panic and despair heading towards fever pitch. She glanced at the clock on the bedside table: five pm. Four hours until the Plaza Asturias across the road opened for dinner. It was going to be a long wait.

*

The room darkened slowly, the grinding and honking of traffic thickened over several hours and then dissipated. At seven thirty Dee reached for the phone.

'¡Hola! ¿Alicia?'

'¡Deirdra!'

She never minded the sound of her full name in the mouths of the Argentineans. Alicia enunciated every syllable in her husky accent, making it sound lilting and musical: *De-i-drra*, with an emphasis on the penultimate syllable and a little roll over the *r*.

'*Acabo de llegar a casa. ¿Cuando llegas?*'

Alicia worked until seven pm most days. She had only just got home.

'I arrived around three.'

'*¿Qué tal el vuelo?*'

'*Muy largo.*' How was the flight? Very long. It was what they always said to each other as an opening gambit.

'¡*Pobrecita!*'

Poor little thing. Dee smiled at the motherly endearment.

'*¿Voy a verte mañana? ¿Vamos a ir a la embajada?*'

'*Sí*. Tomorrow. The embassy. At eleven.'

'*Bueno. Nos econtramos a las diez y media. ¿En el hotel?*'

'*Sí*. Until tomorrow.'

'¡*Hasta mañana por la mañana!*'

It was pointless trying to extend their telephone conversations beyond the bare essentials. With Dee's Spanglish and Alicia's unapologetic disdain for English, things invariably got messy after the introductory pleasantries and confirmation of previously communicated information. In person, mime and body language helped them along. Alicia's ongoing support had been crucial to Dee over the last four years. Their friendship had helped her to understand cultural attitudes and practices that would otherwise have been enigmatic obstacles to her ongoing search. Her dependence on Alicia's goodwill and generosity was, however, deeply unsettling for Dee. It was why, despite Alicia's regular offers of accommodation, Dee always stayed at the Gran Vía and why she generally came laden with several bottles of McLaren Vale shiraz and a large supply of Haigh's chocolate.

After she hung up the phone she rummaged in her suitcase for something suitable to wear to dinner, settling on a pair of black capri pants, a rust-coloured T-shirt and a dark green wrap shot through with silver thread. They were expandable clothes that moulded to the body and did not require ironing. Dee's essential criteria for what she wore included fit, comfort, versatility and whether or not it could be thrown into a washing machine. The comment-worthy things she owned were usually presents from other people. Her friend, Liz, from the school where she worked, had given her the wrap, a souvenir from a trip to Cambodia. Dee gathered up her unruly hair, twisted it several times and caught it at the back of her head with a single clip, threaded some silver earrings through her ears, swiped at her pale lashes with mascara and repainted her faded mouth. She had eschewed lipstick as a young woman, but had succumbed to it in middle age. She just appeared too sad and tired without it. It had become synonymous in her head, of late, with 'making an effort' and 'not letting herself go', of sparing the world the drabness of her encroaching liplessness.

At nine, she was still the first diner to arrive at the Plaza Asturias. A bevy of waiters in black trousers and pale-blue shirts were laying tables, polishing glasses and cutlery, transiting busily between kitchen and dining room. Apart from its convenience to her hotel, Dee liked eating at the Plaza Asturias because, as well as the family groups and couples that frequented the popular restaurant, there were always at least three or four tables occupied by sole diners like herself. A waitress brought her a glass of dry sherry, a bowl of green olives, a saucer of pickled fish and a thick black-bound menu. Dee waved away the menu and ordered a steak and salad.

It didn't take long for the restaurant to fill. The tables were crowded very closely together and the swell of conversation was supplemented by the clatter of plates and the occasional dropped glass in the kitchen. An old woman whose wealth and youthful beauty was strongly implied by her elegant carriage was escorted to a table near the window by a man in his fifties who bore the masculine version of her features and the universal markers of professionalism: an expensive woollen pullover knotted casually around his shoulders, reading glasses balanced on the tip of his nose. A man of about Dee's age in a shabby jacket sat alone reading a book, occasionally scooping forkfuls of rice and sausage into his mouth. A young couple manoeuvred a pram and a sleepy, stumbling toddler past her table just after nine thirty. It had once surprised Dee to see children in restaurants at that time of night, but she had learned that the working day extended until seven or eight for many people and families always preferred to eat together.

She tried not to stare at the other diners, but despite a great deal of practice she always found it difficult to know where to look when she was eating alone. There was only so much interest she could feign in the cantina-inspired décor: the flags and posters, heavy woodwork and medieval-style chandeliers. Her attention kept being drawn back to the family group. The baby slept peacefully. The mother was well groomed and expensively dressed. The little girl, who wore a tiny denim skirt and matching jacket with brightly coloured tights, curled in her father's lap. He reached around her to slice his *milanesa* and sip from his glass of wine. Occasionally he coaxed her to take a piece of meat from his fork. Casting surreptitious glances at them every few minutes, Dee began to experience a familiar wash of sadness. Their calm self-possession and civility reminded her of the idyll she had desired for her own family but had never actually achieved. She had got so many things wrong over the years, right from the very beginning . . .

*

There's no accounting for the movement of the human heart. That was what Sister Mary Frances had observed sadly when Dee, full of moral certainty at the ripe old age of sixteen, had made a scathing comment about Brenda Phillips who had dropped out of school halfway through Year 12 to have a baby.

If the same thing hadn't happened to Dee at the end of her final year of university – if she hadn't *gotten herself pregnant* (this was a phrase she used deliberately because it seemed to imply more personal agency than some of the other unfortunate descriptors, and besides, it wasn't Ross's fault that she had deferred to the Catholic position on contraception while wilfully ignoring its advice about sex before marriage) – if she hadn't *gotten herself pregnant*, would she ever have married Ross? Would he have married her? He had been odd-jobbing his way around the country, having arrived in Sydney from Scotland six months earlier. The cash-in-hand work he picked up at the Gouger Hotel, where Dee also worked on weekends, was to fund the next stage of his journey up through the Alice and on to Darwin.

'Halloo.' He'd appraised her in an open, friendly manner when the manager had introduced them. She was struck first by his beguiling accent, secondly by the blueness of his eyes, and finally by his slow smile.

'Nice to meet you.' She'd stuck out her hand. It had felt like a silly, formal thing to do, but she'd had an urge to touch him. He'd taken her hand in a firm grasp and winked at her. The sleeves of his white work shirt were rolled to the elbows and his outstretched arm was lean and sinewy. She hadn't minded the wink, which might have seemed presumptuous in anyone else. It was continuous with his ease of manner and obvious sociability, but it was not entirely innocent either.

Fridays were always busy. Happy hour stretched to seven pm with the after-work crowd from the mail exchange in the front bar. When it slowed in the front, the manager took over and sent them out the back to the disco: twenty dollars at the door and all you could drink for the night. Sharon, the other Friday-night casual, had called in sick (an act of the gods, Dee thought at the time, because if Sharon had seen Ross first, Dee wouldn't have stood a chance) and she and Ross ran all night.

Bar work, like all work, has its own vanities, even for a casual, and Dee had taken pride in it. There were some people who were useless behind a bar. They held you up, got in your way, interfered with your flow. When you had lines of people, three-deep, waiting for drinks, and they'd paid in advance and wanted their money's worth, you had to keep moving or things got nasty pretty quickly. She and Ross found an effortless rhythm within minutes. It turned into a kind of ballet between the glass racks, the beer taps, the spirit bottles and the mixer dispenser with the music pumping loudly in the background and a wordless competition quickly established between the two of them about who could clear the punters the fastest. He stepped neatly around her as she whirled about to get to the spirit bottles. She ducked as he passed glasses over her head, still keeping a close eye on the beer she was pouring, carefully gauging the final flick of the tap for the requisite half-inch head. She clattered glasses into the dishwasher and slammed the door. He pulled out the steaming rack several minutes later and replaced it with an empty one.

The effects of physical labour are charming on the young. His shirt was drenched in sweat and sticking to his back, her pinned-up hair escaped in damp tendrils and her face was flushed and bright. At the end of the night an undeniable connection had been forged between them. It seemed entirely natural that she would kick off her shoes and rest her legs across his knees as they were sitting at one of the deserted tables in the dark having a knock-off drink, and that he would place his hand under her calf muscle and rub it therapeutically. Comrades in arms. She had never felt such an instant connection with anyone. The mutuality of it made it magical and the magic made her reckless.

Mick and Jim, the two guys who'd picked Ross up hitch-hiking just outside of Melbourne on their way back from the VFL grand final, had offered him a room in their share house at Norwood. Mick worked at the local branch of the Commonwealth Bank and Jim did clerical work for the council, so Dee and Ross had the house to themselves all through the long, hot days of the summer break. Occasionally they took trips to the Barossa Valley and played at being wine connoisseurs or drove to the southern beaches, where they bobbed about in the chill water between the wash of waves and slathered each other in lotion before baking their pale skins red on a bed of warm, white sand. Her VW bug broke down on a regular basis, but it was never anything Ross couldn't fix with a bit of coat-hanger, a squirt of WD40 or a well-aimed blow from a large spanner. Dee felt herself relaxing like a child before his grown-up capacity to deal with all practical contingencies, but when the period she was expecting never eventuated and her breasts started to swell and harden alarmingly, she realised with a jolt that there were certain things that he was just not going to be able to remedy.

'Prairgnant?'

It sounded less alarming in a Scottish accent. Or maybe it was his warmth of tone, the note of indulgent amusement. She had never felt nervous around him before, but had been made so by the awful sense she had of being some kind of supplicant. She couldn't help associating her situation with ignorant, red-cheeked farm girls compromised by the lord of the manor or calculating, would-be wives begging their reluctant boyfriends to 'do the right thing'. There was a large measure of humiliation in it. She was also made miserable by the intractable position she was placed in by her Catholic faith: Hmm . . . let me see . . . will I be a murderess or merely a publicly outed fallen woman?

'What do you want to do?' he had asked her.

She had shrugged. 'Well, I'm not having an abortion, so my options are somewhat limited.'

'Do you want to get married?'

There had been no hint of reluctance in the offer. He had asked the question in the same tone of thoughtful anticipation in which he might have suggested that they take a trip to Kangaroo Island.

'Do *you*?'

'Well, it would solve my visa problems.'

She had thrown him a withering look and he'd laughed aloud. 'What about your trip up north? You wanted to keep travelling.'

'Ach, we've got the rest of our lives to travel aboot.'

He'd hugged her then and she'd felt a little better. The rest of their lives. A mutual endeavour. Shared adventures. They'd take the baby wherever they went. In one of those papoose things. They might have to defer a few plans in the short term, but there would be other possibilities in the long term. She withdrew from her Honours Degree with the English department and enrolled instead in the Diploma of Education. One of them was going to need to earn the money that would be required to keep a family afloat and achieve their future dreams. And it would only be a temporary measure. She'd work her way back to an academic career eventually.

When she'd addressed all the other details she had to steel herself to face her father. He had met Ross and liked him, so she harboured hopes that the encounter might not be as awful as she secretly knew it was going to be.

Her father had pressed his lips together, breathed in through flared nostrils and exhaled slowly, fixing a wide-eyed stare upon the floor. 'This is not what I hoped for you.'

'Look, I know, but—'

'And I know it would have been a cause of great distress to your mother.'

Dee had flinched. Her mother had died five years earlier after a two-year battle with ovarian cancer.

'It is therefore a cause of great distress to *me*,' her father had continued with his doomsday inflexion, 'that I have failed in my responsibility to instil in you the values that she and I both believed in.'

'We're going to get married, Dad. We would have got married anyway. It's just going to happen a bit sooner, that's all.'

'What about your studies?' His face was racked with bitter disappointment. 'You've been invited to do Honours.'

'I've withdrawn. I can always apply again in a few years' time – when Ross gets his visa sorted and finds some full-time work. I've enrolled to do the Dip Ed instead.'

He had shaken his head, his eyes still fixed on the floor.

'I can't say I'm not profoundly disappointed,' he said at last. 'I commend you for trying to do the right thing, but it's not going to be an easy road, you know . . .'

*

Always attend to your baby immediately when she cries. The fear of abandonment is strong in infants and it will take you much longer to soothe her back to sleep once she has worked herself into a state of high distress.

That's what the baby book had advised. It was what Dee's own instincts had compelled her to do from the moment the midwife had slid the petal-soft, exquisitely small creature into her arms and told her that she had a daughter. Dee had been undone by the infant's heart-stopping vulnerability, and had fallen immediately and irrevocably in love. She'd resolved then and there that she was never going to let this child down. She was going to atone for her own failings as well as those of all previous generations through the care of this brand-new, pristine human soul. She would be an exemplary mother – the *perfect* mother – putting paid to any residual speculation that the precipitous circumstances of her marriage marked this child as less loved or wanted than any other.

Corrie's cries shattered the uneasy silence of the dark room. It was five am. Dee lay in bed, clinging to the futile and unsubstantiated hope that the cries might abate of their own accord, but when they assumed their usual rhythmic insistence, she dragged herself up and stumbled across the bedroom to Corrie's cot. Corrie had gone down at nine, after the usual hour of feeding, rocking and patting and had woken, like clockwork, every two hours since: at eleven, at one, at three. Sometimes she would go back to sleep if she was cuddled and rocked, an oversized dummy wedged firmly in her small mouth. More often than not she ended up back on the breast. It was comfort sucking, but Dee did not have the energy or the emotional will to do anything about it.

You may find it easier to tend to baby's needs at night if she is sharing your bed with you. This is, in fact, baby's preferred place, fulfilling her need for physical closeness with you.

Dee had tried this approach in the first few weeks, persuaded by the earth-mother idyll – mother and child snuggled together in mutual harmony, exactly as nature intended. It meant that she did not have to haul herself out of sleepy warmth, that she could just roll over and latch the child onto the nearest breast. Afterwards, however, she lay there tense with worry about Corrie getting tangled in the quilt or ending up face-down on a pillow or Ross accidentally rolling on top of her and crushing her to death. Gradually, this heightened sensitivity and semi-wakefulness meant that it was not only Corrie's full-blown cries that sent a narrow nail of adrenaline shooting up through Dee's innards, it was every snuffle and squeak and cough and gurgle. There were times when Dee awoke to find herself trying to stuff a breast into the mouth of her sleeping child because she had dreamt that Corrie was awake and crying. Thus, within a month, Dee had committed one of the cardinal crimes outlined in the baby book.

Do not, however, confuse your body by keeping her in your bed occasionally, when it suits you, while insisting that she sleep alone at other times.

On the nights Dee stumbled to the cot on jelly legs without a spare ounce of energy to sit upright in the rocking chair, she tumbled them both back into her own bed while she dwelt in the twilight zone between sleep and full consciousness until morning. On other nights she would try to tough out the screaming or droop heavily over the child during the duration of a quick feed, wedge the dummy quickly into the little mouth as soon as she managed to wrest her nipple free and then, with the studied care of the average drunk and anyone else who knows their reflexes are shot to pieces, tip her, ever so gently, back into her cot. She would then creep back to bed and fall into a tense and miserable doze for several hours, at which point the crying would begin all over again . . .

Although you may doubt your capacity to cope with the demands that a new baby makes upon you, be assured that your time and energy will expand in equal proportion to your baby's needs.

That was what the baby book claimed and what Dee so desperately wanted to believe. If other women could cope, why couldn't she? Dee was strong. She would soldier on.

Lesser women might have resorted to a bottle to ensure the baby was comfortably full before she was put down for the night. Not Dee. Formula, she had read somewhere, was just a way of clogging up your baby's insides and stupefying them into a glutted coma, leaving them susceptible to a vast array of insidious diseases later on in life.

Lesser women might have checked into the Mother and Baby Sleep Unit at the local hospital for monitoring and advice, but that would have been an admission of failure. The imaginary whisperings in Dee's mind were too loud: She really wasn't ready for children . . .

Lesser women might have expressed a few bottles of breast milk and prevailed upon their partner to take a turn at the nightshift. Dee *did* express milk, but it couldn't be used at night.

Susan Holoubek

She expressed two bottles a day between lessons at the outer suburban high school where she had secured a teaching position shortly after completing her diploma. These precious bottles were stored in the freezer and delivered to day care along with several changes of clothes, a sun hat and a comfort toy when Dee dropped Corrie there every morning before embarking on the hour-long commute down the Southern freeway.

She had not ceased to be besotted with her daughter – with the sight and touch and smell of her, with her creamy skin and dark feathery hair, with her little bump of a nose and dewy mouth. She was just exhausted, that was all.

Babies who wake constantly in the night for no apparent reason are often seeking out the affection they may be missing during their waking hours. If you are not readily available to attend to baby's emotional needs during the day, she will instinctively try to compensate for this lack of attention by reaching out for proof of your love at night.

Because of the terrible guilt Dee experienced every time she left her daughter at day care, she could deny her nothing in the hours they had together. Unconditional availability had become a default position and she was no longer capable of clearly discerning whether it was Corrie's needs or her own that she was assuaging.

Ross slept on. He had the most extraordinary capacity for sleep. When Dee brought Corrie home from the hospital he had hovered, well-meaning but helpless, on the sidelines, waiting for instructions. Gradually, however, he had relinquished any aspirations of competence in the face of Dee's harried corrections and complaints, and had eventually, given up altogether. 'You're the one with the chebs, dearie,' he would shrug, handing Corrie back to Dee every time she began to cry. Having decided that there was nothing he could do to prevent the night-time disturbances, he slept through them. He'd taken a job with the maintenance department of a major city hospital and started work at seven every morning so he was unable to do the day care drop-off. He finished at three, so he collected Corrie in the afternoon and did a valiant job of keeping her calm until Dee roared up the driveway at four thirty, her breasts feeling like two engorged melons, with a schoolbag full of marking to be completed sometime between feeds and the backlog of domestic chores.

Every night after school, Dee put a load of nappies and another of soiled baby clothes through the washing machine and cooked dinner for herself and Ross, while he played with Corrie. Ross was good at many things, but his culinary skills only extended to baked beans on toast or other things that could be obtained from a can and cooked over a single gas ring. Dee didn't mind. She even experienced a small thrill every now and again at her management of such womanly domestic responsibilities. Ross changed the light bulbs, put out the rubbish bins and fixed the cars when they broke down, which wasn't infrequently. He mowed the lawn on request and ironed his own shirts. Dee was glad of the mutual affection they continued to share, despite their rocky beginnings, and was not inclined to nitpick. She was not about to prove her father right by entertaining the idea of unhappiness.

*

Dee snuck another glance at the handsome Argentinean family. There weren't milk stains down the front of the mother's beautifully laundered rose-coloured blouse. Her eyes weren't cavernous with fatigue. She hadn't run to fat from too much compensatory alcohol and cake. The baby slept on. The toddler played charmingly with a soft toy, rocking it like an infant and singing softly in lisping Spanish.

The narrow front door swung open and her attention was diverted by two newcomers negotiating with the maître d'. One of them was a thin, pale man with rimless spectacles and a mass of flyaway hair springing from a high forehead. His companion was younger and more striking looking, with strongly defined features, a smooth olive complexion and shoulder-length black hair. The waiter directed them to the last available table, which was alongside Dee's. In the process of manoeuvring into his seat, the long-haired man brushed against the wrap she had hung on the back of her chair. It slipped to the ground and he retrieved it with an apology and a smile of genuine warmth. His smile made her realise how lonely she felt.

'*Lo siento.*' I'm sorry.

'*No hay problema.*' She would have liked to have held his attention a little longer, but there was nothing further to be said.

With people beginning to queue outside she was not encouraged to linger over her meal. Her empty plate was whisked away almost as soon as she had finished the last mouthful of steak. Her order of coffee and brandy arrived swiftly. An imperious, elderly man, dressed in a black suit and hunched over a cane, had been moving between tables, exchanging greetings with various customers for most of the evening. Dee noticed him glancing over at her coffee cup as he discussed waiting times with a young couple at the door. She asked for the bill. When the waitress returned with her credit-card slip for signing she attempted to ask if the restaurant would be open for lunch the following day, but the waitress did not understand her halting mix of English and Spanish. The man with the spectacles at the adjacent table glanced up and translated the question for her.

'They are open on weekdays for lunch but only for dinner on Saturdays and Sundays,' he told her.

'Thank you.'

'My pleasure.'

She usually didn't make a habit of pursuing relationships with random English speakers, but the memory of his companion's smile lingered. They seemed like a friendly pair.

'You're English?'

'Yes. And you're – Australian?'

'Yes.'

And then she remembered the other reason that she usually didn't go down this road. *What brings you to Argentina?* Dee stood up quickly, wound her wrap around her shoulders and picked up her handbag.

'Thanks for your help.'

'How long are you spending in Buenos Aires?'

'Not long.'

'That's a shame. It's a great city. You'll have to come back.'

She hoped her retreating smile didn't appear as much like a grimace as it felt.

Chapter Two

Alicia had borrowed her brother's ancient station wagon to drive Dee to the embassy. Dee made this appointment every time she visited Argentina. What had started out as desperate hopefulness four years ago had become a sad courtesy to those who had assisted her through the worst times and whose ongoing presence in her life continued to serve as a tenuous link with her missing daughter.

'¡Hijo de puta!'

Alicia swore percussively under her breath as another car swerved into the only available parking space they had seen on their last four circuits of the block. The cursing was an amusing counterbalance to Alicia's natural elegance. Today she was dressed in jeans with a wide leather belt, a plain but expensively cut white shirt and high-heeled boots. Her only ornament was a bracelet of knotted thread made by one of the barrio children from the parish community centre where she volunteered.

They eventually found a space, half a kilometre away. Alicia nudging the station wagon up against the bumper of a new BMW. Her husband, Juan Pablo, had taken the family four-wheel drive to his office in the city. Alicia's brother, Javier, was a priest and his income didn't stretch further than the clapped-out vehicle common to most Argentinean workers. It was also a practical choice, as it didn't attract too much envy or attention around the barrio where he worked.

'*¿Te gusta el coche prestigioso?*' Alicia banged the bonnet with the flat of her hand as she locked the driver's side door.

'Of course I like your prestigious car. It is the only reason I permit you to drive me.'

Alicia laughed heartily. It had been a relief to them both when Dee when finally managed to move beyond studious politeness and engage in some affectionate teasing.

The sullen sky spat rain as they hurried from the car, dodging pavement puddles and heavy drips from the jacaranda trees. Dee paused outside the embassy gate, struck, as always, by the graceful lines of the white nineteenth-century mansion, a grace that was marred a little by the concrete gatehouse that accommodated security staff, metal detectors and a series of heavy interconnecting doors giving access to the embassy grounds.

Alicia swapped pleasantries with the Argentinean staff, some of whom remembered her from previous visits. A young woman with thick, blonde hair and a strong-boned face pushed open the outer door of the security area.

'Dee Sutherland? I'm Amanda.'

Dee took her outstretched hand and turned to include Alicia in the greeting. 'This is my friend, Alicia. Alicia looked after my daughter when she first came to Buenos Aires.'

Amanda greeted Alicia in Spanish, thrusting a hand in her direction.

'Richard said to bring you up to the house. He thought you might feel more comfortable out of the office environment.'

'That was kind of him.' But Dee suspected something else was being signalled by the change of venue.

Amanda led the way along a narrow path around the side of the main building.

French doors at the rear of the ambassador's residence opened out onto a patio, overlooking a formal garden and swimming pool. The reception area at the back of the house was an expanse of cream and beige with dark wood trim and crystal chandeliers. They sat down on one of two couches facing each other across a highly polished coffee table.

'How was your flight? The weather's been pretty lousy, hasn't it? Have you been following the tennis?' Amanda was tactful and practised at keeping social conversation flowing smoothly. Dee was not as scornful of such small talk as she might once have been. Polite conversation was a dying art and in its death throes she had found herself missing the well-mannered efforts to lay down a cloak of words over the muddy transit between strangers.

'Richard shouldn't be long. He's just finishing up with some people from the wine industry. You've tried the local wines? Good, aren't they? We're setting up some contacts for them with the Australian industry. Ah – here's Richard now.'

Richard Blaine was in his late forties, a delicate-featured man with wavy black hair, greying at the sides. His fine-textured skin retained the imprint of smiles about the edges of his small, bright eyes. His forehead was as smooth as a baby's. There was no weight of consternation there, no furrows of striving.

Dee was always grateful for Richard Blaine's attentions, but she found herself vaguely resenting that smooth forehead from time to time.

'Sorry to keep you waiting.' He had moved swiftly into the room from the patio, but gave no appearance of exertion or strain. His accent was pure private boys' college and law school: languid and slightly effeminate. 'No, please don't get up.' He extended his hand to each of them in turn, greeted Alicia in Spanish.

'Now – tea? Coffee?'

They made assenting noises and Amanda melted away to instruct the appropriate staff.

Richard revisited the litany of flights, hotels, weather, tennis . . .

'Do you play?' Dee asked.

'Used to. The Argentineans are rather serious about their tennis. My wife's arranged for me to have lessons, but I have to keep cancelling because of my schedule. Gustavo, my coach, is beginning to despair of me.'

A white-jacketed waiter brought a tray with a silver service, and a platter each of sandwiches and small pastries. He poured out the tea to their instructions and politely withdrew.

Richard moved delicately to the business at hand. 'So, Dee. How *are* you?'

Dee held his gaze before shrugging lightly and looking away. 'It never goes away.'

'No, of course not.'

Don't bleat, she reminded himself, it makes people feel uncomfortable.

'I guess I'm beginning to resign myself to the fact that there's nothing more I can do,' she continued. 'There haven't been any leads since you called me back for that identification and that was two years ago.'

'Has it been that long?'

Two years ago the body of a young woman without papers had been discovered in one of the inner-city barrios. She had been the victim of a robbery and stabbing. Everything of value had been removed from the corpse, but a police officer had noted the English labels on her clothing and alerted the relevant embassies. Richard thought the description close enough to Corrie's to warrant an identification. In a fog of terror Dee had booked herself onto the next available flight to Buenos Aires, been collected from the airport by Richard himself in an embassy car and transported to one of the large city morgues.

When they had peeled back the sheet from the young woman's face Dee had stared blankly for several moments. It might have been Corrie – the short dark hair, the fair skin, the height, the build. She had to check several times, aware that death can lock familiar, motile characteristics into unfamiliar, frozen parodies – eyes concealed beneath closed lids, the strange manipulations morticians apply to mouths and jaws; these things can be deceptive.

'It's not her.'

'You're quite sure?'

'She had ear piercings and a little stud in her nose. And – may I look at her hands?'

The attendant lifted the girl's hands and placed them on top of the sheet, re-tucking it firmly about the rest of the body.

Her arms had been carefully washed, but there were scratches and grazes where she had tried to defend herself. Her nails were torn and dark with traces of blood beneath them. Her hands were small and short-fingered. Corrie's fingers had been long and fine, almost outlandishly so. 'Like spider's legs,' Dee had teased her once, making her forever self-conscious about them, no matter how many times Dee had tried to undo the damage by rephrasing the descriptor to 'aristocratic' or 'artistic'.

'It's not Corrie.'

'You're absolutely certain?'

'Completely.'

She hadn't been offended by the shadow of disappointment that had flickered momentarily over his urbane features. She understood his need to complete the task and close the file. She understood his flicker of irritation at all the wasted effort and she wondered if perhaps it might have been better to have had a resolution. Even this kind of a resolution.

'Poor girl.' She had rested her hand on the cold doughy fingers. Her head swam and she must have gone pale because Richard had tactfully offered her his arm and organised a cup of tea. The staff of the morgue had hurried to accommodate him and she remembered wondering what it must be like to occupy a position where one could take such alacrity for granted.

She looked at him now: fresh, polished, becalmed, amidst cream upholstery and crystal chandeliers holding court. Richard Blaine was the embodiment of intersecting victories – of breeding, opportunity and informed choice. He was what happened when the complex cams of a social combination lock aligned. Simple passage. Easy access. A falling away of the need to wrestle with a vast array of hidden obstacles.

Despite having dressed carefully to blend into the ambassadorial setting – tailored skirt and jacket – Dee suddenly felt as if she had trailed something unpleasant across the plush carpet. The detritus of her messy history rattled about her, clashing with the décor. She sighed deeply.

'There *isn't* anything else I can do, is there?'

He flexed his bottom lip in grave contemplation and shook his head slowly. 'Nothing you haven't already done.'

'And there's nothing more that you can do?'

There was a shadow of animation around the suggestion that there may have been some dereliction of duty on his part. 'We've done everything possible.'

'I just wondered.'

'Of course we have no control over the diligence of the local functionaries, but we've exerted considerable pressure and there has been no reason to doubt their desire to cooperate. We are, thankfully, not dealing with the complexities of the 1970s and 1980s. As Alicia knows only too well.' He grimaced meaningfully in her direction. 'That was quite a different scenario.'

Alicia caught his gaze and he translated quickly for her. She was intimately acquainted with the horrors of that era. Her brother, Aurelio, had been one of those who had disappeared.

'*No. No está tan mal ahora.*' she murmured.

'How does one stop looking?' Dee turned to Alicia, her voice breaking a little. '*¿Cómo puedo dejar de buscar?*'

Alicia shook her head but said nothing.

Dee knew that the chances of finding out what had happened to her daughter had grown more remote with every passing year. Sometimes she wondered if there had been much hope to begin with. Buenos Aires was a sprawling city of thirteen million people, flooded by refugees and other undocumented residents, encompassing hundreds of neighbourhoods into which even the police wouldn't venture (unless they were in partnership with the reigning drug lords), in a country still reeling from economic collapse, where judicial and police corruption had always been taken for granted.

There was a recognisable Australian artefact on the coffee table – a polished bowl fashioned from the burl of a jarrah tree. Ross would have appreciated the artistry of it. If she hadn't steeled herself against the yearning for her husband's presence years ago, it would have been almost unendurable at times like this. Richard cleared his throat.

'Dee, I think we can take some consolation in the fact that there has been no evidence of any foul play.'

'In the old days the army just dropped the bodies into the river, didn't they?'

'Yes. But they had access to military helicopters.'

'There must be remote areas of countryside where no one goes. Look how long it took them to find Milat's victims. The Truro victims—' Dee stared at the floor.

'I can't pretend that's not a possibility,' Richard said more gently, 'but let's try to keep our hopes up for a more positive outcome. We will, of course, continue to pass on any information that arises, but I need to let you know that we will no longer be making any active inquiries.'

His pronouncement came as no surprise. It was, more or less, what Dee had expected to hear – what she had been toying with announcing herself: I won't be coming back anymore. It just felt more dismissive coming from somebody else.

Alicia could sense the tension in their conversation, but was chewing tactfully on a sandwich and gazing out over the wet garden.

'I appreciate your frankness,' Dee said at last. 'And I appreciate all that you've done for me over the years.'

Richard Blaine held her eyes intently for a moment. 'You know I took a very strong personal interest in your case. I did everything I could.'

'But it's time to move on. I understand that.'

Amanda materialised from a door at the rear of the room. Dee, ever obedient to social signals, a habit she despised in herself even as she succumbed to it, picked up her handbag and rose from the sofa.

'Thanks, Richard. It won't be easy to cut ties completely. It feels strange. Like losing the last thread of connection . . .' She petered out.

'By all means keep in touch. If we can be of any further assistance, don't hesitate to let us know.' He clasped her outstretched hand in both of his, then made his formal farewells to Alicia in Spanish. Amanda stepped forward and led them out the French doors, back down the winding path and waved them through security.

They had only taken a few steps down the street before it began to rain.

'*Hijo de puta*,' Alicia declared, hunching her shoulders against the steady spatter of heavy drops.

Son of a whore. It was an attempt to cheer Dee up. Alicia's husband, Juan Pablo, had taught Dee a few basic curses in Spanish ('so you will not feel left out of our rich cultural exchanges') and this phrase had become a running joke between them.

'*Hijo de puta*,' Dee echoed and forced herself to smile.

As the downpour intensified, Alicia linked her arm through Dee's and pulled her at a run in the direction of the parked car. She fumbled with the keys, laughing and cursing her own clumsiness. They were both soaked by the time they fell into their seats and slammed the doors behind them. Alicia put the key in the ignition and then turned to look at Dee.

'*¿No es fácil, Dee?*'

'No. Not easy. But it's what I was expecting.'

'*Eres una madre. Siempre vas a tener la esperanza.*'

'Yes, I will always have hope, but I need to focus on Luke and Ben now.'

Alicia nodded her understanding then started the car. They drove back to the hotel with the radio playing, bridging the silence between them.

There was no parking anywhere outside the Gran Vía. Dee scrambled out of the car in the middle of the road while making effusive thankyous to her friend. Alicia waved them away.

'Dee. Saturday. At my house? *Asado*. You come?'

'I would like that very much. Thank you, Alicia. *Muchísimas gracias.*'

'*De nada ¡No olvides que sos nuestra amiga!*'

Don't forget that you are our friend. It was a gracious declaration in the wake of the turmoil Dee was conscious of having added to the Torres family's life.

'*Y nunca voy a olvidar tu amabilidad.*'

And I will never forget your kindness. That was what she wanted to say, but by the time she had composed the sentence in her mind, the slow stream of traffic was inching forwards and her words were lost in the honking of horns and revving of engines.

Chapter Three

Breakfast was being cleared by the time Dee emerged from a long shower and laboured efforts to doctor her puffy eyes with make-up, but the waiter brought her a plate of hot *medialunas* and refilled the coffee pot.

She took her second cup to the booth where the terminals for internet access were located and, after negotiating the quirks of the Spanish-language keyboard and the inevitable connection dropouts, she eventually gained access to her email account. There were four new messages. Two from Luke, one from her friend, Liz, and something tagged, 'Forward to 10 great women!' She checked the messages from Luke first.

> *Hi, Mum. How ya doing? Where's the sandwich maker? Also how do you make your hamburgers the boys are coming over for a BBQ on Saturday. You wouldn't know where dad's old tackle box is would you? What's the weather like over there? It's pretty good here but still no rain. Belinda says hi. Love your son Luke.*

Hi Mum. Found the sandwich maker.

Love your son Luke. It was an old joke. He had been signing off like that since the first Mothers' Day card he dictated to his kindergarten teacher, tickled for some reason by the notion of being 'a son'.

> *Dear Luke,*
> *Glad you managed to locate the sandwich maker. Hamburger recipe: 1kg mince, one finely diced onion, six slices of bread sprinkled with ¼ cup water and squeezed out, salt, pepper, oregano, one egg. Squelch it all together with CLEAN hands and make into patties. Good to hear you are having a stab at cooking and not leaving it all to Ben.*
> *I haven't seen that tackle box in years, but I suspect it's behind the old paint tins in the shed. Are you planning on going fishing? I hope this doesn't involve a boat, a mob of scungy mates and too much alcohol.*

She deleted the last sentence. Retyped it. Deleted it again. Retyped it, but added a softener:

> *Don't tell me. I don't need to know. Wear a life jacket and catch lots of fish.*
> *Lots of love, Mum*

When she and Ross had decided that they should provide Corrie with a sibling, they had, of course, not been anticipating twins. It had taken some years for them to feel brave enough to face the prospect of another child. (Surely second-time around would be easier? After all, they were old hands now. Corrie was starting kindy, and becoming more independent, and they didn't want to leave too big a gap.) Then at around about the eighteen-week mark of Dee's pregnancy they were hit with news of the double whammy. Back they went to Your Child's Nursery to buy the second cot and the second bassinet, two more car seats and the double pram. There were no baby bonuses in those days and paid parental leave was the stuff of utopian fantasy. Ross was barely pulling down enough money at the hospital to cover the double cost of child care that they were going to be up for, so, in the end, they decided that it made more sense for him to quit his job and stay home with the new babies. Dee returned to work, milky, tired and teary. Ross embarked on the steep learning curve of caring for not one but two infants. Somewhere along the line, the travel dreams had been quietly shelved. Dee had been offered a permanent position and promoted to English Coordinator. They'd taken on a mortgage and proceeded to live from one pay packet to the next. Life slipped by in an exhausted haze.

The day Corrie started school, Dee was running a staff in-service on literacy and had to be at work early. She'd laid out the pristine new uniform the night before: the little checked dress and the snow-white socks, the polished black shoes and the broad-brimmed hat.

'Please take a photo of her in her new uniform,' she'd urged Ross, but he forgot.

'Look – I had everything ready, but Ben shat himself just as we were getting in the car and by the time I got him changed we were running late and I just forgot, all right?'

'You're always running late,' she replied between clenched teeth.

On Sports Day Corrie was picked for the relay team. Dee had drilled Ross about the time he had to be there.

'It's at 12.45 – just before the barbecue lunch. Try to get there early in case they're running ahead of schedule. Please. Someone needs to be there for her. She's so proud to have made it into the team.'

When she got home that evening, Ross was asleep on the bed, Luke nestling in his crooked arm. Ben was in his cot and Corrie was watching *Rugrats* on the television. Her mouth was smeared with red iceblock stains, which were also blooming on her school uniform around the bright-blue 'second' ribbon pinned to her chest.

'You came second! Wow! Was Dad proud?'

Corrie shrugged. 'I dunno. He didn't see me. He couldn't find a parking spot and Luke fell out of the pram. Mum, when are you going to do canteen? Everyone else's mum does canteen and they get a lunch order and chips and a drink at recess.'

'I can't do canteen, darling. I have to work every day. But I can give you some money for a lunch order.'

You never get that time back again. Dee found herself staring sadly into space. Even as she had lived it she had known that. But she had always imagined that respite was somewhere just around the corner. When the boys are in kindy, Ross can pick up a few shifts somewhere. I'll cut my time back at work. I'll put my name down for canteen. I'll come to Sports Day and I'll cheer like crazy. But the years had slipped by so quickly and, before she knew it, she was no longer required at any more sports days.

Dee clicked on the email from Liz.

Dee! Mate! Olé! Yes, I've had a drop or two. Or three, but who's counting? I hope the flight was bearable, hotel appropriately swanky, and that you choke on those glazed croissant things you bang on about ad nauseum whenever you come back from Arggggghentina. Spare a few thoughts for those of us still slaving away at the chalkface while you swan around the globe on long-service leave.

Took a relief with that Year 10 Religious Education class of yours the other day. I think they're eating your replacement alive. I notice your absence conveniently coincides with the Human Sexuality unit. Whoever decided to call that unit 'Made in the Image of God' has obviously never attempted to front up with anatomical diagrams to the likes of Danny Centofanti and Co, but let's not go there.

ANYWAY, this is just to pass on the news that we are missing you, fearless leader, and also because I know, from bitter experience, that once you have run the gamut of third-world internet servers, it is imperative to have some reward apart from spam for your efforts. Hope all is going well. You just go ahead and enjoy yourself. Don't worry about us. And don't forget to check out the talent. I'm prepared to go guarantor on an Australian visa in exchange for sexual favours with anyone who looks like Gael García Bernal.

L x

Liz was one of the few people who could distract Dee from herself and make her feel less like an aberration from the rest of humanity. It was she who had encouraged Dee to apply for the Deputy Principal's position at St Catherine's seven years ago, ignoring Dee's protestations that they'd never give her the job. 'You need something to get your teeth stuck into. And if you're going to work like a donkey you may as well earn some decent money for it,' Liz had argued, and she had been right. Dee had found a new lease of life in the more varied challenges of leadership, but the extra income had been the most significant boon when everything else in her life had started to fall apart. It made it possible to keep the family afloat after Ross died. It had funded her regular trips in search of Corrie.

She'd never cared about money as a young woman, trudging through the decade between 1983 and 1993 in a state of catatonic oblivion. By the time she had the energy to notice what everyone around her was up to, she discovered that the whole country had suddenly abandoned casks and was drinking expensive bottled wine from boutique wineries in the Coonawarra or Margaret River, putting in a second bathroom and pushing out the back wall of their kitchens to make glassed-in entertainment spaces. The 1971 Ford Laser that Ross had managed to keep operational for her since they had got together had become a quaint anachronism amongst the shiny new vehicles in the staff car park and every second person was off to Bali or Thailand or a Gold Coast time share in the school holidays. She remembered how, gradually, she had moved from mild curiosity about these new social indulgences to active interest to irritable envy, but was unable to pinpoint the exact moment at which she had started to feel diminished by her lack of access to them. Nor could she remember when she had begun to turn her resentment upon Ross.

Ross hadn't returned to regular employment when the twins started school. He'd lost confidence, lost contact with his former networks. Every workplace seemed to have put in a computer and he didn't know anything about them. His ignorance made him angry so he turned back to what he could control with his own two hands and a knowledge of observable mechanics: he fixed things. He put up a pergola and built a chicken coop. He laid slate pathways and created ornamental garden beds.

He dug a pond and populated it with exotic water plants. He did an adult education course in furniture construction and made an ornate rosewood coffee table. Visitors to their home were impressed by the meticulous craftsmanship. They asked him if he would make similar things for them. They passed on his details to their friends. He argued his case with Dee for a lathe and a bandsaw. He expanded into bookshelves and cabinets, outdoor furniture and kitchen suites. Over time it became something of a backyard business, but Ross was fussy about his materials and painstakingly attentive to detail, so his margins were low even without the added expectation of selling to everyone at 'mate's rates'.

'It's not a job, it's a bloody hobby,' Dee had flung at him on more than one occasion, but he had shrugged away her resentment and gone back to his shed. Afterwards she would feel sorry, follow him out there and stand silently in the doorway, watching him while he planed the edge of a tabletop or lathed an intricately turned chair leg, oblivious to her presence, absorbed in his craft.

'Is that red gum?'

'Yeah.'

'It's a really nice piece of wood.'

'Yeah.'

'Do you want a cup of tea?'

'What? Yeah all right.'

*

Someone coughed politely behind her, bringing her back to the present. Dee turned to see a young man waiting to use the computer. She closed Liz's message, logged out of her email account and took her empty coffee cup back to the dining room.

It was Saturday, the day of Alicia's *asado*, but that was scheduled for late afternoon. In the meantime Dee decided to clear her head with a long walk through the city.

When she stepped out onto the street she was struck once again by the distinctive smell of the place. She always forgot about this between visits, but it was so different to the smell of Australian cities. Buenos Aires smelt of caramel. It was woven between the cigarette smoke, the car exhaust fumes and the richly sour emanations of restaurant bins. It infused the clouds of sweet cologne attendant on the businessmen she passed in the streets, lingered about the doorways of shops and smudged the clearer ring of disinfectant slopped into gutters.

The rain had cleared. The sky was the blue of the national flag it inspired, with puffs of light cloud and a brisk breeze, perfect weather for Alicia's barbecue. The wide median strips on Avenida 9 de Julio were a chaos of wire fencing and churned concrete. Dee headed up Mayo towards San Nicolas. The jumble of Spanish colonial, neoclassical and nineteenth-century European architectural styles, the private mansions and the public edifices all bore witness to the great wealth of the past and the jostling for personal status and public glory. Recent social history had, however, taken a toll and while many such buildings had been re-imagined and restored as shops, hotels and museums, there was still a lingering aura of grime and decrepitude in many backstreets and lanes.

On a patch of bare earth in one of the gardens near the Plaza del Congreso, a group of *cartoneros*, collectors of the city's waste, had built a fire on the ground with pieces of scavenged wood. They squatted beside towering hessian bags crammed with recyclable refuse retrieved from the streets during the night, drinking from tin cups. Outside the Teatro Liceo, a young man was asleep on a piece of raw foam rubber, a blanket pulled up to his chin. He had a strong jaw, with an even grazing of black stubble, high cheekbones and a swathe of ink-black hair falling across his forehead. His skin was toffee coloured, and despite his rough living conditions, retained the glowing patina of youth. Dee noticed in herself a soupy mixture of maternal and sexual feeling. His face could have been from one of those magazine advertisements for a new cologne, but there were black rims under the fingernails that gripped the blanket beneath his chin and he looked vulnerable and exposed against the filthy stone pavement and the garish advertisements plastered to the wall of the theatre. She experienced an almost irresistible urge to caress his sleeping cheek but she checked herself, resumed her brisk walking pace and turned the corner into Avenida Callao.

Fragrant gusts of butter, yeast and warmed sugar drifted from the bakeries and cafés, where a smattering of breakfast customers hunched over their newspapers and *cafés con leche*. In the Plaza Rodríguez Peña, a young woman adjusted the leads of the six large dogs she was walking. She glanced up as Dee paused to read the graffiti scrawled across the pedestal of the old military hero's statue.

Aparación con vida ya de Jorge López.
We want to see Jorge López alive immediately.

These regular slashes of graffiti on public monuments and exposed concrete walls throughout the city seemed to echo Dee's own inner anguish.

30,000 ¿Donde están?
The 30,000 – Where are they?

30 Años. ¡Nunca Más!
30 years. Never again!

There was a dignified determination in the statement 'Never again', but it occurred to Dee that she had nothing so concrete against which to set her will. Only the blank impotence of the question, 'Where is my daughter?' The plaintive vulnerability of someone constantly broadcasting absence. *¿Dónde están?*

Over thirty years had passed since the city had lost thirty thousand of its bravest and brightest young people. The laments had become muted with the passing of time, but the popular commitment to protest and resistance remained undaunted. Last night the *murga* drums had pounded in the streets around Dee's hotel until three am. When she mentioned it to the concierge in the morning he told her that there was an election looming and there would be more protests and street marches in the days and weeks ahead. Thirty years ago Dee would have been excited to be caught up in such a wave of collective rebellion, but now it struck her as strident and futile. She had lost faith in popular protest a long time ago. Perhaps she had been beaten into submission by her own history or perhaps that was what happened to everyone eventually: loss of faith, a narrowing of allegiance to the parsimonious hopes of the lone and struggling self.

There was a trickle of people emerging from the Basílica del Pilar next to the famous cemetery at Recoleta. Dee supposed that morning Mass had just finished. The small church had high white walls, dark wooden pews and a red-tiled floor. Heavy columns on either side framed alcoves in which statues of the saints and various manifestations of the Virgin all but disappeared amidst Latin excesses of gold filigree and ornamentation.

'The great thing about the Catholic Mass,' Dee's father had

regularly declaimed to Dee and her brother, 'is that it's always the same. Wherever you are in the world you can go into a Catholic church and feel at home.'

This church was not like those Dee had attended as a child in Australia. Religious décor had gone minimalist there in the 1970s, informed by fashion as well as the democratic surge of the second Vatican Council. Looking around at all the gold and gilt, the effigies of saints caught in gestures of long-suffering piety, the heavy crucifix weighted with the tortured body of the Christ, Dee had to acknowledge that it was, nevertheless, very familiar. Too familiar. All that sacrificial imagery had taken up permanent residence in her imagination, reinforcing the ubiquitous sense of her own unworthiness. She worried now about the effect of dragging her own children off to Mass and hauling them through the Sacraments during their tender, formative years. By the time they hit high school they were refusing to go and she had only put up a token resistance to their rebellion. Her certainties were crumbling by then, but perhaps the damage had already been done. She had asked Ben recently, 'Did you hate being forced to go to church?' He had looked blank. 'Did you force us to go?' But her anxieties weren't only about church attendance, were they? They were about how deeply she had infected her children with her own sense of never being good enough. They were about hounding her daughter in a way that she had never hounded her sons – over petty failings and lapses of good taste and deportment and the evasion of domestic responsibilities; they were about the way she had not been able to resist attempting to conscript her daughter into the double bind of being female: you must sacrifice more but expect less.

On the lawns opposite the cemetery, the *artesanos* were setting up their stalls. An old man dressed in black with a battered guitar was playing tango favourites from the Carlos Gardel days, trying to catch the eyes of the tourists, his volume and passion swelling with any hint of passing interest. Artists hung their brightly coloured depictions of tango dancers and the colourful portside suburb of La Boca on easels and scaffolds.

It was the sort of place that had enchanted Dee when she was young. She had always loved the bohemian atmosphere of weekend artists' fairs. They were like pieces of a child's dream that had escaped into the dreary adult world and set up shop. Here, as everywhere, the silverware, bangles and beads were accompanied by fortune-tellers, puppeteers and buskers. Lean young men in black T-shirts, reeking of dope and patchouli, rolled their own cigarettes and stared at passing females with mocking intimacy. Plump, frizzle-haired women knitted behind piles of misty mohair shawls and rough-spun cardigans. Grey-bearded men with deft hands created miniature sculptures out of nails and coins and wire. One elderly woman presided over a stall where all the wares – little figurines and boxes – were made of orange peel. '¡*Cáscara de naranja!*' she declared proudly, almost defiantly, waving her arm over the goods on display. Dee never failed to be touched by such obsessions.

Corrie and Ross had both had something of this in them – artistic absorption in small things. In Corrie's case, it was the study of people, their dress and gesture, facial expressions and vocal intonation. Even before she took up formal drama studies at school, from the time she was quite young, she had demonstrated a remarkable capacity for observation and mimicry, amusing the family with her impersonations. She emerged from the bedroom once dressed as their Indian neighbour, Mrs Bhandari, wrapped in coloured scarves, a large red dot painted on her forehead, making inquiries in a singsong accent. She could similarly evoke a number of her primary school teachers: Mr Scribner, who constantly ran his hands through his hair and grinned inanely, Ms Cootes, with her darting eyes and pursed lips. Ross and Dee had also featured in her repertoire. Ross she always did goofy and chuckling, one arm wrapped affectionately around someone's shoulders. She had a particular signature gesture for Dee: slightly bowed head, thumb and forefinger pinching the bridge of her nose, eyes closed, eyebrows hauled high on her forehead. Dee hadn't realised how frequently she adopted this theatrical stance of constrained pain and irritation, but had recognised herself instantly. Ross, Luke and Ben had been hugely amused. Dee had laughed too, not wanting to appear a bad sport.

*

She was one of the first to arrive at Alicia's *asado*, having overestimated the commuting time from the city, but she did not mind being early in the way she minded being early to similar events in Australia. Socialising in the last few years had become an awkward process. Being a widow was difficult enough, as many women will attest. You are the odd person around the table, the one who must be matched with someone. Your hosts feel compelled to invite their longstanding bachelor friends or the recently divorced or those resonant with other forms of loss or social liability.

Corrie's disappearance had added another layer of awkwardness. People were overly solicitous, their eyes a little too curious. She was 'that-woman-whose-daughter-went-missing-in-South-America'. She came with a small thrill of tragedy, a poignant reminder of the 'Moving Finger, You Do not Know the Day nor the Hour, There But for the Grace of God,' etc. etc., and there was a little touch of something that was not quite smugness but, well, a sort of gratitude in their demeanour towards her – a relief that it was her and not them.

In Argentina her story was not so novel. Everyone had lost somebody and the particular hardship of unresolved endings was something she shared with many others. When people referred to such things, the allusions were formal and studied, but they did not isolate her in a sticky fog of pity, in the manner of: *Oh, you are so brave. I would never have the strength* . . . Such responses unwittingly held her at a distance. Under the guise of sanctifying her, they quarantined her. There was a stronger sense of communal responsibility here. *Los acompaño en su sentimiento.* I am with you in your sadness. *Estoy a su disposición aunque mas no sea para sentir la cercanía del cariño*. I am at your disposal if only so you might feel the nearness of affection.

It was a warm spring afternoon. Yellow sunlight fell in folds across the green lawn; the air was rich with the rich odours of seared meat. Flamenco-jazz guitar wafted from speakers directed through the French doors at the rear of the house.

Alicia's husband was preparing *asado*, cooking plump chunks of sausage, offal and marbled slabs of fillet on an impressive brick barbecue he had constructed himself at the back of the garden. Juan Pablo was a solidly built man, Germanic in appearance, with a round, ruddy face and thinning blond hair. As a grain exporter he was one of the few who had done well out of the 2001 economic collapse. Dealing in foreign currency gave him a certain advantage over those who were obliged to rely on the savaged local peso.

'Juan Pablo, I bought some bottles of that Wirra Wirra shiraz you enjoyed last time I was here.'

'*¡Qué bárbaro!* And Dee, look, I have bought extra *morcillas*, especially for you!' Juan Pablo held a fat, claret-coloured sausage aloft with long tongs.

'But there are only two dozen. What will everyone else eat?'

Juan Pablo was amused by the fact that Dee ate the local blood sausage. When he'd first offered them, she had been reluctant to appear squeamish and confirm his prediction that she would reject them like most foreigners. She had hoped to become accustomed to the rich, coagulated texture and sweet, metallic flavour, but there were still times when they almost made her gag. Now it had become a point of pride. She refused to let Juan Pablo know that she had been affecting enjoyment of them for the last four years, as this seemed a greater character weakness than refusing to try them in the first place. At the same time, she suspected that he already knew, and found her stoicism endearing rather than contemptible.

'Dee, can I trust you with my *morcillas*? They must go into the oven now – no eating them on the way to the kitchen, you understand?'

'*Sí, comandante.*'

'I know of course that it is nearly impossible for women to resist my sausage, but you will have to control yourself a little longer.'

She was not good with cheap double entendre, even when she had the advantage of being more fluent in the language in which it was framed. She lacked the requisite boldness, was too cautious with her own and others' feelings to join in the banter. The best she could manage in this instance was a hackneyed roll of the eyes before making a quick retreat to the house with the plate of sausages.

Alicia and Juan Pablo's back room, the room where they entertained, was decorated in a rustic style with rendered walls and stone floors, folkloric rugs, cushions and an array of indigenous artefacts and carvings. There were also many framed photographs of their children and grandchildren. Set prominently on the mantelpiece was an enlargement of a grainy black-and-white photograph in which a young man with long hair and a wispy beard waved a cigarette at the camera, laughing. With his other arm, he hugged the shoulders of a teenage Alicia who was also laughing. Dee knew from previous inquiries that the photo was of Alicia's brother, Aurelio. He had disappeared one night in 1976 following an anti-government demonstration and had never been found. A candle in a small glass was kept alight beside his picture. A statue of *La Virgen de Luján* kept vigil. Whenever Dee had been left alone in this room she found her attention returning obsessively to Aurelio's image. No one believed he was still alive and Alicia was resigned to the fact that, after thirty years, they were unlikely to find any physical remains. All she hoped for now were fragments of his story. Someone who had seen him or spoken to him or heard of him in those last days. Words. Images. Clues to the state of his heart. Mementos of ordinary human feeling to relieve the weight of the monstrous unknown. Something by which she could follow him down that last, dark tunnel, could at least be present to him in imagination, because the spectre of his loneliness at the end could still cause her to wake weeping in the haunted hours of the early morning.

Alicia and Graciela, the family's long-serving nanny and housekeeper, were at work in the kitchen. Alicia was making *empanadas*, sealing up the last of the pastries before putting them in the oven. Graciela was preparing a dessert. Her round face and clay-coloured skin hinted at Guaraní ancestry. She was a solid, quiet woman who seldom smiled. Alicia had assured Dee that this was not due to animosity but embarrassment over her missing front teeth.

'*Hola, Graciela.*' Dee made an uncertain movement towards her.

Graciela offered her cheek without expression and hastened to take the tray of *morcillas*.

'*¿Dulce de leche?*' Dee asked about the soft caramel Graciela was spooning into the flan.

'*Sí.*'

'*¡La comida favorita de Argentina!*' Argentina's favourite food!

'*Sí.*'

Perhaps Graciela sensed Dee's desire to demonstrate her egalitarianism by conversing with the help and refused to indulge it. Or perhaps it was just her teeth.

'*¡Ya está!* Dee, *¿vino?*' Alicia filled two glasses with a generous flourish of local syrah as the front doorbell rang.

She moved quickly to answer it and Dee heard her enthusiastic greeting, answered by a quieter male voice, which, while speaking fluent enough Spanish, did not resonate with the same rhythmic percussiveness as a native speaker's.

When Alicia brought her guest into the lounge room, Dee was startled to see the pale, bespectacled man from the Plaza Asturias, dressed casually in black trousers and a colourful shirt.

'*De-irrr-dra, Me gustaría presentarte a mi amigo, Esteban—*' Alicia held up a finger in self-correction, '*No – en Ingles* – I present to you my friend, Stee-phen.' Dee wanted to tell her the translation was not necessary. She liked the way Argentineans immediately turned English names into their Spanish equivalents, the way they renamed you as one of their own.

'*Es de Inglaterra. Él está trabajando en la parroquia de mi hermano.*' Alicia paused after the announcement that this Englishman worked in her brother's parish and Dee could see that she was scrolling through her limited repertoire of English. 'A very beautiful man!' she finished triumphantly.

Stephen waved away her compliment. 'Alicia thinks everyone is very beautiful.'

Dee took his proffered hand. 'I think we've met before. In the Plaza Asturias, last Thursday evening?'

He touched his glasses and looked at her closely. 'Oh, yes. I remember. Deirdre is it?'

'Deird*ra*. A piece of whimsy on the part of my father. Some Irish ancestor. But everyone calls me Dee.'

'Got to watch those Irish ancestors.'

'Personal experience speaking?'

'Oh, no. English as far back as anyone cares to remember.'

Alicia pressed a glass of wine into Stephen's hand and spoke to him in animated Spanish for several minutes. He nodded and asked questions, his eyes averted, blinking rapidly as he processed what she was telling him. Alicia eventually ended the conversation with a decisive '*bueno*' and turned back to Dee with her laughing smile. 'Now you talk *Inglés*.'

'Alicia was just telling me about one of the boys in the parish,' Stephen explained. 'She's worried because his mother's new boyfriend has thrown him out of home, which leaves him enormously vulnerable to reviving the *paco* habit he's been struggling with over the last few months.'

'*Paco?*'

'It's the rubbish left over from processing cocaine for the international market. At fifty centavos a hit it's the drug of choice for the completely destitute. But enough of all that. What brings you to Argentina and how do you know Alicia?'

The dreaded question. But somehow his calm familiarity with desperation and damage made it easier for Dee to confess.

'I hosted Marco when he was studying in Australia—'

'That was good of you.'

'No, wait. As they say in the commercials, there's more.'

The assumed flippancy helped propel her towards the darker material. A style she'd learned from Liz.

'My daughter, Corrie, came over here to visit Marco in 2005, but not long after that we lost contact with her. There's been no word since. I've been back and forth a lot over the last few years, looking for her.'

It was a great conversation stopper and she no longer waited for the hurtful inanities and platitudes that people reached for to fill the awkward silence.

'Alicia has been so kind. I don't know what I would have done without her,' she continued briskly.

Stephen acknowledged her clunky segue with a twitch of a smile and hastened to smooth over her discomfort. 'She's an extraordinary woman. You know she went through something similar with her brother? But I'm sorry to hear about your daughter. It must be very difficult.'

'And what about you? What's your interest in Argentina? You seem very at home here.'

He swirled the wine in his glass. 'I had a stint out here as a young curate back in the early eighties. I was studying liberation theology. Fell in love with the people and the culture. Kept coming back. They can't get rid of me now.'

'You're a priest?'

There was a shadow of hesitation before he answered. 'Yes.'

'You don't have parish responsibilities in England, then?'

There was a longer pause and he did not meet her eyes as he answered. 'I'm taking extended leave at the moment.'

Dee furrowed her brow sympathetically. It was nice not to be the only one harbouring conversation spoilers. She wondered if the beautiful young man in the restaurant had any bearing on his current status.

'Really?' She knew it was crass to fish, but her curiosity was piqued.

He sipped his wine slowly. 'What part of Australia are you from?'

'Adelaide. South Australia.'

'Oh, yes, I have friends in Adelaide. Progressive little place by all accounts.'

'Used to be. Back in the seventies. And you? Where are you from?'

'I'm a London boy.'

'The big smoke.'

'Indeed.'

The conversation stalled. They sipped self-consciously from their wine glasses and then spoke over the top of each other.

'I'm sorry – you first.' He blinked apologetically and encouraged her to continue with a roll of his hand.

'I just said it's a nice drop – the wine. Can't believe they don't have more of an export market.'

'Yes. It's a common theme. Lots of natural resources, but they don't capitalise on them as much as they could. Borges claimed Argentineans have a basic mistrust of the state. He said they could only conceive of personal relations, not civic ones. Therefore acts of civic subversion for personal gain were seen as heroics rather than crimes. There's a lot of corruption and a great deal of disorganisation.'

'Yes.' Her tone was pointed, but Stephen seemed not to notice.

'I've told them, you know, they should have embraced British rule when they had the chance. They made a big mistake when they repelled our advances on Buenos Aires in 1806.' A self-parodying smile flickered on and off like a faulty fluorescent light.

'Don't worry. You've still got the Falklands.'

He grimaced, enacted a stealthy look over his shoulder and spoke in a stage whisper. 'Ssh! Nobody likes to be reminded about that.'

It made her laugh.

'Speaking of which, I need to go and trade a few insults with my great adversary, Juan Pablo. How do you feel about lurking around the barbecue with the menfolk?'

'You go. I've already run the gauntlet of Juan Pablo's sausage humour.'

As he got to his feet Alicia re-entered the room with her daughter, Paola, son-in-law, Diego, Marco and his girlfriend, Sylvia. Marco moved forward to brush Dee's cheek with his own, the usual look of apologetic anguish on his face.

Poor Marco, she thought. It wasn't fair that he'd had to carry the weight of her family's tragedy. He was too young.

She embraced him lightly. 'Lovely to see you.'

Alicia cradled her daughter's new baby in the crook of one arm and held the hand of a three-year-old boy with dark hair and wide brown eyes.

Dee bent towards the boy with an exaggerated smile, and attempted to take his hand in greeting, '*¡Hola Rafaelito! ¡Qué alto que estás!*' But he moved quickly behind Alicia and stared mistrustfully out of the corner of the eye not pressed into her trouser leg. It saddened Dee. Children seemed particularly sensitive to her aura of suppressed anguish, so she usually avoided them. This was not something she could easily explain to her Argentine friends, for whom children were the delightful centrepiece of every social gathering.

'*¡Lito! ¿No te acordás de Deirdra?*' Alicia stroked the little boy's hair indulgently. 'Don't you remember Deirdra?'

Graciela had finished distributing the first round of empanadas to everyone and swooped upon him. Rafaelito raised his eager arms to hers and was carried into the kitchen for the sweets he knew she always kept hidden for him.

The house gradually filled with people, loud conversations and intermittent laughter. Juan Pablo eventually invited the guests to be seated at a long table on the back patio. Bowls of salad and baskets of bread were placed at even intervals along the white cloth, flanked by cutlery, generous wine glasses and linen napkins. They were twelve at the table: Juan Pablo and Alicia, Paola and Diego, Marco and Sylvia, Stephen and Dee, Agostina, one of Alicia's friends from the parish community centre, Agostina's husband, Claudio, Lucas Morales, a business partner of Juan Pablo's and his young wife, Cecilia.

Alicia assisted Graciela to bring in the five meat courses, starting with the sausages: paprika-flavoured *chorizos*, followed by the *morcillas*. Then there was the offal course – the sweet and soft-textured *mollejas*, then ribs and finally the spectacular Argentinean fillet steak.

'A vegetarian's worst nightmare, really,' Stephen murmured to Dee as he mopped up the sweet, oily juices of the *mollejas* with a chunk of bread.

Alicia had placed Stephen next to Dee, with Agostina, a faithful churchgoer, on his left. On Dee's right she had seated Cecilia, who was studying tourism and had, consequently, excellent English.

The afternoon wore slowly and luxuriously away. As the shadows of the jacarandas lengthened across the garden, Alicia brought out woollen shawls, products of one of the weaving workshops she ran with a group of Paraguayan women who had recently arrived in her parish. Dee's Spanish had improved considerably with the many glasses of *vino tinto* she'd imbibed and she believed herself to be making great strides in her conversation with Cecilia, who was actually speaking to her in English. An enthusiastic *porteña*, Cecilia was filling Dee in on some of the things she might like to see in Buenos Aires during her stay. Dee found herself blithely exclaiming, '¡*Qué maravilloso!*' every time Cecilia paused for a response.

'On Sundays there is a very nice antiques fair in San Telmo – at the Plaza Dorrego. I think that it would be interesting for you. There are also artists and music groups. If you like, I could meet you there tomorrow.'

Dee acquiesced readily. She was generally very social after a few drinks, less sensitive to the complicated nuances of human interaction that, in more sober circumstances, reduced her to wary passivity.

'¡*Qué maravilloso!* I would love that!' She leant across Stephen, interrupting his conversation with Agostina. 'Stephen, have you seen the Feria San Telmo? Come with Cecilia and me tomorrow!'

'I can't I'm afraid. Sunday Mass. But you heathens trot right along.'

She gave him a playful slap. Watched herself giving him a 'playful slap'. Noticed the delay in becoming aware of his slightly startled look. Noticed herself feeling amused by his startled look. Felt glad to feel amused and not worried about her presumptuous behaviour. Knew also, somewhere in the back of her mind, that she *would* feel worried about her presumptuous behaviour when the wine wore off. But because the alcohol made it difficult to hold more than one thought at a time, this latter idea slid away without leaving the usual stain of apprehension.

'We could meet after Mass is finished. What time does it start, Cecilia?'

'From about ten o'clock, but the stalls are open until five or six.'

'Why don't you meet us for lunch, Stephen?'

He grimaced in a show of disappointment. 'We have our big football match in the afternoon. We're trying to get a neighbourhood competition going – give the boys something to do apart from theft and vandalism.'

'I guess that's too noble to argue with. Maybe I should come and watch you play football instead?'

'Oh, I don't play. I just run up and down with a flag.'

'That's still impressive.'

'Here, this will make you even more impressed.' He threw her a wink, topped up her wine glass and refilled his own.

Agostina seized his elbow and started to berate him about something, bursting into great gusts of open-mouthed laughter every so often, which triggered his own laughter – a sudden, abruptly abbreviated trumpet blast of mirth. The whole table joined in and even though she had no idea what the joke was about, Dee mirrored the collective jollity with her own polite giggles.

'Agostina!' Juan Pablo put a *cumbia* track on the stereo and pumped up the volume, holding out his arms. Agostina laughed and waved one arm dismissively while continuing her conversation with Stephen. Juan Pablo came and threaded her out of her chair anyway, despite her loud but not especially sincere protests.

It didn't take long before Paola had prevailed upon Stephen and Diego had drawn Dee up with a questioning hand and a gesture of his head towards the others.

'*No sé bailar muy bien,*' she apologised in advance, noting Stephen's shambling arrhythmic movements out of the corner of one eye.

'It is expected that we *gringos* should dance badly!' Stephen proclaimed, his own pomposity roaming free since its bashful keeper got knocked temporarily unconscious by red wine. 'Never apologise, Dee! Dance as badly as possible, but always with panache!' This last pronouncement was followed by an ungainly twist of his narrow hips, applauded delightedly by Paola.

It was after midnight when the party started to wind down. Paola and Diego carted away their sleeping children, Agostina hugged everyone many times, Marco and Sylvia left for a nightclub and Cecilia took pains to ensure that Dee understood the time and place of their rendezvous at San Telmo the following day. Juan Pablo disappeared in the direction of the bedroom and did not return. Stephen, Dee and Alicia finally fell semi-comatose into soft armchairs surrounded by wine-stained glasses and half-eaten slabs of Graciela's *dulce de leche* tart.

Alicia gave Stephen a *mate* gourd full of *yerba* and a thermos of hot water, telling him to act as *servidor* while she cleaned up in the kitchen and stacked the dishwasher. She joked that she didn't want to risk Graciela's anger on Monday morning. Stephen added water to the *mate* and passed it to Dee. The brew was slightly bitter. Like drinking mown grass steeped in hot water. But Dee knew from previous experience that it was not so much the drink as the camaraderie that mattered.

They sat in comfortable silence by the light of a single lamp, listening to Mercedes Sosa's husky clarion tones playing on Juan Pablo's expensive sound system.

'So. What are your plans for the rest of your time in Buenos Aires?' Stephen asked eventually.

Dee thought for a while. 'I don't know. I think it's becoming clearer to me that this is a farewell of sorts. A journey of letting go, if you like.'

She cast her mind back to the earlier trips she had made. In the beginning there had been such urgent and painful purposefulness – retracing Corrie's steps, talking to as many people as she could find, bus drivers and tour guides, hotel receptionists, waiters and shopkeepers, hounding police and officials. In those days her daily life was full of the memory of Corrie, full of hope for a future that would still include her. Over time, however, the inexorable weight of ongoing existence had carved out different patterns of expectation and feeling; hope had become more of a burden than a promise. She had continued to move doggedly forward but only because it had kept her one step ahead of the more terrifying prospect of giving up altogether. The year before she had noticed that her annual visit to Buenos Aires had started to assume the character of a pilgrimage – a simple act of fidelity to Corrie's memory.

'I don't think I've really allowed myself to confront the fact that I may never see Corrie again. Perhaps that's what I'm working my way towards on this visit.'

'And what do you think you need to do to come to terms with that idea?'

'Well, Alicia and I saw the ambassador on Thursday. He let us know that the inquiry has well and truly wound up on the official level. Pending any further information, I guess.'

Stephen topped up the *mate* with more water and passed it back to her. 'That must have been difficult.'

'I guess I already knew it at one level. There really hasn't been any activity on that front for a long time. But, yes, it's different when someone officially announces the fact. It means that anything that comes to light from now on will be pure happenstance: a chance sighting; an intersection with some other crime or event.'

'An act of God's grace, maybe?'

'If you like.' She passed the *mate* back to him.

He looked at her thoughtfully for a few seconds. 'Dee, what do *you* think has happened to your daughter?'

She met his eyes steadily. 'I can't let go of the belief that she's still alive. Perhaps it's just what I *want* to believe. Perhaps it's because I can't bear the alternative. But it's what I feel, in my bones. In my waters, as my grandmother used to say.'

'Alive but not able to make contact with you?'

She shrugged. 'Unable. Unwilling. I don't know.'

'That can't be easy either.'

'I don't need her to be dead so I can feel better about myself.'

'No, of course not. But it would be hurtful, nevertheless.'

'It happens. We can live whole lifetimes not knowing what we've done to the people we love. I wasn't a perfect mother. I made mistakes. Those mistakes might have been unforgivable.'

These were things that she did not often voice. How susceptible she was to priests and nuns, she thought, how much access she allowed them to tender, concealed places. Bless me, Father, for I have sinned. It has been thirty-five years since my last confession and these are my sins . . .

'No such thing as an unforgivable mistake.'

'That's a nice theory, but children are vulnerable creatures and mothers have a lot of power. I have no way of knowing how much damage I did or didn't do. The police pursued that line of questioning pretty vigorously: Did we have a fight? Was she upset about anything? Had I tried to force her to do something she didn't want to? It was quite the opposite actually. I was the one who suggested she might like to get away for a while. She had a pretty hard time of it when her father died—'

'Your husband died?'

'Yes – I'm a walking soap opera, aren't I? Ross died nine months before Corrie disappeared. They were very close. She was devastated by his death and she didn't settle into university well. Marco had gone back to Argentina and I thought she might have been missing him so I encouraged her to take a break from her studies and pay him a visit. She'd always wanted to travel and I thought she'd be safer in a place where she knew someone. Ironic, isn't it? You can't imagine the number of times I've gone over all this in my head. And then I find myself wondering – maybe she thought I was trying to get rid of her. Maybe she felt rejected. Maybe she felt that she wasn't wanted or needed. But I thought I was doing the right thing. I was always careful not to cling to my children. I didn't want to saddle them with my needs.'

Stephen stretched his legs out in front of him and took a long sip of *mate*. 'Why was that a particular concern? Not appearing needy?'

'Trying to avoid the patterns of my own upbringing, I suppose.'

'You had a needy mother?'

She found herself flinching against this characterisation, even though it was what she had implied. 'She had a lot of sickness.'

'Is she still alive?'

'No. She died when I was sixteen. Ovarian cancer. She'd been having chemo on and off for about two years. I wasn't as attentive or as kind as I should've been. Consumed with myself. Feeling resentful about having missed out on all the normal teenage stuff my friends seemed to be enjoying.'

'Pretty normal sixteen-year-old behaviour, I'd say.'

'I often point that out to myself. It's a convenient excuse.'

'Well, it's an excuse.' He passed her the *mate*. 'It's like passing a bong around, isn't it?' he observed, smiling.

'Was that a part of your misspent youth, Father? I wouldn't know about such things.' But she smiled to show that she was only enacting primness. That she too may once have been a bohemian.

'You know, you probably weren't half as bad a mother as you seem to think you were.'

Alicia came in from the kitchen and sat on the arm of Dee's chair.

'What do you think, Alicia?' Dee asked her '*¿Qué piensas?* Do Argentinean mothers feel guilty about everything? Or is it peculiar to the neurotic west?'

She looked blank.

'*¿Las madres argentinas se sienten culpables por todo lo que hacen?*' Stephen translated.

Alicia frowned and shook her head vigorously in disagreement. She spoke at length, directing the flow of rhetoric to Stephen but casting pointed glances at Dee by way of punctuation. When she finished Stephen blew out his breath in a long stream.

'As you may have gathered, Alicia has strong feelings on this topic. Firstly she says that of course there are many women who feel guilty, especially poor women who want something better for their children but know that they can never achieve this. For middle-class women there is guilt, too. They strive for the careers and opportunities that their mothers never had, but then they are torn between their careers and their families. There is never enough time to do everything properly. We always want so much for our children. She thinks maybe it is the wanting that is the problem. Maybe we should focus more on the love that underlies these hopes. Not the sentimental feelings – but the daily sacrifices, the active works of love that help our children to take their places in the world. This is the sacred work of the mother, but also a task that must be shared. It is not only the mother's responsibility.'

'Phew!' Dee laughed and performed a charade of mental reeling. 'That's a step up from the sort of social banter we Australians are used to.'

'*¿No estás de acuerdo?*'

'*Sí, sí.* It's true. You are right. *Es verdad. Tenés razón.*' But Dee continued to hold Stephen's gaze and smile at their shared joke, which exasperated Alicia even further.

'*¿De qué te ries?*' Why are you laughing?

'Nothing. *Nada. Los ingleses, no somos tan intelectuales como los latinoamericanos.* We English aren't as sophisticated as Latin Americans.'

But Dee could tell that Alicia still felt patronised. She didn't know why she was making such a joke of what Alicia had said, but perhaps it was because it felt like another impossible ideal. She would have liked to believe that she had created such a legacy of love for her own children, but her belief faltered around that question. She could not find herself in Alicia's description of motherhood. She could only find more traces of absence.

Her watch read two am.

'I guess I should think about leaving.'

'*Puedes quedarte aquí.*' Alicia's invitation to stay was issued in the bossy maternal tone that made Dee feel more welcome than any amount of solicitude.

'Thanks, Alicia, but I arranged to meet Cecilia in the city tomorrow.'

She shrugged. '*¿Quieres que llame a un taxi?*'

'*Gracias.*'

Stephen got up to retrieve his jacket from a hook by the front door. 'We won't be seeing you at Mass, then?'

'Maybe some other time.'

Alicia and Stephen waited with her out the front of the house until the taxi arrived.

'*Llamame.*'

'Yes, I'll call, Alicia.'

'Call me, too,' Stephen insisted.

'Too.'

It was pretty lame, but Stephen laughed as they traded phone numbers.

Jolting around in the back of the apparently suspension-less taxi on the return journey to the city, Dee replayed the images of the day in her head, recalling the moments of laughter and kindness, scanning the vista of interactions for false notes or little slippages that may have revealed too much of her own weaknesses or the intensity of her desire for acceptance. Days like this one were rare, days on which she was able to transcend the barriers between herself and others and simply revel in their company. The sociability of her Argentinean friends made it easier for some reason, but camaraderie was something that she had never been particularly good at.

A scene sprang to mind. She was looking out of the kitchen window at home onto the back garden. Ross had made a set of soccer goals and was trying them out with the kids. The light, gold-saturated from the setting sun, was making all the greens glow like a picture book. She remembered thinking how beautiful it was. Had she been yearning to join in the game with Ross and the kids? Not really. She'd come to know herself better than that. She'd learned that her self-consciousness and tendency towards high seriousness were spoilers. She always competed too fiercely or failed to take the game seriously enough. She could never find the right rhythm for playfulness, flailing between various modes of excess, ultimately alienated and bored by the effort. There were no such complications in Ross – no layers between himself and his children. No panes of glass. No pain.

So she'd arrived at the decision to leave such things to him – the play, the make-believe, the silliness that was so crucial to childhood. Her contribution was to keep the household running smoothly, facilitate the necessary activities, clean up the mess. *Have you done your homework? What do you want on your sandwiches? Have you fed the cat? Turn the television off and go outside and play. There's fruit on the table. No, you've had three pieces of toast already. It's bedtime. No – not at the next ad break – now!* The background static of their lives. It wasn't her only mode of communication with them. Just the primary one.

She could see the scene so clearly now: Ross weaving the ball expertly between the children's lunging attempts to intercept it, passing it off to Ben, who immediately lost it to Corrie. Luke stealing it from her and scoring. The four of them running in circles around the yard with their T-shirts pulled over their heads before they purposely collided and ended up in a heap on the lawn. Even then she had known: this is what they will remember when they are old – these are the moments that will stay with them. Long summer evenings, soccer games in the backyard, the smell of grass, their father rolling on the ground. That was the stuff of the heart, the stuff that sticks.

She could have removed her dishwashing gloves that evening. She could have walked away from the sink, hurried out to the garden to join them. She was trying to imagine it, but the scene still played false. She couldn't do it then and she couldn't imagine it now. The dishes needed to be finished and then there would have been school lunches to organise for the next day, probably a load of ironing and then a pile of marking and lesson preparation for the week ahead. There was always something to do. Some act of defiant organisation to keep the chaos at bay.

It had been exhausting. And the exhaustion had turned to resentment and the desire to prickle and punish. Ross and the kids had learned to skirt around her outbreaks of nastiness, to ignore the tight-lipped fury and scathing remarks. They had learned to lie low, awaiting the ricochet into repentance and compensatory kindness. They went outside and played soccer. And she watched them through the window.

Chapter Four

Dee set out at lunchtime the following day to meet Cecilia. Just past the basilica of San Francisco on Avenida Defensa, she noticed the first street-sellers, squatting on the kerb behind white groundsheets on which their wares were displayed. After a few blocks there were no gaps between the street-sellers. A long multicoloured carpet of crafts and bright baubles for the tourists extended down both sides of the street for several kilometres. The road was closed to traffic and buskers of various kinds had set up in the middle of the thoroughfare. She stopped to watch a tango orchestra made up of seven bearded youths, who possessed the sort of attentiveness to their craft and cool detachment from their audience that marks serious musicianship. They had somehow managed to manoeuvre an upright piano onto the cobblestone streets. It rhythmically underscored the warm lament of the cello, the swooping violin melodies and the eerie hurdy-gurdy tones of the *bandoneónes*. The players' facial expressions were deadpan, but the music wept and whirled.

As she approached the Plaza Dorrego, she noticed an increasing number of antique shops. One in particular caught her attention. It boasted a treasure trove of posters, magazines, comic books and sheet music. Luke and Ben would love this place, she thought. Overlapping layers of plastic-wrapped pictures lined the walls from floor to ceiling and there were many more piled on tables, chairs and every other available surface. She sifted cursorily through the nearest stack uncovering some old Cream and Hendrix posters that were too good to walk away from. The assistant, a stockily built man in jeans and an old grey pullover, balanced a lit cigarette in the corner of his mouth as he rolled the posters expertly and slipped a rubber band around them.

'*¿Para vos?*'

'*No, para mis hijos.*' For my sons.

It had always been easier to buy things for the boys. Dee had agonised over gifts for Corrie and never got it right. Their aesthetic preferences seemed diametrically opposed. By design or accident? Dee was never sure. From kindergarten days they had battled over clothing choices. It had caused Dee particular anguish when, at a time when they were really struggling financially, a friend had delivered several boxes of good-quality hand-me-downs from her own children and Corrie had refused to wear any of them. Sadness that they were reliant on this sort of charity wrestled with common sense, and then segued into anger over Corrie's intractable stubbornness. Dee had ended up throwing the offending items in her daughter's face and marching from the room. Things didn't improve much when she could afford to pursue her own choices for Corrie.

'Are you doing this on purpose, Mum?'

'What do you mean?'

'I would *never* wear anything like that.'

'Oh, for God's sake, I'll give you the money and you can do your own shopping from now on.'

No matter how hard she tried, she and her daughter always seemed to deeply disappoint each other. The boys' utilitarianism was much easier to deal with. Even when they tossed things aside with cavalier indifference it never felt like the same indictment of her taste and capacity for discernment. Was it because they were easier to please? Or because Dee's self-conception was less wedded to their reactions?

Two mime artists had taken up position in a frozen tableau opposite the poster shop. A few metres away, a living statue of the 1920s tango singer, Carlos Gardel, made a stylised shift in posture. His coat of white body paint was relieved by a single red rose in his lapel and a black band on his chalky fedora. Dee contributed generously to the cache of coins and notes in his velvet-lined collection box, recalling that her daughter had applied herself with similar seriousness to her own performance skills, a seriousness Dee had, on occasion, been unable to resist subverting.

In Year 10, Corrie had won a place with a highly regarded youth theatre company. 'Pulse' survived on a plethora of government grants, making it somewhat susceptible to collaborations on various health and wellbeing campaigns. Dee couldn't remember whether the particular play she was recalling was the one about youth suicide or binge drinking. Corrie's performance had been excellent and there were moments when Dee had felt genuinely absorbed in the action. She and Ross waited with the other parents in the foyer afterwards and when Corrie eventually appeared, still in costume and smeared with hastily removed stage make-up, Ross was ebullient with praise.

'That was fantastic! You were amazing!'

'What did you think, Mum?' Corrie had turned excitedly to Dee.

'Look, I was pleasantly surprised.'

Her face had fallen. 'Why? Did you think it was going to be crap?'

'No! It's just that, well, I felt somewhat beaten over the head by the last one. There was a tad too much vomit. Or something. But tonight was great. I thought your performance was excellent – really subtle and nicely judged. I mean, compared – to that other lass – the one who played Rebecca – Ms Hysterical Monotone. How did she get that part? Daddy must have made a whopping donation.'

'That's not how it works, Mum. I've told you that before. She wasn't that bad. She worked really hard on that part.'

'Anyway, you were great. You really lifted the standard.'

'What do you mean? What standard? Absolute rubbish? Is that what you're saying?' Corrie looked away with a pained expression. Ross moved quickly to smooth over the moment.

'I thought it was phenomenal, sweetheart. It blows me away how you can do that stuff – get up in front of people and remember all those lines – cool as a cucumber.'

'I didn't feel as cool as a cucumber. Did you see that bit when I banged into the refrigerator?'

Dee had jumped in quickly, trying to redeem herself. 'You pulled it off brilliantly. It looked like it was intentional.'

'No,' Ross said firmly. 'Didn't see a thing.'

Dee always got it wrong. She and her Asperger's-like compulsion to tell the truth, the whole truth and nothing but the truth.

Enough. She could feel her equilibrium wilting under the barrage of self-reproach. Cecilia had arranged to meet her outside the Café Dorrego, and there she was, hurrying forward to curtail Dee's anxious scanning of the crowded plaza.

'¡Hola, Deirdra!'

Cecilia was the epitome of casual elegance in a simple, white linen dress, strappy sandals and bold silver jewellery. Her blonde-streaked hair was loose and hung past her shoulders. Dee was suddenly conscious of the middle-aged bulk of her hips in her well-worn jeans, the faded quality of her T-shirt, the riot of carnival colour in her beads and earrings.

'What a gorgeous bracelet,' she said, touching the two-inch band of roughly beaten silver on Cecilia's wrist.

'Yes, I love it. It's from one of my favourite designers in Palermo Viejo.'

'Gorgeous,' Dee said again, not sure why she kept repeating a word that sounded so affected, even to herself, and feeling suddenly inadequate about the absence of 'favourite designers' in her own life. Well, the absence of designers in general.

'Are you hungry?'

'I had a late breakfast.'

'Good. Me too. Shall we walk?'

The bric-a-brac stalls in the square were cluttered with the usual array of flea market wares but with an interesting Spanish or Gaucho twist. Cecilia chatted away happily about the immigrant history of San Telmo, its development from an industrial, cholera-ridden slum to a trendy bohemian neighbourhood. She pointed out unfamiliar items, explaining their use and significance. They spent an hour or so browsing before wandering back down Defensa for a late afternoon snack. Over coffee, Cecilia asked Dee what else she would like to see.

'Do you have any suggestions?'

'A friend of mine told me about an exhibition of contemporary photography close by. Is that something you would find interesting?'

'Yes, I love photography.'

It was not a place that she would have been able to locate on her own. Cecilia referred to a scrap of paper on which her friend had written the number of the empty *conventillo* in which the exhibition was being housed. The only signage was a computer printout just inside the front door that directed them up a dark stairway where they encountered a scruffy youth lolling in an armchair, who pointed to another sign announcing a five-peso entry charge. Dee thought it was characteristically Argentinean to go to the trouble of mounting an exhibition without bothering to promote it in any way except through word of mouth. Cecilia paid for them both and made inquiries of the young man, who waved his arm in the direction of several rooms on either side of the landing.

'This group is a collective that includes students as well as teachers from the art school and some of their professional associates,' Cecilia explained. 'They exhibit here several times a year. This exhibition is called *Los Invisibles*. It was a kind of photographic challenge – to make visible the invisible. The photographers were free to interpret it in any way they wanted, but many have constructed a political reading and focused on the situation of people who are invisible to the mainstream – those who are relegated to the margins, the ones we choose not to see, even when they are right in front of our eyes.'

It was rhetoric that bored Dee a little in the English-speaking world, always tinged as it was with a note of hysterical self-righteousness, but for some reason it was more tolerable in a Spanish accent. It felt more authentic.

The first series of images they encountered had been taken in the women's prison at La Plata. One photograph showed a wild-haired woman staring past the camera with a look of angry perplexity, clutching a baby whose tiny hand flexed against her mother's heavily tattooed arm.

Another depicted a woman on the day her daughter, who had reached two years of age, had been taken out of her custody and placed in foster care. The woman rested her head on the breast of her cellmate, her eyes closed in pain. Her cellmate's arm curled around her head, one eloquent hand, cigarette balanced between two fingers, caressing her friend's cheek.

Dee stared at this image of maternal loss for a long time, stoic and unflinching. Watching the mother's grief, she mentally tested the seals on the place where she had stuffed her own.

The last in the series was of a window made up of fifty-four panes of frosted glass. There was a dark and ominous shadow behind the frosting, but one pane was missing in the top right-hand corner, revealing the tips of tree branches, poignantly clear and distant.

The photographer's tenderness for her subjects was evident, the patterns of their pain evoked in different densities of shadow and stolen light, but it was that pattern of branches against a white sky, framed by fifty-three squares of smudged glass that Dee found most affecting.

The next series of photographs focused on the *cartoneros*, the city's refuse collectors and recyclers. There was a long-haired woman, smiling shyly as she posed with two of her teenage children beside a cart laden with neatly stacked sheets of cardboard and another of an old man taken at night under a streetlight, bending over to retrieve bottles out of the gutter. A third image had been taken on a train, shot into the light of a window, framing three boys and a girl. The boys were bare-chested, their shirts tied around their waists; they gripped a pole against the lurching of the train. The composition of the picture was exquisite: the angles of their bodies, the gestures of their hands, the play of light between their limbs.

The same photographer had taken a series of pictures at a food-distribution centre in one of the southern *villas miserias*. Dee could feel her attention waning and was about to hurry ahead to find Cecilia when something caught her eye. Instinct registered before recognition. Surveying the last portrait in the series, a study of two Paraguayan women and their babies, it took Dee some moments to realise what it was that was niggling at her. The women were in the foreground, facing the camera, but they stood at the back of a long queue, the head of which receded into the background of the picture towards a shadowed doorway. There were two figures standing away from the queue engaged in earnest conversation, a man with a beard and a young woman, slightly taller than he. Her face was averted from the camera but there was something very familiar about the line of the jaw and cheekbone and the fine dark hair that fell around her face in blunt-cut layers. But that was not what had made Dee look twice. It was the jacket that the girl was wearing. The photograph was in black and white, but the style of the jacket was distinctive – it was a zip-up leather bomber jacket with a fur collar. Corrie had one just like it – one of those triumphant finds that vindicated the regular garage sale expeditions she and Ross used to undertake on weekends. It had become something of a signature piece of hers throughout the winter months. After Ross died, it acquired even greater significance, as he had been the one who first spotted it, jammed under a pile of suit coats in a box of old man's clothes.

At first the image didn't seem like anything of great importance, just another familiar figure in a long line of familiar figures, another object, of no particular rarity, evoking the style and taste of her daughter. Dee walked away, to shake herself free from the cloying fingers of nostalgia, but something made her return. And return again. She felt her emotions shift in slow motion, from objective curiosity to puzzled semi-recognition to fearful excitement. But even as she experienced these shifts and the bodily sensations that accompanied them – the thumping heart, the sudden chill – she could not discern if they were real or if she was willing them into being. Was she seeing what she wanted to see, or what was actually there? How much did height count? Build? Posture? What was it about the posture that was familiar? That hint of a slump in the shoulders, the folded arms, weight dropped back onto the right haunch, left leg brought forward and slightly bent.

It could be anyone. The hairstyle was different, but the hair was the same. Apart from the jacket there was no other clothing that she recognised – the short skirt, the heeled boots were generic to the fashions of the day. There was no visible jewellery. What was there, really? A girl of about the same height as Corrie, with the same coloured hair, wearing a jacket that resembled her favourite jacket. It was nothing and it was everything.

She noticed Cecilia walking back from the other room to find her and moved quickly, almost guiltily, away, focusing her attention on another picture.

'You like this series, I think?' Cecilia observed.

Dee smiled vaguely, making a non-committal noise and strolling casually into the next room. Perhaps a change of focus would help her put things into their proper perspective. But she found that she could not concentrate. She made a show of scanning the remaining pictures and then asked Cecilia if she had had enough.

'Yes, if you're ready. I need to visit my mother-in-law in Belgrano later, but I have another hour or so if there is something else you would like to see.'

Dee grasped at the chance to be alone with the picture. 'You go ahead, Cecilia. I've had a lovely day. Thank you for showing me around. But I might make my way back to the hotel for a siesta.'

'*Bueno*. We can walk together to the Plaza de Mayo and I can take a taxi to Belgrano from there.'

Dee's heart sank, but perhaps it was for the best. She had had a good, long look at the picture. What else could be revealed by further scrutiny? Distance would serve her better than obsessively revisiting the same ambivalent detail. After walking Cecilia back down Defensa, she waved her off in a cab. As soon as the cab was out of sight, however, Dee hightailed it back to the old building that housed the exhibition, only to find the heavy wooden doors firmly locked and bolted. It was closed for the day, and there was nothing to indicate when it might be open again. She banged her fist so hard against the door the impact jarred her whole arm.

*

Dee sat in the downstairs bar of the Gran Vía, evading the confronting isolation of her room. Alcohol was not a puritanically allocated commodity in Buenos Aires. Two lavishly overflowing measures of whisky had been poured ceremoniously into her glass before the barman had raised his arms in a theatrical shrug of surrender and thumped the whole bottle down in front of her.

She raised her eyebrows at him and downed half the contents of the glass in one gulp. He smiled knowingly and went back to watching a football match on a large screen hung at the other end of the bar. She knew this kind of drinking wasn't wise. She was in one of those moods in which half a bottle of scotch wouldn't even touch the sides – would leave her absolutely stone cold sober – but the next measure would knock her entire evening into oblivion. She would wake several hours later in a state of high paranoia, not remembering how she had got to bed and wondering whether or not she could make it to the bathroom in time to throw up. It was a well-worn path, albeit one she hadn't trodden for a while. The last of the whisky in the glass burned down her gullet and brought a flush to her cheeks but failed to mute her restlessness. The next two didn't help either. She decided to walk instead.

Cardigan crossed tightly across her chest, shoulders hunched, she headed south towards the Plaza de Mayo. Feeling like a cliché. Feeling like someone emulating all the cinematic gestures of a protagonist in crisis. What exactly was she in crisis about?

I thought I saw a photo of my daughter.

But it isn't Corrie, is it? It's just a girl wearing a jacket like hers.

Yes. No. It could be her.

It probably isn't.

But it might be.

It might be.

There was a large rally taking place in front of the presidential palace. The muffled roar of a rock band boomed down the avenue from the distant stage. Red banners bearing the black-stencilled image of Che Guevara and the ubiquitous slogan, '¡Hasta la Victoria Siempre!' were stretched across the plaza. Groups of young people swayed and staggered up the street, dropping beer bottles that smashed in the gutters and left trails of broken glass and sour-smelling froth. A fire had been lit in the middle of the road. A young bearded man performed a slow zorba around it, his arms raised above his head.

Dee turned away from the plaza towards the theatre district. Despite it being Sunday night, animated family groups, perambulating couples and clusters of young people crowded the streets. Two men hailed each other on a corner, embraced and exchanged exclamations of delight at their unexpected encounter. Dee noted their camaraderie sadly. She would have liked to have been large-spirited and expressive like the South Americans. She would have liked to speak a language that filled the mouth and emerged in strong rhythmic currents and musical dynamics. She would have liked to have known the personal certainty that surely underpinned their free flow of expression. How otherwise would they dare such frank and unqualified statements of feeling and opinion?

If she had been capable of such unmediated feeling would she have been a better mother to Corrie? Over the years, she had observed the spontaneous flow of affection between other mothers and daughters with envy and perplexity. What was it in her that prevented the same ease of relationship? But the more she second-guessed herself, the worse it got. Would that last year with Corrie have been less fraught with pain and misunderstanding if Dee had been able to express the real love she had for her daughter in straightforward, uncomplicated terms?

Dee had told Stephen that she believed Corrie was still alive. Now that, for the first time in four years, she had seen a shadow of proof that this might actually be the case, she was dumbfounded with disbelief. It was too cruel. It was completely ridiculous to think that for all these years Corrie had been living in Argentina, had been wearing that goddamned jacket, had been carrying on a normal life of everyday banalities while her family had been locked in grief over her absence. It was simply not possible. She *must* be dead. Why couldn't Dee just accept the fact that Corrie was dead? The country was groaning with the weight of ghosts like hers. She was merely one of a multitude of spectral hopes. It was time for Dee to come to grips with that. It was long past time.

If you were with me now, Corrie, what would I tell you? I would tell you that I was sorry for all those times I shouted at you, all those times I turned away when you were waiting, excitedly, then hopefully, then sadly, to be hugged. And then not waiting at all anymore. I would tell you that you were a sensitive, loving child who deserved more encouragement than I ever gave you. That you had so much to offer. That you were creative and clever and kind and imaginative and funny and – and I loved you.

It had begun to rain. She lowered her face against the spatter of raindrops but her cheeks were wet with tears anyway.

That's what I wanted to tell you before you got on that plane to go away. But I never got around to it. That's what I was planning to tell you when you came home. But you never came home. Did you? Damn you, Corrie. You never came home.

Chapter Five

Dee woke at three am before drifting into a semi-comatose state in which she returned again and again to the exhibition, mounting the dark stairway that got longer with every attempt to climb to the top and each time she stood before the picture it was different, until eventually it was Corrie who was featured in the foreground, Corrie holding a baby, Corrie queuing for food and Dee became tormented by her previous ambivalence. How could she not have seen it? How could she have been so obtuse? And then she was jolted into full consciousness, relieved and disappointed in equal measures, staring into the darkness.

She hauled herself out of bed at nine, thickheaded with tiredness and intensely irritated for having succumbed to the befuddlement of pre-dawn emotions. Too much whisky. She should have been more careful.

She needed to go back and view the photograph again, but it was unlikely that the exhibition would be open before lunchtime. She stood under the shower for a long time, stretched out her breakfast with so many coffees she began to feel sick, then loitered in the hotel foyer, picking her way, word by word, through the front-page stories in *La Nación*.

By the time she left the hotel several hours later it was raining heavily. Deep puddles added another challenge to negotiating the cracked and broken paving. Umbrella salesmen had appeared from nowhere, intoning '*paraguas, paraguas*' at passing pedestrians. She purchased a small umbrella, which was only marginally effective in keeping off the rain, as she was obliged to keep moving it to one side to avoid entangling it with the umbrellas of pedestrians hurrying in the opposite direction. Stepping off the kerb to cross Avenida Defensa, she sank ankle deep in a torrent of gutter water and the strap of her sandal broke. She squelched and shuffled the remaining six blocks to the old *conventillo* that housed the exhibition. The door was shut fast. She searched in vain for a sign detailing opening hours and then began to pound the door with her fist, more in frustration than any real hope that it might be answered. A woman opening the shop next door glanced in her direction.

'*¡Disculpe!*' Dee pointed to the locked door and shrugged her arms heavenwards.

Not open Mondays, the woman explained dismissively, come back tomorrow. Dee looked down at the sodden hems of her trousers and shivered against the cold. She slammed a fist hard against the door in one last act of defiance and leant her head against the wood. Her wet handbag started to vibrate. She scrabbled for her phone.

'Hello?'

'Dee? Stephen.'

'Stephen! I'm so glad to hear from you!'

'I wondered how you were getting on.'

'Not so great, as it happens.'

'Why's that?'

'Well, I'm standing outside an old *conventillo* in San Telmo. The exhibition I wanted to see is closed. It's pouring rain, I'm soaked through and—' She paused, feeling foolish.

'And?'

'Stephen, are you busy for lunch today? I really need to talk to someone.'

'Funny. I was ringing to ask *you* about lunch. I'm in the city today, taking one of Javier's Pastoral Praxis classes at the university.'

'Pastoral Praxis?'

'Yes, he teaches at the Catholic University – at Puerto Madero. There's a good Italian place around the corner. Fancy something like that?'

'Sounds perfect.'

'I can meet you out the front of the university in about an hour.'

'Is it hard to find?'

'Head towards the canal and ask a local when you get close. Call me if you get lost.'

'You're a lifesaver.'

'We aim to please.'

Dee didn't mind the rain so much now that she had a firm destination and an offer of company. She limped back to Calle Florida, purchased a cheap pair of sandals from the first shoe shop she could find and then headed east towards the river. She reached the entrance of the university within twenty minutes, and waited by the main doors, watching the students wandering in and out and around the plaza. They appeared earnest but untroubled: fresh faces, faded jeans, jackets buttoned against the rain, hands thrust in pockets, backpacks stuffed with books, lives stuffed with promise. They were easy with each other, couples holding hands, groups of friends trading friendly insults, unconscious of their youthful beauty, stretching out into new freedoms, inhabiting that halcyon, timeless space between childhood dependence and adult obligation. Oh, Corrie.

'You found your way, then?' Stephen touched her on the shoulder.

'This is so good of you.' She almost threw her arms around him in relief.

'Enough, enough. Got to eat lunch. May as well eat it with you.'

'I'll stop feeling grateful then.'

'Please. I'll feel so much more comfortable if you do. Now – Italian?'

'Sounds good.'

As they walked he pointed out the Arts Pavilion and, when they turned on to the street that ran in front of the canal, the asymmetrical sweep of The Women's Bridge. When they reached the restaurant, they joined the queue for a table. It was a large, casual eatery, with windows facing the water.

'Popular place,' Dee observed.

'Handmade pasta, big serves, reasonable prices. We won't have to wait long. They have a quick turnover.'

He was right. A table became available almost immediately. They were waved to their seats by a waiter with a brusque manner and a completely deadpan expression.

Comfortably buffeted by the drone of conversation and the clatter of plates, Dee settled back in her chair and let out a deep sigh.

Stephen glanced at her as he consulted with the waiter. 'Are you drinking?'

'Are you?'

'Red?'

'Sounds good.'

'Glass or bottle?'

'Bottle.'

He raised his eyebrows in surprise and turned back to the waiter and made a rapid selection from the wine list.

'I've had a rough couple of days,' she explained when he'd finished with the waiter. 'How did your football match go yesterday?'

'We lost. But we put up a valiant fight. Four goals to three.'

'And how come you had to take Javier's class today?'

'He's dealing with an emergency in the parish, trying to find accommodation for a family who needs to move rather urgently. The father's been in prison for sexually abusing several of the children, but he's being released tomorrow and will probably head straight back to the family home.'

Dee winced. 'What are the chances of relocating them?'

'Javier's going to talk to the priest in the next parish over. We're hoping there's a family there who can put them up for a week or so. Just until we find something more permanent.

'There's nothing that can be done to keep this thug away?'

'Odds are the mother will go back to him anyway. It's tough trying to cope on your own.'

'It's good that the parish is there to help her.'

'We had to do a hospital run last night for a mother whose baby was running a temperature of 103. This afternoon I'm taking Alejandro – that lad I was telling you about at Alicia's – to go and pick out a new guitar for the parish rock group. The other one got stolen last week. Never a dull moment.'

'I don't know how you keep going. It all seems so futile and depressing.'

'No, not really. There's a lot of resilience out there, more laughs than you'd expect. And the people are great ones for parties. Any excuse for a fiesta.'

'And, no doubt, a few drinks?'

'Speaking of which.'

The waiter returned with a bottle of merlot and a basket of bread. He poured them each a glass.

'What are you having?' Steven asked her over the top of the menu.

'I'll have the ravioli alla panna.'

'I think, perhaps, the seafood.' He ordered for them both. Dee admired Stephen's easy flow of banter with the waiter. He seemed more animated and responsive in this setting. It reminded her of the first time she had seen him with his attractive young friend at the Plaza Asturias.

'So, Dee,' he said, turning back to her after the waiter had gathered up their menus and hurried off to the next table. 'To what happy misfortune do I owe the pleasure of your company and this fine bottle of red?'

She suddenly felt sceptical of her own experience and flushed a little. 'Oh, I don't know. I'm probably overreacting.'

'Overreacting to what?'

'Do you remember Cecilia saying that she was going to take me to the antique fair at San Telmo yesterday? Well, we also visited a photography exhibition.'

She took a sip from her glass of wine and then eyeballed him with a look of apologetic confession. 'Stephen, I feel like an idiot. I thought I saw Corrie in the background of one of the photos.'

His eyebrows climbed cautiously up his forehead. 'Really? What made you think it might be her?'

'Height, build, hair colour. Her face was turned away from the camera, but she was wearing a jacket identical to one that Corrie used to own.'

'In combination, those facts seem quite compelling.' He paused. 'Have you had these sorts of experiences before?'

Dee flushed again. She didn't feel like recounting the numerous embarrassing episodes in which she had furtively pursued young women, sometimes for miles, along crowded city streets.

'I often see girls who look like her.'

'How do they resemble her?'

'Similar things: build, hair, dress, gait. The shape of a face in profile. Sometimes I can be completely fooled by a trace of the perfume she used to wear, floating by me in a crowd.'

'What is she like, your daughter?'

'Do you mean her personality?' Dee paused, aware that for every generalisation she was about to name she could describe an equally pointed exception. She felt as though she no longer had any coherent sense of Corrie – only fragmentary impressions and memories that didn't quite fit together. She remembered the aspects of her daughter's personality that had generated strong feelings of pride or hurt, the things that had seemed to manifest Dee's own successes and failures. She felt ashamed to realise how frequently Corrie had been refracted through the distorting prism of her own fears and desires. She felt that she had missed the opportunity to get to know her daughter properly because she, Dee, had kept getting in the way. She sat at the table, trawling through scraps of memory, hoping to convince herself, and Stephen, otherwise.

'She was quiet – but not shy, lost in her own world a lot of the time, but also capable of quite sharp and astute observation. She was something of a chameleon really, like most actors. Eclectic. She collected gestures and mannerisms and different personas. She played with style and fashion a lot. She liked clothes that told stories – op shop finds, unusual fabrics, antique jewellery. She looked like a bohemian, but she wasn't the sort of person who drew attention to herself just for the sake of it. There was a kind of diffidence about her. Preoccupation. She got absorbed in particular ideas and projects. Forgot everything else. Consequently there was always a trail of minor disasters following in her wake.'

'She sounds lovely.'

Dee glanced up at him and smiled wryly. She *was* lovely. Why was it that she could describe her now in a manner that evoked her loveliness but when Corrie had been with her she'd persecuted her for the very things she now eulogised? *For God's sake, make up your mind . . . Oh, let me do it . . . Could you please get a wriggle on? . . . You look like you've raided the local Salvo's bin . . .* But she was weary of these old tapes, of the records she kept against herself. Surely it was part of the normal badinage of family life. She had had her own struggles. Children are not porcelain china. *Yes, very good, but every second word is misspelt.* Corrie folding up the story she had written and walking away with a blank expression on her face. The pages ripped into tiny pieces in the rubbish bin.

Dee straightened her cutlery, parallel, equidistant, bases aligned.

Stephen cleared his throat to gain her attention. When she met his gaze she could see the shadow of her own discomfort in his furrowed brow.

'Tell me more about the picture.'

She sighed and shrugged her shoulders. 'The shape of the face was familiar. The contour of the cheek and jawline. But I've been deceived many times by a profile or the back of a head.' She stopped to gather her thoughts.

'There was also something about the way that she was standing, something familiar about the posture. And the jacket. The girl in the picture was wearing Corrie's favourite jacket. It was a present from her father. She wore it everywhere.'

'What sort of jacket?'

'A leather bomber jacket.'

'They were very popular a few years ago.'

The waiter delivered their pasta dishes with a flourish and deposited a bowl of salad between them.

Stephen flicked his napkin over his knees. 'So what are you going to do?'

Dee deferred her response as the waiter reached across her with a pepper grinder the size of her arm.

'I suppose I could try to track down the photographer.'

'The organisers of the exhibition would have the contact details.'

'She was only a background figure in the picture. The photographer probably has no idea who she was.'

'Maybe. But he or she will be able to tell you where the picture was taken.'

'Yes.' She pondered the long and potentially futile line of investigation. Part of her wilted before the prospect of another wild goose chase.

'You could see if anyone who lives in the vicinity remembers her.'

'It's a bit of a long shot.'

He shrugged. 'But it's bothering you.'

'I'm wondering if it's worth it. I can't keep chasing down blind alleys forever. I'm so tired of the crucifying disappointment.'

Stephen put down his fork, wiped his lips with his napkin and took a sip of wine. 'You'd rather live with the doubt?'

Dee contemplated the question. She had never been able to walk away from anything. She was a picker and a pedant. Which was why, she decided with sudden conviction and purpose, once this last thing was tackled, it was over. It was time to stop coming back to Argentina. It was time to stop peeling off the scab.

'What was the photographer's name?'

'I don't know. Julio someone or other. I was so caught up with the image and then Cecilia interrupted me and I was trying to act normal. I forgot to check.'

'Go back tomorrow and have a look. The Australian Embassy might be prepared to make some inquiries on your behalf.'

'I don't really want to involve them at this stage. I'll take your first piece of advice and start with the exhibition staff. If they ever open again.'

It had occurred to her that the exhibition might be over. Perhaps it was all dismantled by now, packed away into boxes, dispersed back to the artists along with their identifying information. That would be just her luck.

'How's your pasta?'

She pushed a few pieces of ravioli around her plate. 'Rich. I don't know why I went for the cream sauce.' She forced herself to swallow a mouthful.

Stephen topped up his wine glass and then her own. 'What's wrong?'

'What if the exhibition is over? Then what?'

'Then, between us, Cecilia and I can help you to find out who the organisers were, and we'll take it from there.'

'Really? You wouldn't mind?'

'Um, let me see. I suppose I *could* try sleeping at night knowing that, with minimal effort, I might have eased a mother's anxiety over her missing daughter, but passed up the opportunity because it was too much bother.'

'But you have so many other things on your plate.'

'No, you do.' He glared at the mound of pasta before her. 'EAT!'

She scooped up a forkful, her confidence and, consequently, her appetite suddenly returning, rekindled by his kindness.

'Stephen?' she kept her eyes firmly fixed on the salad bowl as she helped herself to a serving.

'What?'

'What are you doing in Argentina?'

He paused so long she was forced to hazard a sidelong glance at his face.

'I thought I had already explained that.'

'In part. You said you were taking a break. Is it some sort of sabbatical?'

'You could call it that. But it hasn't been entirely of my choosing.'

She pulled apart a bread roll and pressed a chunk into a patch of salad oil on her plate.

'I've been asked to undertake some discernment about my ongoing vocation.'

'Because?' She smiled encouragingly.

'Because I was in love with someone.'

'Does this have anything to do with the man I saw you with at the Asturias?'

'What? You mean Sebastián? Good heavens, no! But yes, it was a man I was involved with.'

'I thought so.'

'I don't try to conceal it, but it's not always politic to trot it out immediately.'

'It's an awkward thing to be—' she blotted the oil from her lips with a napkin, leaving mauve smudges on the white linen, '— a gay priest.'

'Well, to the extent to which one is prepared to play the game – bow to the charge of being fundamentally disordered, shut up about it and submit to the prescription of celibacy – it's manageable.' It sounded like a well-rehearsed speech.

'And are you and do you and is it?' The wine had loosened her tongue along with the vague awareness that according to the usual social transactions it was now his turn to be vulnerable.

'Am I?'

'Fundamentally disordered.'

Even though it was his own characterisation she could see that he still smarted at the description on someone else's lips. 'I like to think I'm no more fundamentally disordered than anyone else.'

'Then why do you submit to an authority that says you are?'

'Ah well,' he replied thoughtfully, 'there you have my current problem in a nutshell. I haven't been submitting enough for their liking. Hence my current – um – hiatus.'

'I see.' Then something occurred to her. 'I thought you said that you were celebrating Mass yesterday. Do they still let you do that?'

His tone became even more irritated. 'I wasn't celebrating Mass. I was assisting. I help out where I can. Javier has been kind enough to let me be part of his team.'

'But—' She was not sure how to phrase the question.

'You want to know why I bother with the priestly thing at all? Why I don't just leave?'

She shrugged. She had waded into choppy waters and had probably pushed him to the edges of what was permitted by polite conversation. 'It's your business.'

He took his time answering while he poured himself another glass of wine. 'I suppose the only thing I can say is that I feel called to it. I don't think it's a choice. I think it's what God wants of me. I know that's not language that sits comfortably with the modern sensibility, but I can't explain it in any other way.'

His humility tempered her reflexive contempt at the concept of a 'calling'. She had no inclination to make him suffer through further explanations.

'Fair enough.' The response was too flippant and sounded like an insult. 'I mean – you're right. There are some things you can't explain. I know what that feels like.'

They both fell on the remains of the salad with sudden diligence. But, despite his discomfort with the subject, she couldn't stand the silence and decided to press on to a more satisfactory resolution.

'What did you do exactly? Did you have an affair with this guy?'

He laughed aloud then, a gesture of gracious surrender as well as amusement. 'Is that an example of Australian tact?'

His show of good humour made her bolder. 'In my experience, most men are flattered that you think them capable of it.'

'Is that so? Well, the short answer is yes. Not just an affair. A serious relationship with someone I met here. His name was Felipe. The love of my life. But he died two years ago.' He pushed his empty plate to one side and took up his wine glass.

'I'm so sorry.'

He swirled the wine in his glass, took a long draught.

'Tell me about him.' She knew only too well that unwitting

intrusions into grief stung less than the suddenly slammed door and hasty retreat. She was pleased to see a nostalgic smile creep across his face.

'Oh, he was quite beautiful. *El guapo* – the handsome one. I used to joke with him about that. He had all the women swooning. And he had an equally beautiful manner – gentle and calm and very thoughtful. You can imagine how stunned I was that he even looked twice at me.'

'How did you meet?'

'He was a project officer for Caritas – the Catholic aid agency. Alicia has done bits and pieces of consultancy work for Caritas over the years. She introduced me to the local director when I told her that I wanted to research some of the capacity-building projects in the local barrios. The director suggested a number of projects I could look at and one of them was Felipe's. Anyway, you know what the Catholic scene is like – one degree of separation – if you're lucky.'

'Was it love at first sight?'

'Everyone fell in love with Felipe at first sight. Not that I had any plans to act on that. Not that I would have imagined I had a snowball's chance in hell – even if I were so rash.'

'But?'

'But we spent a night together in a casualty ward after taking in a woman who'd been badly knocked around by her husband. We got talking and then we kept talking and then we went out for breakfast and by the time poor Belen was released with her arm in a cast and twenty-four stitches in her head, I think we both had some intuition that we'd found a soulmate.'

'Does it upset you to talk about what happened to him?'

'Felipe was working in one of the barrios on the south side of the city. They're quite violent places – much worse than the suburban and rural ones. He'd been working there for a number of years, trying to set up employment projects for the young men in the area. I don't know what went wrong. We think he might have fallen foul of one of the drug syndicates. He was trying to get the kids away from dealing.'

'Pretty gutsy.'

He sighed deeply, rubbing a hand over his face in weariness.

'He was attacked one evening. They had knives. There was more than one person involved, apparently. Sometimes I wonder if he was the victim of a queer bashing gone wrong, but I don't think so. I think it was as simple as being in the wrong place at the wrong time.'

'It doesn't make it any easier though.'

'I was devastated – completely devastated. It had taken such a long time to open myself up to the possibilities of that relationship – to accept the gift that it was. We'd begun to talk about a life together, to believe in our unlikely happy-ever-after. And then everything got snatched away.'

'Yes. I know what that feels like.'

'I still find the violence of it completely surreal.'

'How did you cope?'

He shrugged and looked at her ruefully. 'I can't pretend I coped especially brilliantly. Had something of a breakdown. Got shipped back to England. I think it was tacitly assumed that once I recovered I would just take myself off quietly. They didn't count on me applying to resume my ministry.'

'They knocked you back?'

'As I said, I've been counselled to "continue my process of discernment". It's quite a complex business to strip someone of Holy Orders.'

'So you're in something of a no-man's land?'

'Yes. Or an every-man's land, if you like. There seem to be an awful lot of us not fitting into our prescribed places at the moment.'

She thought about that for a while, approved his instinct to generalise his experience rather than use it to claim special status.

'So what will you do?'

'My diocese continues to pay my stipend so I try to make myself useful. It's something of a privilege to be able to work here. Javier has generated some interesting initiatives in the parish: adult training programmes, micro-credit schemes. He needs all the support he can get. I like to think I'm helping to make a difference.'

'And the celibacy thing? How do you cope with that? Surrounded by all these hot Latin men? That Sebastián is a bit of all right.'

He smiled. 'Yes, he is, isn't he? And very happily involved with Benito, another friend of mine. As I said, I'm not immune to the odd crush, but even that has been significantly tempered since Felipe died. Perhaps it's a new kind of grace I've been given. But while we're on the subject, what about you? You haven't mentioned a current partner.'

'I've had a few other things on my mind since Ross died.'

'How long has it been?'

'Since he died? Five years. Corrie was halfway through her Year 12 exams and Ben and Luke were in their first year of high school. Ross died in November. Corrie left for Argentina in July the following year.'

'You must have been very strong to cope with the double loss.'

She shrugged, rolling a lone olive around her plate with her fork. 'What choice do you have? I had Ben and Luke to look after. There were no family savings to fall back on. No super. No life insurance. I had to earn a living. And I had to do everything I could to find Corrie. I didn't have time to sit around feeling sorry for myself.'

'Did you ever feel angry with your husband for dying and leaving you to deal with everything on your own?'

'Of course I did. But I'd had lots of practice dealing with things on my own. It's not as if I wasn't used to it.'

'So things weren't all that great between you and Ross when he died?'

She drained the last of her wine and thought about the question for a while.

'We were coming out of a difficult patch. I'd been appointed Deputy Principal twelve months earlier. It was a steep learning curve and I was working long hours, but we were doing better financially and that had taken a lot of the pressure off. I'd gone through a stage of feeling pretty disgruntled about Ross's contribution to the family income but I'd got over that. And I was slowly coming to terms with the fact that he was never going to clean the toilet or acquaint himself with the vacuum cleaner. But I was also learning to appreciate the other things he did around the place. The traditional blokey stuff. And he was a great dad. He adored the kids. That counts for a lot, you know.'

'How long had you been married?'

'We were about to celebrate our eighteenth anniversary.'

'That's no mean achievement.'

'No, I guess not.' She smiled a little grimly.

The waiter returned to clear their plates.

'¿Postre, café?'

Stephen deferred to her.

'No, gracias,' she told the waiter. '*La cuenta, por favor.*'

'*Bueno.*'

When the bill arrived Dee quickly passed the waiter her credit card.

'I was going to shout you,' Stephen protested.

'Next time.' She shrugged.

'Thank you.'

'Thank *you*. I was beside myself when you rang. I'm feeling better now.'

Dee and Stephen collected their jackets from the backs of their chairs and exited by the door onto the canal. It had stopped raining and the clouds were beginning to clear.

'Are you heading back to the parish?' Dee asked.

'Yes. What are your plans?'

'No plans. A nanna nap, maybe. I didn't sleep so well last night.'

'You'll go back to Plaza Dorrego tomorrow?'

'Yes. Hopefully the exhibition will be open.'

'Let me know how you get on, won't you?'

'Of course.'

'Well. Good luck.'

There was a moment of awkwardness as they both considered whether or not to enact the Argentinean ritual of a farewell kiss, and both rejected it as a potentially weird affectation between two Anglos. Dee scratched her nose with the hand that she had partially raised in readiness for an embrace and Stephen turned his gesture into a wave.

'You too. I'll be in touch.'

She smiled ruefully at his retreating figure as he turned and walked away from her along the waterfront.

Chapter Six

On Tuesday morning, when Dee returned to the *conventillo* in San Telmo, she was relieved to find the door propped open. The woman who greeted her pleasantly at the top of the stairs asked if she would like a catalogue, and handed her a photocopied pamphlet.

For some reason, Dee felt obliged to enact a leisurely interest in the first roomful of photographs, although she wasn't sure what she hoped to gain by doing so. Credibility as a potential buyer, perhaps – someone who had the right to ask questions afterwards? When her casual stroll brought her in line with the picture she had come to see, she raised her eyes slowly, trying to take the most objective view possible. It yielded nothing more, however, than it had two days ago: a young man with a kindly face talking to a girl of the same height and build as Corrie, who was wearing a jacket very similar to the one that she always wore. There was no more shock in it, just confirmation of the frustrating non-specificity of the image. Dee opened the catalogue slowly, as if stealth would alter the contents, as if care and deliberation were more likely to be rewarded with revelation.

There was a biography and a headshot of the photographer: Julio Ruiz, a former teacher at the Escuela Bellas Artes and a freelance photographer whose work had appeared in journals in Argentina and the United States. He currently resided in Uruguay. Dee nearly stamped her foot in frustration at the final sentence, but there was a website address included, and if there was a website, there would almost certainly be an email contact. The pamphlet was a photocopy of a photocopy and Julio Ruiz's image was not especially clear. He had a voluminous mass of light-coloured hair that might have been white blond or grey and which looked like a halo at first glance. He could have been thirty or fifty. It was hard to tell from the picture. The strong line of his dark eyebrows was clear against the background static. One eyebrow was cocked and he was smiling, but Dee could not tell if the smile was benign or mocking.

Glancing quickly from left to right, she extracted her camera from her handbag and took a photograph of the picture. As hastily as she could, she zoomed into the figures in the background and snapped off several more pictures.

The girl at the door looked up from her novel with a polite smile as Dee paused on her way out.

'Julio Ruiz?'

'¿*Sí*?'

'Is he in Buenos Aires at the moment? For the exhibition. *¿Está en Buenos Aires ahora? ¿Para la exposición?*'

'*No sé. ¿Quisiera comprar una fotografía?*'

Dee hesitated. '*Sí*. I would like to buy one of his pictures, but I would also like to see more of his portfolio. *Quisiera ver más de sus obras.*'

The girl reached into the drawer of a small table and brought out a bundle of business cards secured with a rubber band. Flicking through them, she located the one she was looking for and handed it to Dee. *Julio Ruiz, fotografía.* A telephone number, a website, an email address.

Back at the Gran Vía Dee waited impatiently for an elderly woman to finish with the public computer. She hovered in the woman's peripheral vision, deliberately communicating her impatience with floor pacing and watch checking, but she was calmly ignored. After ten minutes of futile low-level harassment she decided to make a quick visit to the lavatory. When she returned a young man had taken the woman's place. Anticipating greater efficiency on his part, Dee planted herself in a nearby chair and kept close watch but was obliged to wait another twenty minutes before he concluded his business and she could, finally, gain access to the precious computer.

She had rejected the option of telephoning as she knew she wouldn't be able to communicate clearly enough over the phone. Stephen or Alicia would have been happy to help her, but she wanted to see how far she could get on her own. If there was another humiliating disappointment in store, she didn't want to experience it in the presence of others. Dee opened her email account and typed in Julio Ruiz's address. A simple note in Spanish could be managed with her basic vocabulary and an internet translating tool. If the correspondence was stilted, so much the better. It might prompt a quicker response if the photographer thought she was a rich *gringa* interested in purchasing some of his works. Did she dare imply such a thing?

Estimado Señor Ruiz,

And then she stalled. What next? It was important to get the tone right. He might not reply if she came across as gauche or ill educated, if she bored him or inadvertently offended. Artists could be so touchy.

> *Dear Señor Ruiz,*
> *I recently saw some of your photographs at an exhibition in San Telmo. I liked them very much and am interested in seeing more of your work, with a view to purchasing some prints. I am from Australia, holidaying in Buenos Aires for several weeks, and would like to meet you personally if you have the time. The themes you explore in your photographs hold particular interest for me.*
>
> *Your work displays both elegance of design and sensitivity to the shifting patterns of contemporary human subjectivity.*

Thankfully, the Spanish language lent itself well to vague abstractions. She added her hotel address and mobile phone number at the bottom of the page. In the subject box she typed, 'From an admirer of your work' and hit 'Send'.

Then she prepared herself to wait. She was good at waiting. Waiting had become her permanent mode of being. Even before Corrie had gone missing, the habit had been inscribed in her bones. Dee knew that she didn't have a monopoly on this. Waiting was what women did.

She couldn't remember exactly when youthful action and self-determination had mutated into endless attendance on the actions of others, but she suspected it dated back to her first pregnancy. 'She's expecting,' they used to say in the old days, which aptly characterised the profound bodily and emotional orientation towards a distant arrival that was ultimately beyond her control.

The waiting, through both her pregnancies, had been simultaneously anxious and hopeful. Dee had anticipated all the gestational misfortunes for which she had been tested at various intervals, with the inevitable drawn-out delays between medical tests and the communication of results. When the children were born she continued to watch and wait. Were there underlying problems to which she was oblivious? Things that would manifest later as mute condemnations of her earlier ignorance and unwitting neglect? She waited for signs and symptoms. She waited for confirmation of normality.

She waited in doctors' rooms and emergency departments and by sickbeds when they ran fevers or split open their flesh or broke their bones in various childhood accidents. She waited on the sidelines of the boys' soccer games in freezing winds and stinging rain, idled in cars in the dark outside Corrie's inevitably extended drama rehearsals. And when her children were old enough to drive themselves, she waited in an even greater agony of anticipation, through the long evenings and early mornings, for the peppercorning of their car tyres on the gravel driveway, the scrape of their key in the lock. As the slow drip of scalding seconds hit the frayed edges of her nerves late at night, Dee had tried in vain to repel the parade of imaginary horrors – road carnage, overdose, date-rape, abduction, murder – and Corrie had copped the worst of Dee's fear-fuelled anger whenever she was late home.

Perhaps it was because she was the eldest or because she pushed the boundaries harder than the boys. Did she push harder? Or did it just appear that way because she was a girl and Dee expected different things of her? When Dee considered her reactions to the twins' early forays into the adult world of parties and dating, she had to concede that there was a palpable difference. Corrie had stirred a kind of wordless terror in Dee about the dangers and vulnerabilities of femaleness. She feared for her daughter and she feared for herself. For the weight of tragic consequence they would both, potentially, be left to endure.

'Where have you been? It's one thirty! I told you to be home by twelve thirty at the latest.' Dee recalled one evening when she had blocked the kitchen doorway, trembling with rage, assessing Corrie's state of inebriation by the light of the open fridge into which her daughter was staring.

'Is it one thirty? I didn't realise.'

'How did you get home?'

'With Liam.'

'You told me you were going to get a lift with Sara's parents.'

'Sara went home early. I didn't know she'd gone until I tried to find her. So Liam offered to drop me but I had to wait until he was ready to go.'

At the time Dee had suspected the whole tale was an elaborate fabrication. 'You had no intention of getting a lift home with Sara's parents, did you?'

Corrie had slammed the fridge door and swung around to face Dee with a look of outraged innocence on her face.

'I did so. You can call them if you like.' She'd fumbled in her bag for her phone. 'I've got their number here.'

'Don't be ridiculous. I'm not going to ring them at this time of night. You always do this to me. Tell me you're doing one thing and then go off and do something completely different.'

'Things happen, OK? What was I supposed to do? I didn't have any money for a cab.'

'I've told you I'll always pay for a cab if you need one.'

'It's a waste of money. Liam was happy to drive me.'

'I'm sure he was. I'm sure he'd be happy to do a lot of things for you, but what does he expect in return? He's an odd character and I don't like you hanging around with him.'

Corrie had tried to push past Dee to get to her bedroom, but Dee shot out a hand and gripped Corrie's bare arm so tightly that her fingers made white marks in the skin.

'Let go! That hurts!'

'I've been wide awake for the last hour worried sick about where you were. You wouldn't even answer your phone—'

'I didn't hear it!'

'It's your job to make sure you hear it. I don't ask much, but if you can't manage that one small thing you won't be going to any more damned parties.'

'What! Why not? Why can't you just trust me? Let go. You're hurting me!'

Dee had tightened her grip. 'I'd like to trust you, Corrie, but how can I? You never do what you say you're going to do and as for that Liam, well, I wouldn't trust *him* as far as I could kick him.'

She'd let go of her daughter's arm but continued to block the doorway to the hall. 'He can't look me in the eye. He can't string a coherent sentence together. He looks like a druggie and he smells disgusting.'

'He does *not* smell disgusting!' Corrie's voice had risen to a shriek of outrage.

The absurdity of the level to which the exchange had sunk suddenly struck Dee and made her laugh through her anger. Her tone softened.

'Corrie, I'm just worried about you. I don't want you to find yourself in a situation that you can't get out of. I don't want you to—'

'End up getting pregnant like you did?'

Dee was brought up short by the sneer on her daughter's face.

'Among other things,' she had muttered, casting around desperately to find a way of explaining what she really meant.

'Because I guess it must have really wrecked your life having me?'

'You know that's not true.'

But Corrie's eyes were alight with triumph and she wasn't about to concede the high moral ground she had accidentally stumbled upon.

'Don't worry. I'm not going to get pregnant. I'm not that *stupid*.'

Dee had stepped aside then, hurt and confused, as Corrie pushed past her, giving off waves of cigarette smoke and the pungent residue of vodka cruisers, clumped down the hall in her elevated party shoes and pulled her bedroom door shut with a defiant thud.

Dee shook off the memory and braced herself, once again, for another round of waiting. She didn't stray far from the computer that day. She bought herself the thickest piece of English detective fiction that she could find in one of the big city bookshops and lounged in her hotel room, reading, drinking cups of tea and checking her emails religiously every two hours. On the second day she packed a picnic of bread, cheese and fruit and trekked to the Botanical Gardens, in order to forestall her compulsive checking. Five hours later when she returned to the hotel there was still no reply from Julio Ruiz. The following morning, she decided to give him one more day before throwing herself upon Stephen's mercy. She took herself off to a cinema on Avenida Corrientes to see *The Curious Case of Benjamin Button* with Spanish subtitles and then decided to fill in some more time by visiting the Museo Evita

Peron in Palermo. The museum housed a well-curated exhibition that explored the life of the controversial former First Lady. The rags-to-riches story and displays of haute couture were a welcome distraction for Dee but the final room of the exhibition was more confronting. It contained a projected image of Evita's embalmed and battered corpse. The accompanying commentary explained that her body had been stolen from the presidential palace and desecrated by sexual as well as other forms of violence. The extent of the hatred directed at the woman's defenceless body sickened Dee and stirred all her old terrors about what might have happened to Corrie. She made a hasty exit from the museum and turned the long walk back to the hotel into a piece of hard physical exertion, trying to exorcise the image from her mind.

She arrived around five pm in high colour, perspiring from the long walk, but feeling better. Jorge, the barman, greeted her with cheery familiarity and poured her a generous gin and tonic in a long glass. She took her drink to the computer in the foyer, logged on to her email account mechanically and froze in surprise when she saw Julio Ruiz's name in her inbox. The message was in fluent English.

Hello, Mrs Sutherland,
My studio is in Colonia. It is a short journey across the river. There are ferries three times a day from the Buquebus terminal at Puerto Madero. There are many tourists here on weekends so perhaps you would prefer to visit on Monday.
   Julio Ruiz

He had added his address and telephone number. Dee closed her eyes and blew out her breath in a long relieved stream.

Chapter Seven

There was a ferry leaving for Colonia at seven on Monday morning. The clerk at the terminal who sold Dee her ticket told her that she would need to allow at least an hour to check her baggage and clear Immigration. She went to bed early on Sunday evening but slept badly, anticipating the five am start. Her dreams were full of abortive preparations, clumsy attempts to dress, losing shoes, missing the ferry or being barred from boarding, choking with frustration. When the alarm buzzed her into full consciousness, she pulled on jeans, a shirt and a light cardigan against the chill of the morning, double-checked her bag for her ticket and passport and hurried out into the darkness.

Several hours later, following the inevitable sequence of creeping queues, form-stamping, X-ray machines and official checkpoints, she stood by one of the thick, plate windows on the lower deck of the ferry and watched Buenos Aires recede surprisingly quickly into the distance beyond the choppy expanse of brown water. The weather had cleared and the sky was a bright and cheerful blue, but the view of the city was smudged with low-lying smog.

Dee purchased a coffee at the onboard kiosk and collapsed into a stale-smelling chair in the economy-class section. The safety announcements and waves of conversation washed over her. Children played on the floor. A wall-mounted television broadcast the day's news but the sound had been muted. Spanish text scrolled across the bottom of the screen. She dozed in an uncomprehending cocoon of foreignness, alone and, for all practical purposes, deaf and mute.

The journey passed quickly. In less than an hour she was disembarking in Colonia. There were several buses waiting to take passengers on to Montevideo. In answer to her query about the direction of the town centre, an official pointed up the hill from the quay and gestured to the left.

The contrast with Buenos Aires was profound. The streets of the little riverside town were deserted, save for the trail of passengers strolling up from the ferry. It was not long before Dee encountered cobblestone streets, the crumbling remains of an old Portuguese fortress and little stone houses with red-tiled roofs.

There was not a car to be seen, but an old woman in a headscarf putted past her on a scooter. The air was clear and cool and the whole place felt like the memories of childhood holidays – shady streets, sleepy patches of sunlight, a breeze blowing up from the river, sailboats bobbing on the harbour.

It seemed too early to call on Ruiz so, after making a circuit of the town, and obtaining a map from the local information office, Dee ordered breakfast in a café overlooking the water. According to the map, Ruiz's studio was located just off the main street. She stretched out her breakfast, picking at the crumbs of *medialunas*, letting her coffee turn cold, watching the seemingly immobile minute hand of her watch creep slowly forwards. Just after nine thirty she gathered her things together and, despite rising impatience, forced herself to maintain a casual strolling pace as she headed in the direction indicated on the map.

The studio was housed in a geranium-coloured stucco building fronting on to a small plaza. A middle-aged man with white curly hair, wearing jeans and a dark pullover, was sitting at a table by the front door, smoking a cigarette and scanning a newspaper. She paused, taking stock of him. He was about her own age, but asserting a youthful style. He turned the pages of his newspaper unhurriedly, taking long drags on the cigarette that he held close to his lips. He wore a signet ring on his forefinger and a thick silver band on his thumb.

'Señor Ruiz?'

He turned at the sound of his name.

'*¿Sí?*' His eyes were long and dark. They flicked briefly over her whole body and then settled on her face. He raised his eyebrows in inquiry but did not smile.

'I'm Dee Sutherland, I sent you an email.'

He closed his newspaper and stubbed out his cigarette. 'You caught the early ferry.'

'Yes.'

His head was inclined as if waiting for her to say something else.

'It was good of you to invite me at such short notice. I was really impressed with the photographs that I saw at the exhibition in San Telmo.'

He continued to appraise her silently, then nodded to himself and smiled a half smile that seemed to indicate he was prepared to progress their interview to the next stage.

'Please.' He stood up and gestured for her to precede him into the house.

It took a few seconds for Dee's eyes to adjust to the dimness. The room was cluttered with furniture: a low sofa, a coffee table, several freestanding lamps, miscellaneous armchairs and bookshelves of varying sizes. Newspapers and items of discarded clothing were scattered over the chairs. There was an empty wine bottle, several stained glasses and an overflowing ashtray on the coffee table. The curtains were drawn against the morning light.

'My studio is out the back. Please go through.'

The narrow corridor opened on to a brightly lit space at the back of the building. It was obviously an addition to the original house, almost as big again with a high sloping ceiling and a number of strategically placed skylights.

'So,' Julio Ruiz waved his arm around the walls that were lined with pictures. 'You want to buy a photograph? As you can see, you have many to choose from. Also, of course,' he pointed to a series of albums displayed on a long counter against the wall, 'I can enlarge any of those if you prefer. Perhaps you can tell me the themes you are interested in so we know where to start.'

Dee wondered if she should affect some interest in the photographs on display. She glanced around the walls, took a few steps towards an image of an old man behind the counter of a kiosk, and then spoke with her back to Ruiz, trying to keep her tone casual.

'The series that you are exhibiting at San Telmo is interesting. There is a portrait of two women, waiting in a queue.'

'You like that one?' He flipped through an album until he found a print of the picture, and then handed the open album to her.

The figures in the background were even more obscure in the smaller photograph. Dee studied it for a long time then, conscious of Ruiz's attention on her, turned the page of the album and pretended to peruse the next set of photographs. She nodded over the images and turned back to the original picture.

'Where was this taken?'

He moved closer to her, redolent with smoke and sweet cologne, and peered over her shoulder to look at the picture more closely. 'This one? Villa Soldati, near barrio Ramón Carrillo on the south side of the city.'

'What sort of an area is it?'

He glanced at her curiously, apparently intrigued by her interest.

'It is a very poor area. A lot of the residents were resettled from a nearby slum that was torn down in the 1980s to make way for the freeway. There are also many *cartoneros* who take the train back and forth to the city. I had in my head an idea to document the different layers of struggle in the area. There are the two groups I have just mentioned and then there is a third group – the *paco* addicts. Do you know about *paco*?'

Dee nodded.

'They call them the living dead. That's how they end up.' He paused. 'I never finished the series. I could not work out how to take that last set of images. It did not seem right to point a camera at so much degradation.'

Dee was pleased that she had touched on a line of inquiry that engaged Ruiz's attention but also disturbed at his unsettling narrative and its implications for her real area of interest. Her uneasiness made her press ahead with less subtlety.

'This girl, here.' She indicated the background figure with her little finger, not meeting his gaze. 'Do you know who she is?'

He frowned. 'The girl? I have no idea. Why do you ask?'

Her plunging disappointment was difficult to conceal. 'She looks familiar.'

'Someone you know?'

'I thought it might be.'

He studied her then with narrowed eyes and a disdainful lift of his top lip as he began to intuit the signs of a hidden agenda.

'It is possible. She was also a *gringa*.'

There should have been rumbling timpani, a sudden squeal of high brass. But there was only the sound of a scooter sputtering past the building, changing gear, and receding into the distance, of Ruiz tapping a cigarette out of its crumpled packet and into the palm of one hand.

'What do you mean *gringa*? North American?' Dee's voice was sharper than she'd intended.

He kept her waiting for a reply as he lit his cigarette.

'I don't know where she was from,' he said eventually. 'She spoke English but I did not recognise the accent. I did not take much notice of her. I was busy setting up my picture.' He indicated the Paraguayan women in the foreground with a wave of the hand that held the cigarette. Dee moved her head back to avoid inhaling the acrid side-stream smoke.

'How long ago did you take the picture?'

He reached over and relieved her of the photograph album. 'I take it you are not really interested in the picture. It is the girl you want to know about?'

'Yes.' Dee's words tumbled out urgently and apologetically. 'Look, I'm sorry. I intended to buy the picture from you. I'm not here to waste your time. But I also need information and I was hoping you could help me. My daughter, Corrie, has been missing for four years. She came to Buenos Aires for a holiday and then we lost contact with her. She just disappeared. I don't know what happened to her. I've been looking for her ever since. The girl in your picture reminded me of her. I know it probably isn't her. I know it's a ridiculous proposition, but I needed to find out if you knew who she was and where she might be found.'

Ruiz folded his arms and leaned back against the counter with a look that was still more offended than sympathetic. 'I told you, I wasn't very interested. Some foreign do-gooder. They come and they go. Why should I care?'

'What about this man? The one she's speaking to?'

He shrugged. 'A social worker maybe. He was organising the food distribution that day.'

'What food distribution?' Dee seized on this evidence of order and bureaucracy, the potential that there might be records, some sort of paper trail.

'The parish hands out donated food several times a week.'

'So this man was from the parish?'

'Or from one of the charities. Caritas perhaps.'

'Maybe he's still working there? Maybe he can tell me something about the girl. He might know where she lives. Or how to find her.'

He drew slowly on his cigarette. 'Perhaps she doesn't want to be found.'

Dee slammed an open-palmed hand on one of the counter tops and addressed him in the sarcastically measured cadence she used in the classroom when provoked beyond all measure.

'Yes, Señor Ruiz, that is entirely possible. It is also possible that she is in some kind of trouble and needs to be found. Or that this girl is not my daughter at all. My daughter might be dead, Señor

Ruiz. That is not an unlikely scenario. And I might spend the next ten, twenty years – whatever time I have left – waiting for someone who left this world long ago. Someone who I have the right to grieve over if that is the case. And it seems to me a monumental act of arrogance for you to stand there and imply that you have the right to withhold information that might be of some help to me in establishing what has happened to my daughter. I don't see how anyone can believe that they have such a right.' Dee's voice cracked, but she stared Ruiz down, her throat working valiantly to swallow the rising waves of emotion.

He shrugged. 'I'm not trying to withhold anything. I'm just saying that if someone doesn't wish to be found, all the information in the world isn't much good to you.'

'What would you do in my place?'

He let the question hang in the air, smiled a little ruefully. 'Would you like a glass of water?'

Dee swallowed again and nodded.

'Come and sit down.' He led Dee back down the corridor to the dim front room and waved her towards one of the couches. She moved some sticky cushions and a scattering of magazines to one side and sat gingerly on the couch that reeked of dope and something slightly doggy. He left her for a moment, returning with a glass of water, which he handed to her before taking the chair opposite.

'So you have not heard from your daughter in four years?'

'No.'

'You went to the police?'

'Of course.'

'What did they say?'

'They think, in the absence of any evidence to the contrary, that she might still be alive. And that is what I want to hear so, mostly, I believe them. How long ago did you take that picture?'

He stroked his chin, thoughtfully. 'Two years?'

'And is it a very dangerous place, this villa?'

'Well, it's not a place I would encourage a young woman to visit on her own. Especially a foreigner.'

'But she wasn't on her own. She was with the parish workers, wasn't she?'

'She seemed to be.'

'Was she helping with the food distribution?'

He frowned, considering the question. 'I assumed so. What else would she be doing there?'

'You didn't speak to her?'

'No.'

'Then how do you know she was a foreigner?'

'I overheard her talking to that guy. I thought maybe she was English.'

Dee leant forward and placed her hand on his knee, holding his gaze, willing him to know something. 'What was she talking about?'

He shook his head. 'It was over two years ago and I wasn't really paying attention. Something about the *paco* addicts. That was probably what caught my attention. She seemed upset. I thought maybe she was a little naïve, someone who had been shocked by what she had been exposed to. I remember thinking that.'

He looked down at her hand on his knee and then back at her face with a quizzical smile. She quickly withdrew her hand.

'And the man she was talking to? You think he worked for Caritas?'

'Maybe. I've seen him distributing food in other villas.'

'You don't know his name?'

'Favio? Federico? We only spoke a couple of times. I am not so good with names. Faces, I remember, but not names.'

Dee scrabbled around in her bag, looking for the photograph of Corrie that she always carried with her. 'This is my daughter. The girl in your picture has her face turned away from the camera, but perhaps you can remember what she looked like.'

He took the photograph from her, examined it carefully, and then looked up at Dee with more interest. 'Her hair was different but sure, it could have been her.' He passed the photograph back to Dee.

She sat very still, staring at the image in her hand. Her emotions were not keeping pace with what she was hearing. It was the first time since the early days of Corrie's disappearance that Dee had encountered someone who thought they actually might have seen her. She leant forward again.

'Is there anything else you remember? Anything at all?'

He shook his head apologetically. 'I'm sorry. I was concentrating on other things. But you could ask the priests who work in the parish. They might know something.'

'How can I get in touch with them?'

'The parish is Our Lady of Fatima. It's not far from the metro line.'

'Señor Ruiz – Julio—' Dee searched in her satchel for her notebook. She tore out a piece of paper and wrote her name and mobile number on it. 'If there's anything else you remember, you'll let me know, won't you?'

'Sure.' He took the paper from her, folded it several times and slipped it into his shirt pocket.

She hauled herself up awkwardly from the couch. 'I won't hold you up any longer. There's a twelve thirty ferry.'

Traces of Absence

He stood as well. 'I hope I have not raised any false hopes.'

'I guess that's what I have to find out.' She paused. 'I would still like to buy a photograph from you. There was another picture that I really liked. The boys and girl on the train – with the light from the open door behind them.'

Ruiz looked at Dee with a flicker of renewed interest. 'You like that one? I also like that picture very much.'

'I'd be glad to have a print.' She wasn't being entirely disingenuous but she was also conscious of deliberately shoring up his continued cooperation.

'Of course. But it will take me a few days to prepare. Perhaps when you come back to collect it you could arrange to stay a little longer. I could show you the town.'

Dee's face lit up spontaneously at the unexpected invitation. 'And I need payment in advance.' She felt immediately foolish at her blushing, girlish assumptions.

'How much?'

'For you, 1200 pesos.'

Dee thought that it was rather a lot of money for a photograph. 'Will you take it in US dollars?'

'Sure.'

She rummaged in her bag for her purse. 'I only have three hundred.'

He pocketed it casually. 'You can pay me the other hundred on collection. When you come back perhaps we can have that conversation you requested in your email? The one about my compositional elegance?'

Dee flushed, remembering her fabricated interest. 'Oh, yes.'

He opened the front door for her. She turned back to him and held out her hand. When he extended his own, she gripped it tightly.

'Thank you. Thank you for your help.'

'*Suerte*. Good luck. I'll see you next week?'

'Yes. I'll be in touch.'

As she walked away she thought she could feel his eyes on her back, but when she snuck a look behind her his door was closed.

Around the first corner and out of sight of the house, Dee sat down heavily on an old bench under a spreading shade tree. Ruiz had seen Corrie. Or *was* it Corrie? He hadn't been a hundred per cent sure. But he was pretty sure. She had been wearing that distinctive jacket. It had to be Corrie. *Didn't it?* Then she remembered Stephen's casual remark: *They were very popular a few years ago.* There was room for doubt but there was room for great hope as well. Did she dare hope? Did she dare to believe that her worst fears were unfounded and that Corrie was alive and well and living in Buenos Aires somewhere? Maybe even working for Caritas or a local parish, devoting her life to saintly service to the poor? Maybe she'd had some kind of a breakdown? Dee had heard about people who were so profoundly affected by their first encounter with extreme poverty that they completely lost the plot. Like St Paul on the road to Damascus, they would experience an overwhelming desire to rub out their former lives and reinvent themselves as champions of a better way. But without telling their families? Perhaps Corrie had been persuaded by some kind of cult to cut off contact. Perhaps she had lost her memory in an accident or as a result of some deep trauma.

The photograph was two years old. The trail, if there was one, would be very cold. If Corrie was alive two years ago, could Dee necessarily assume that no harm had befallen her since? Two years was a long time. Corrie could be anywhere by now. But there were people Dee could ask. That man in the photograph must know something. And he was traceable. He had worked for Caritas. Perhaps he was still working for them. Stephen had some connection with Caritas, didn't he?

She sat on the bench for half an hour, wrestling with her conflicting feelings. Sudden flares of rejoicing alternated with plunges into perplexity. She was accustomed to deferring hope and censoring expectation, but her habitual caution seemed to have broken its reins. Painful speculation was propelling her full tilt towards something that could break her completely if she wasn't careful. She took a deep breath and expelled it slowly. Then another. She tried to focus on her surroundings. The sun was high in the blue sky. Two old men wandered past with *mate* gourds and thermoses. A young boy drove by on a scooter with fishing rods slung across his back. Dee rose purposefully, if a little unsteadily, to her feet and began to walk slowly back to the dock.

Reality had sharpened, but she felt removed and disconnected from it. When she purchased her return ticket at the ferry terminal, her voice sounded overly loud, her gestures exaggerated. She sat jammed among the other passengers in the narrow boarding bay, feeling like an anomaly amongst so much human ordinariness. Eventually, in response to a muffled announcement that she did not understand, her fellow passengers stood and queued. She followed them, shuffling obediently down angled corridors and walkways, halting, waiting, pressing forward again, until eventually they reached the ferry's boarding ramp. People then dashed to claim their preferred seats. Dee would have liked a window seat, but they were quickly taken. She took one on the aisle. After a while she became aware of the people next to her. A teenage girl rested her head on her mother's shoulder and murmured something that made her mother smile as she turned the pages of a magazine.

Dee got up to go to the toilet. Afterwards, she found herself a seat on the other side of the boat.

Such mother and daughter tableaux never failed to disturb her. When did her relationship with Corrie start to falter? When did she first notice that they seemed only to communicate in snappy, reciprocal recriminations? When did Corrie start interpreting every remark as a criticism? When did Dee start taking more and more respite in the affirmations of her professional life?

She thought things had been getting better just before Ross died. Marco had come to board with the family when Corrie was in Year 11. He and Corrie had got along well and he'd been a good influence on her. She had gradually begun to separate herself from Liam and his dodgy crowd. The whole family had pulled together to show Marco a good time. His presence became a catalyst for activities that Dee and Ross had had neither the time nor the energy to tackle for many years. They went up to Cleland Wildlife Park to pat the koalas and take photos with the kangaroos. They drove to Port Noarlunga for snorkelling. They trooped up to Hahndorf for a German lunch and took the scenic route home through the Adelaide Hills. They planned day trips to Victor Harbor and the Barossa Valley and spent the Labour Day long weekend on Kangaroo Island. Seeing Adelaide through Marco's eyes helped them all to rediscover the wonder of their own place. More importantly, Marco gave Corrie an incentive to participate in family excursions she would otherwise have been inclined to shun. Ben and Luke adopted him as their 'big brother' and, for the first time in years, Dee and Ross found themselves relaxing into leisurely endeavours. Sharing those outings had reminded them of their early days together and the things that had drawn them to each other in the first place. Looking back, Dee often wondered if the fates hadn't conspired to grace the family with these experiences as some sort of pre-emptive consolation for all that was subsequently snatched away.

There had been eight missed calls from Corrie on Dee's phone the night Ross died. Three hysterical voice messages.

'Mum! Answer your phone. It's an emergency. I think Dad's having a heart attack. I don't know what to do!'

'Mum! Dad's collapsed! I've called an ambulance. You have to come home. Oh, God, he looks terrible. I'm so fucking scared. Where are you?!'

'Mum! Answer your phone! Answer your fucking phone! I can't do this by myself! Mum, please. Oh God, oh God, oh God. What are they doing to him?' Followed by a long wail of despair before a calmer adult voice intervened and the phone clicked off.

There were so many 'if onlys' afterwards:

If only Dee had cancelled that dinner date as she'd intended.

If only she hadn't switched her phone to silent.

If only she hadn't lingered so much longer than she should have.

She hadn't checked her phone until she was walking back to her car. Her stomach had turned to water when she listened to the messages.

'Corrie – what's going on? Is Dad OK?'

'Where *were* you?'

'Corrie, I need to know what's going on. Where's Dad?'

'They've taken him to the RAH. They said I should stay here to look after the boys.'

'OK. I'm going there now.' Dee hadn't thought to ask Corrie how she was. Her focus had narrowed down to the one essential thing that needed to be done. She had been in the city's restaurant precinct, only a few blocks from the hospital. She ran the whole distance.

'My husband's been brought in. Ross Sutherland. He came in by ambulance. Half an hour ago.'

The receptionist behind the desk seemed to stare at Dee for a fraction too long before shaping her mouth into a perfunctory smile and retrieving a piece of paper from a pile in front of her.

'You're Mr Sutherland's wife?'

'Yes, I am. I only just picked up my daughter's message. She thought he was having a heart attack. Is he OK?'

'Mrs Sutherland, would you like to take a seat for a moment?' The receptionist pointed her pen towards a row of chairs at a distance from the desk. 'I'll just ring through to the clinical staff and let them know you're here.'

Dee didn't feel like sitting down, but the receptionist kept an odd smile fixed on her until she obediently moved in the direction indicated by the pen.

She saw the young woman pick up the telephone and turn her face away as she spoke quietly into the handset. The waiting room was crowded with dull-eyed parents of small children flushed with fever or racked with phlegmy coughs. A baby screamed and screamed. A young man reeking of alcohol clutched a bloodstained T-shirt to a gash on his face, while a woman in a tight black dress that barely made the distance from crotch to upper thigh tottered over him in four-inch stilettos, dabbing ineffectually at the other scratches on his face with a tissue.

'Mrs Sutherland?' A plump, red-haired nurse with a consoling smile, stopped by her chair.

Dee looked up eagerly, spoke a little too loudly. 'Yes!'

'Mrs Sutherland. I'll just take you through to our relatives' room. The doctor would like to have a word with you.'

'Is my husband OK? Can I see him?'

'Doctor Wu will let you know what's going on. He'll be with you very shortly.'

The nurse waved her into a small room, furnished with a faded couch and a couple of upright chairs in clashing colours.

'Can I get you a cup of tea? Glass of water?'

'No. No thank you. Could you just tell me —?'

'I'll let Dr Wu know you're ready to see him. Please take a seat.'

Dee couldn't decipher the nurse's smile. It didn't look like a smile of commiseration, but it wasn't particularly encouraging either. She returned within minutes, in the company of a young, smooth-skinned doctor whose look, however, was much more readable. His face was grave and his eyes were slightly widened with anxiety. Dee knew then. She knew, but she continued to hope that the bad news he was about to deliver would be tempered with some small opportunity for her to influence a more positive outcome: to contract the services of the best specialist in town, to summon a range of alternative therapies, to keep a bedside vigil with the full force of loving intent, to coax Ross out of whatever coma or semi-living state he had slipped into —

'I'm so sorry to have to tell you, Mrs Sutherland. Your husband passed away an hour ago. We did everything we could.'

Dee had stared at him.

'The paramedics did all the right things, but there were no vital signs by the time he arrived here. Because of his age, we rushed him into re-sus and kept trying for another twenty minutes, but he didn't respond.'

Dee kept puzzling over the words. 'Ross is dead?'

'I'm so sorry.'

The nurse sat next to her and put an arm around her shoulders. 'Is there anyone we can call for you?' she asked.

'Can I see him, please?'

'Of course.'

The nurse took her arm and Dee leant against her gratefully. She was steered down a long corridor and through a set of double doors, past bays cluttered with machines and monitors and peopled with comatose patients sprouting various tubes, past busy staff in blue scrubs with scarves tied pirate-style over their heads. Eventually they stopped at a small bay located at a distance from the nurse's station and the bustle of medical activity. The nurse pulled the blue concertina curtain aside.

And there he was. Dee had last seen him when she left for work that morning, lying in their shared bed, tousle-haired and sleepy but reaching a warm arm out of the rumpled blankets to draw her down and kiss her goodbye. And now they were both here, together again, but teleported into a completely alien world, where a stranger had dressed him in a hospital gown, smoothed down the bedding around his immobile arms and closed his eyes against her. She moved to the bedside and placed her fingertips on his cheek. Already the warmth had gone out of him; the texture of his skin was dense and heavy. His cheeks and lips were pale and bloodless, his hair and brows and lashes, brushstrokes of dark colour against so much whiteness. She touched his hair. It, at least, felt the same. She bent to kiss him but it was like kissing a lump of plasticine. She put her arms around his neck and put her cheek against his unyielding one and understood that he was gone. He was irretrievably beyond her reach, beyond her care, beyond her capacity to redeem any of the old hurts and grievances, beyond her gratitude and beyond her love. He was gone and she had been too late to say goodbye.

The children's distress had been profound. Attending to their grief had distracted Dee from her own during the months that followed. Focusing her attention on the children made it possible to survive the trauma of the funeral and the cemetery and the loneliness that eventually descended when friends and relatives reclaimed their casserole dishes and cake-tins and returned to the lives they had put on hold to help the family through its immediate crisis.

The twins had rallied from their disbelief and shell-shocked distress quicker than Corrie. They had the resilience common to thirteen-year-old boys and they had each other. Corrie, however, was halfway through her Year 12 exams. She scraped through one but bombed badly in the other. In the end she got a medical certificate and was awarded enough points to get into the drama course she had applied for, but her confidence was severely shaken and her motivation stripped back to nothing.

Towards the end of April, Dee had come home late from work one night to find Luke and Ben prowling the kitchen, complaining of hunger and Corrie locked in her bedroom.

'Corrie!' Dee had banged angrily on the door. 'Corrie, I asked you to make the boys some pasta for dinner! Corrie, open the door!'

She heard her daughter fumbling with the latch and then the sound of the bedsprings creaking. When Dee opened the door Corrie was lying on the bed, face down.

'Was it so much to ask? All you had to do was boil a pot of water and throw a jar of sauce in a pan.'

Corrie didn't answer.

'Corrie?!'

She turned a tear-stained face towards Dee and stared at her with a strange combination of pain and accusation.

'Are you not well?'

Corrie shook her head slowly.

'What's wrong?'

She shrugged and dropped her gaze to the wall behind Dee's right leg.

'Has something happened?'

After a long pause Corrie answered in an expressionless tone. 'I miss Dad.'

'We all miss Dad, Corrie.'

Corrie had looked at Dee then with pointed scepticism.

'You think I don't? You think it doesn't break my heart every single day?' Dee's voice rose to an angry pitch. 'It tears me apart Corrie, but I have to keep going. I have to earn a living and look after you kids and you know what? I don't think it would kill you to stop wallowing in your own self-pity and lend a hand.'

Corrie had continued to stare at the wall, swatches of rough-cut peroxided hair flopping over her face, her blue eyes glazed with tears.

Dee sighed and sat down on the bed, picking at her nails in silence for several minutes as she composed herself.

'It's not easy for any of us, Corrie,' she sighed, 'but I know it was even harder for you because you had your exams to deal with at the same time.'

Tears began to spill over and run down Corrie's face.

'I think maybe you need a break. You need something to look forward to. Something apart from the study treadmill. Something completely different. What about going to see Marco in Buenos Aires?'

An almost imperceptible flicker of interest had passed across Corrie's face.

Dee had pressed on eagerly. 'I'll pay for your ticket. I'm sure

Marco's family would be happy to put you up. What do you think?'

Corrie had not responded, but Dee could see that she was silently chewing over the suggestion.

'Get in touch with Marco. See what he says.' She stood up and pushed back the fall of hair from Corrie's face. 'Think about it.'

As she turned to go, Corrie had said quietly, 'You left your phone at home today. It's on top of the fridge.'

Dee smiled at her daughter. 'Thanks. I wondered what I'd done with it.'

She supposed it had been an oblique attempt at conciliation. They had struggled so much with communication in those last few months, struggled to bridge the growing distance between them, but they had kept falling short. There are such deep rifts, Dee thought, between what we mean and what we say, what is said and what can never be said, between the veiled insinuations and the questions we cannot bear to ask.

The ferry slowed as it approached the terminal and Dee joined the queue at one of the exits. She was carried along by the crowd, up and down ramps, into the echoing concourse and out into the smoggy afternoon. With a dozen or so other commuters she headed back towards the city centre, jaywalked across eight lanes of traffic, stood in the middle of the road, skimmed by darting taxis, and awaiting an opportunity to dodge around the banked-up semi-trailers.

The crowd flowed up Córdoba. Dee followed them for a few blocks before veering down one of the narrow lanes that led back to Plaza de Mayo. The usual dark and ragged beggars were working the stone steps of the Metropolitan Cathedral, calculating the charity of the pious. A lank-haired woman in ill-fitting clothes mumbled something with averted eyes and held out her hand. Dee didn't really believe that there was any virtue in giving to beggars, but she felt suddenly superstitious about the need to assuage the gods, to purchase some karmic points. She stopped and opened her purse, remembering too late that she had given all her money to Julio. The young woman was limp with lack of expectation and not surprised by the pitiful handful of centavos, but Dee blushed with shame as she dropped them into her hand.

'I'm sorry.'

The woman didn't look at Dee, just folded her fingers over the coins, slipped them into her pocket and moved towards the next person mounting the cathedral steps.

Inside the church, Dee sought out a pew tucked away by one of the side altars and surrendered to tears.

'Corrie? Where are you? What happened to you, love?' she whispered into the shadows. 'What happened to you? Whatever happened?'

It was cold. She hugged herself and rocked in the pew. I am like one of those mad people you see in churches sometimes, she thought, unable to shut off the flow of self-conscious commentary. Like those people who appear to be on day release from the local psychiatric hospital. The lucky ones who have transcended the need to appear normal, the need to ease the anxiety of casual onlookers . . .

Her handbag started to play 'Nutbush City Limits'. The ring tone was Luke's idea of a joke. Dee scrabbled for her phone, embarrassed, as other visitors to the cathedral searched out the source of the noise with hostile stares.

'*Hola, Deirdra, ¿que tal?*'

'*Alicia. Un momento por favor.*'

Dee slid out of the pew and hurried outside.

'Alicia, I have received some very strange news.' She tried to explain in her halting Spanish, stumbling over every second word. I saw a photograph in an exhibition. There was a girl who resembled Corrie. I talked with the photographer. There is a possibility the girl is Corrie. The photograph was taken in Villa Soldati.

'¿Donde?'
'Villa Soldati.'
'¿Villa Soldati?'
'Sí.'
'You tell Stephen?'
'Not yet.'
'Dee. Is necessary you tell Stephen.'
'I will. Of course. But why?'
'Deirdra...' She spoke very slowly in Spanish, ensuring that Dee understood each phrase before she continued. 'Do you know this place?'
'Not specifically, but I have seen areas like it.'
'It is a very dangerous place.'
'Sí, sí, I am aware of this fact.'
'Stephen has told you about his friend Felipe?'
'Felipe? Yes. What about Felipe?'
'Deirdra, this is the villa where Felipe was killed.'

Chapter Eight

When Dee arrived at the *conventillo* in San Telmo the next morning, Stephen was already waiting for her.

'It's good of you to meet me, Stephen.'

'How are you?'

Dee shook her head. 'All over the place. One minute I'm convinced I'm on to something, then I think I'm deluded. When I'm certain it's Corrie in the picture I start to get angry about her being OK and not telling me. But when I convince myself it's probably not her, I just feel bitterly disappointed all over again. I'm a mess, basically.'

'The fact that she was at Villa Soldati and may have met Felipe is the thing that's making *my* head spin.'

'Perhaps it's one of those "grace of God" things you were talking about?'

Stephen gave a short laugh. 'While, of course, I'd love to seize on the opportunity to proselytise, I think we can put it down to the fact that most people who work for the Church here have some kind of connection with each other. If Corrie had any contact with Caritas it was bound to get back to Alicia or myself eventually.'

They climbed the stairs and paid the admission fee to the young woman who had been there the last time Dee visited. She looked at Dee curiously and asked if she had been able to get in touch with Julio Ruiz.

'Yes, thank you.' Dee flushed, feeling embarrassed by what was beginning to look like a strange obsession. She hurried Stephen through the first room of the exhibition and into the second.

'This is it.'

Dee glanced from the photograph on the wall to Stephen, who was contemplating it with an abrupt and frowning stillness. He lifted his glasses and moved forward so that his face was only inches from the picture, then turned back to Dee with a look of intense confusion.

'What is it?'

'That's Felipe. It's definitely Felipe.'

'You're sure?'

By way of an answer, he withdrew his wallet from a pocket inside his jacket. He opened it and passed it to her. In the little window reserved for such things there was a snapshot of a young man with shoulder-length black hair and a closely cropped beard. His skin was the colour of polished walnut and his eyes were nearly black. He had a generous smile and his teeth were very white and even. He looked like a children's picture book Jesus.

Dee held the snapshot close to the other photograph and studied them side by side.

'Even without knowing him, I'd be pretty confident it's the

same person. I can see why he was known as *el guapo*.' She passed the wallet back to Stephen and he returned it to his jacket, shaking his head in disbelief.

'Notwithstanding what I said about the size of Catholic circles, I'm completely stunned.' He stared at the photograph on the wall.

'I wonder what they were talking about.'

'I know that look on Felipe's face and it would suggest to me that she was confiding something quite serious to him.'

'He never mentioned anything to you about meeting an Australian girl?'

'Never. Although it might have been a matter of confidentiality. He was quite scrupulous about those sorts of things.'

'But surely he would have remarked on such an unusual encounter!'

'Unless – when was the picture taken?'

'Julio couldn't remember exactly. He thought it was about two years ago.'

'It might have been while I was away. I went back to England for several months that summer. I only saw Felipe briefly after I returned and we had a lot to catch up on.'

'I wonder if it's just coincidence.'

'What do you mean?'

'The fact that they're both in this picture. She's gone missing and he's . . .' Dee trailed off.

'Let's go and sit down somewhere,' Stephen suggested. 'I need to get my head around all this.'

Dee clutched the banister and kept her eyes on her feet as they slowly descended the old staircase. When they pushed open the external door her darker speculations retreated a little before the innocence of bright sunshine and geraniums spilling through wrought-iron balconies. They crossed the road to a café and claimed a table by the window. Dee ordered tea with lemon and Stephen watched as she added several spoonfuls of sugar.

'I feel a bit faint,' she explained.

'You and me both.' He added milk to his own cup and stirred it thoughtfully. 'Going back to your question, I suppose it's possible that there's a connection between the two events. It's not an everyday occurrence to find a foreign woman in the middle of one of the villas. Even the locals think twice before venturing into those areas and you certainly wouldn't want to go there on your own.'

'So what are you thinking?'

'I'm thinking that she must have known someone there. Someone must have been looking after her. Therefore, someone in the villa will know about her.'

'What should I do next? Will you come with me to see the priests?'

'Well, you can't go alone. Besides, you'll need a translator. They don't speak a word of English at Our Lady of Fatima.'

'Would you mind?'

'I'd mind if you didn't ask. I have something of a vested interest now.' Stephen took out his mobile phone. 'I used to have the number of the parish in here . . . Pedro and Carlos are the two parish priests – or they were. The diocese might have appointed a new team by now, but we'll soon find out.'

He put the phone to his ear. 'Pedro?'

Dee's head shot up in surprise. Stephen's conversation proceeded in rapid Spanish. She strained to catch the gist of it. There was a great deal of laughter and bonhomie. When the call was over he turned to her with a look of playful conceit.

'He's got a few appointments today, but he's happy to squeeze us in.'

Dee leant forward eagerly. 'You didn't get straight on to the actual parish priest?'

'That I did.'

'Did you ask about Corrie? Does he know anything about her?'

Stephen shook his head. 'He said that it's not unusual for North Americans or Europeans to be helping out with the Caritas projects from time to time. He doesn't recall meeting an Australian, but he said that there's a woman in the parish who's been there forever and who was very close to Felipe. She might know more.'

They finished their drinks quickly and Stephen led Dee back to Plaza de Mayo where they caught the *subte* to the end of the line and boarded the *premetro*, a spartan tram with moulded plastic seating and plenty of room for straphanging. Dee gazed out of the window at a landscape that soon left city parks behind and became increasingly impoverished. Between the freeways the opportunistic construction on vacant blocks of land proceeded apace: precarious multi-storeyed dwellings made from slivers of orange brick, sandwiched together with oozing layers of grey mortar, a hotchpotch of exposed concrete pillars, galvanised iron roofing, unglassed window holes and a crazy network of illegal cables syphoning off electricity from the major power lines.

They alighted opposite an enormous warehouse that occupied a vast area of vacant land. A group of teenagers hung around a kiosk on the opposite side of the street. Stephen led the way across the road, steering Dee around the dried-up corpse of a dog tossed into the gutter.

The 'roads' leading into the barrio were rough dirt tracks, relieved occasionally by patches of broken brick. There were muddy potholes everywhere, filled with stagnant brown water and floating rubbish: disposable nappies, grey plastic bags, torn rags and food wrappers.

But it was not as menacing as Dee had expected. During the last stages of their journey, Stephen had located a clerical collar in one of the pockets of his jacket and attached it to his grey cotton shirt.

'What's that for?' she had asked.

'It gives you an instant identity. People feel less jumpy if they know who you are.'

As they navigated the dirt roads, Dee realised that he was right. People glanced at them, noted the collar, looked her up and down, but then went back to their business. A couple of gaunt youths with closely cropped heads and oversized jeans lolled past them. One of them whistled at Dee and called out something in Spanish that made his friend break into appreciative laughter. Dee didn't need a translation. The intonation had the same lewd, jeering note as its English equivalents. But, at her age, it wasn't the sexual objectification she minded so much as the note of sarcasm. Either way, she thought, you ended up feeling diminished. It must have shown on her face.

'Don't worry about it. It's just the usual machismo posturing.' Stephen was smiling as if he found the episode amusing.

'I'm not worried.' The words came out more sharply than she intended.

The church was situated about five hundred metres from the main road, flanked by a well-secured priests' residence and community hall. There was a scattering of people gathered in the plaza in front of the hall, sitting on benches or standing about in groups. Stephen acknowledged those they passed with a cheerful greeting. Dee also nodded and smiled as they made their way to a small office located just inside the main doors of the hall.

Padre Pedro was sitting at a table in the cramped confines, drinking *mate* with a couple of officials who had briefcases at their feet and notepads in their hands. Pedro acknowledged Stephen enthusiastically when he spotted him peering around the doorjamb and assured him that he wouldn't be long.

'You can tell there's another election coming up,' Stephen murmured to Dee. 'All the bureaucrats are out in force with their usual offers of local grants. Of course, they seem to develop amnesia after the elections are over.'

They returned to the courtyard to wait. Stephen's collar gave him easy entrée to the waiting supplicants and he struck up a conversation with some of the women, inquiring about their children, where they had come from and how long they had lived in the area. They responded with warmth and friendliness, happy to be acknowledged by 'the Father'. Dee wished that she had a similar way of engaging with them, but all she could do was smile inanely and tickle the babies' chins.

Despite Pedro's assurances that he wouldn't be long they waited half an hour. Dee retired to one of the benches, isolated by her lack of language and her increasingly nervous restlessness. Eventually, Pedro emerged with the officials, all smiles and embraces. As their retreating car lurched cautiously around the potholes, Pedro rolled his eyes at Stephen.

'They mean well,' Stephen translated his laughing remark for Dee. 'And sometimes the money even comes through, but it always runs out before the parish is able to achieve anything of lasting significance.' He and Pedro spent a few minutes making what Dee imagined, from all the embracing and backslapping, were the usual observations about how well they both looked and how it had been too long. Pedro had a round face with a full-lipped mouth and thick hair curling on his collar. He welcomed her in Spanish and asked if she would like to see the church. Dee and Stephen followed him into the white-rendered building. The light, airy space, with its neatly swept, tiled floor, new pews and striking stained-glass windows had a peaceful ambience about it and Dee was glad that she could be genuinely appreciative of what was obviously Pedro's pride and joy. They settled themselves on the ends of the rear pews while Stephen explained to Pedro the background events to their visit.

Pedro's frowning countenance hinted at the reply Stephen eventually translated.

'He says he never met a girl of this description, but he agrees with me – someone must know something. There's a local woman called Fidelina who worked quite closely with Felipe. She looks after one of the community centres and knows everything that goes on around here. If you don't mind a bit of a walk, he'll take us round to her house and introduce you.'

Dee turned to Pedro. '*Muchísimas gracias, Padre.*'

'*Pedro,*' he corrected her. '*Por favor, llameme Pedro.*'

He gestured at Dee's handbag. She looked at Stephen in puzzlement.

'It's better that you don't take that. It's like a red rag to a bull, walking around these streets with valuables in full view. The local people respect the priests but only up to a point.'

Dee removed a handkerchief and the photograph of Corrie that she always carried with her and handed the bag to Pedro who took it back to the presbytery to lock away. When he returned he led them out onto the main road, which they followed for about half a kilometre before turning down a narrower dirt thoroughfare. Teetering two- and three-storey structures jammed up against each other. Tiny shadowed alleyways ran between the buildings and they were obliged to pass through in single file. At various points the alleyways ended in high, locked gates.

'Ostensibly for security but mostly to keep out the police,' Stephen explained.

Dee felt safe with the two priests, but there was no visible evidence of danger. When they were back on the main roadway, they encountered a series of women sitting on their front doorsteps who waved to Pedro and Stephen. They, in turn, called out greetings or teasing remarks that made the women laugh. Children and teenagers wandered through the dusty streets in a manner that evoked the inhabitants of a sleepy, rural township. The dwellings, painstakingly assembled over time from recycled objects, displayed little homely touches: checked curtains at the windows, well-tended gardens struggling out of the poor soil. Women diligently swept their cracked patios and concrete courtyards. Laundry, scrubbed fresh and clean, billowed on lines strung between rooftops and balconies. But the piles of rubbish shovelled into gutters and spilling out of torn bags on the footpath signalled the extremity of their collective hardship.

'Does the municipality not collect the rubbish?'

Pedro understood the question and answered via Stephen.

'Yes, sometimes, when the roads are not too muddy for the trucks to get through. But it is a question of education. The people just put the rubbish in the streets and the dogs get to it.'

'There are a lot of dogs.'

'Yes. Their owners sleep next to them at night to keep warm.'

'Really?'

'So I've heard.'

They passed an expanse of open ground, where half a dozen *cartoneros* were unloading their carts next to high mounds of sorted objects – piles of wooden planks and assorted building materials, a collection of old computers, stacks of bundled cardboard and cartons. A little further along, in the burnt-out chassis of a car, a boy, so filthy and ragged as to be almost unrecognisable as human, was lying passed out, his head flung back, his mouth open.

Pedro shook his head sadly.

'*Paco*,' Stephen explained. 'It's an epidemic.'

They turned a corner into another open area, less cluttered by housing. There was a sprawling single-storey dwelling set apart on a patch of land enclosed by high wire fencing. A black V8 with sleek American lines was parked outside, its windows down, its stereo blaring. A group of rough-looking men perched on upturned crates around a fire and stared them down.

'Dealers,' Stephen murmured, but both he and Pedro smiled and waved at the men who acknowledged them with nods and disdainful laughter.

'It must stick in your throat, having to be pleasant to them after what happened to Felipe.'

He shrugged. 'There's nothing to be achieved by antagonising them.'

Around a corner and down another alleyway they arrived at a dwelling with high gates and a courtyard full of potted plants and semi-tropical trees. In the middle of the courtyard there was a salvaged table and a selection of chairs. Through an open door Dee could see a neat and serviceable kitchen, plastic cups and old crockery arranged on benches, a concrete sink, jars of jam on a windowsill.

A woman, who Dee hoped was Fidelina, hurried out when she saw them peering through the gate. She was a sturdy, large-bosomed woman; her strong arms were bare and her hair was pinned up in a tight bun. She laughed happily at the sight of Pedro and quickly unlocked the gate, pulling the rickety chairs into a little circle so everyone could sit down together.

It took a while to go through the round of greetings and pleasantries and Fidelina was full of excited news that she wanted to relay to Pedro, but eventually he steered her towards the subject of Felipe and the foreign girl.

Fidelina studied Dee curiously before replying and then launched into a long and animated diatribe, occasionally turning to Dee and addressing her as if she could follow the conversation. Stephen became more alert and attentive, leaning forward, his brow furrowed but his eyes bright with interest. Several times he opened his mouth to ask questions, but on each occasion Fidelina gathered pace and raised her voice, forestalling him. Fidelina's Guarani accent was so thick Dee could barely understand a word. She kept looking from Pedro to Stephen for clues about what they were hearing. Eventually the narrative flow trickled into a series of musings and cross-questionings by Pedro. Only then did Fidelina turn to Stephen and motion with her head that it was time for him to translate.

Stephen blew air out of puffed cheeks and shook his head. He took a few moments to mentally sequence what he had been charged to pass on.

'Firstly,' he began, 'she remembers a girl – a foreigner but not North American. She knows the North American accent. Fidelina believed the girl was English.'

He paused.

'She came to the barrio with a man called Niko. No point in glossing it. Niko, in Fidelina's words, is a very bad man. He supplies the local dealers here with *paco*. She was at pains to tell us that she stands up to the dealers. She has kept them away from her own children and she tries to help out her neighbours' as well. If the dealers come near her house she gives them a bit of a blast. She says she is not frightened of them, but many people are.' He smiled. 'Fidelina is a bit of a matriarchal battle-axe. It's a good thing you can't speak much Spanish because her language would curdle your ears.'

'I think I'd cope.' Dee was irritated by the interruption to Fidelina's account. Being locked out of these crucial exchanges made her feel like a deficient child awaiting the picked-over crumbs of adult information. She guessed from Stephen's lightness of tone that Fidelina had not communicated any definitive tragedy concerning Corrie, but what he had just told her left open a number of unsavoury denouements and she was already anticipating several of them.

'So this Niko – what was his relationship with Corrie?'

Stephen glanced at her apologetically and quickly resumed his narrative.

'Fidelina says Niko was often in the company of foreigners, dealers from the States. They swan around like businessmen, apparently: sharp suits, expensive jewellery. She thought at first the foreign girl might have been a girlfriend of one of the North Americans, but after a while it seemed pretty clear to Fidelina that she was with Niko. He only brought her here once, seemed to be showing off in front of her. Fidelina says that the girl seemed unhappy. She was angry with Niko. He laughed at her. They had a fight. She thinks perhaps this was the first time the girl had seen this side of Niko's business. Maybe she didn't realise that these were the sorts of activities her boyfriend was involved with. Niko fancies himself as something of a ladies' man apparently. He's very good-looking and he can be quite charming although Fidelina has other less flattering characterisations of him. Anyway, she only saw the girl one other time. She remembers her because she did not seem like the usual, um – I won't repeat her word – like Niko's usual girlfriends, and she felt sorry for her. The girl came back on her own a week later. She had noticed that Fidelina wasn't afraid to confront Niko and she came back to ask for her help. She wanted to get away from him. Fidelina encouraged her to make the break. She told her about some of Niko's less savoury activities, which include – sorry Dee – arranging for people who interfere with his business to be removed.'

Dee pressed her fingertips hard against the bone of her forehead. 'Go on.'

'Fidelina told the girl that she should talk to Felipe. That he would be able to help her find a place where she would be safe. The girl tried to give Fidelina money but she wouldn't take it. She says the girl was very nice, very respectful.'

With shaking hands, Dee held out the well-worn photo of Corrie. '*¿Es está la chica?*'

Fidelina took the picture from her and studied it closely. She smiled and nodded. '*Sí, está es la chica. Es Corazón.*'

Corazón? Corrie had Latinised her name. Or her friends had. It meant 'heart' and was used as a term of endearment. It was consoling to know she had inspired such tenderness.

'*Sí.*' Fidelina continued to smile and nod as she looked at the picture. '*Sí. Corazón.*'

Stephen asked her another question and she gave an extended answer. When he turned to Dee to translate his voice was scratchy with emotion.

'She doesn't know if the girl ever saw Felipe because she never got to ask him. She thinks it might have been a week later that Felipe was murdered. She knows who did it, but there was no point in going to the police. They are all being paid off by Niko. Sorry – this is quite difficult for me.' His mouth began to tremble. Dee bit her lip in concern and passed him her handkerchief. He wiped his eyes and blew his nose, stared into the middle distance as he composed himself. 'The priests and some of the Caritas workers had signed an open letter to *La Nación* condemning the activities of the dealers and calling for a clampdown. The dealers made death threats. Nobody thought they'd dare act against the priests, but – she is wondering now – maybe they saw Corrie with Felipe. That might have given them the excuse they needed to go after him. They might have persuaded Niko that there was something going on between Felipe and Corrie.' He broke off and put his head in his hands.

Pedro placed a reassuring hand on Stephen's back. He explained to Fidelina that Felipe was a close friend of Stephen's, which immediately prompted Fidelina to throw her arms around him and begin a broken-hearted litany of praise for Felipe while tears ran down her face.

Dee picked up the photo of Corrie that had fallen to the ground from Fidelina's lap and gazed at it, her own eyes blurring.

Stephen sighed deeply, rubbed definitively at his nose with Dee's handkerchief and sat with his shoulders hunched, staring at the ground. Fidelina brought him a bottle of warm Coca-Cola from the dim recesses of her kitchen. He nodded his thanks and took a few swallows.

'Does Fidelina know where Corrie might have gone?' Dee asked, '*Fidelina, ¿Adónde se fue?*'

Fidelina shook her head sadly, but Pedro exchanged a few words with Stephen.

'Pedro thinks that it might be worth trying the Sisters of Mercy in Barrio Moreno,' Stephen explained. 'That's where the parish often refers women who are trying to get away from violent partners. There are other agencies, but that one is a good option for women from this area because it's on the other side of the city and therefore more difficult for their partners to track them down. He thinks that is where Felipe would have referred her.'

'How far away is it?'

'Two hours by car. Maybe a little more.'

'Do you think she would have managed to get away from this Niko character?'

Stephen shrugged his unwillingness to speculate.

Fidelina reached for Stephen's empty cola bottle and asked if Dee would like a *gaseosa*. She shook her head. Fidelina started conferring with Pedro in Spanish, but their eyes kept drifting over to Dee.

There were a hundred questions competing for consideration in Dee's brain. How did my daughter look? Was she in good health? Was she unkempt or abused? How did Niko treat her? Did he show her any affection? Fidelina had said they'd had a fight. Corrie had taken him on. Did that bode well or ill? Fidelina stood up to him and he left her alone. Did this Niko like strong women or did he punish them?

'Have you seen Niko recently?' she asked Fidelina.

Stephen translated Fidelina's reply. Niko had not been seen in the barrio for a long time after Felipe was killed, but Fidelina had seen him occasionally during the last year. He came and went, but not as often as before. She had never seen Corrie again and she had not asked about her because she did not want Niko to know that they had spoken.

Dee found herself wanting to squeeze more information out of Fidelina. She felt cheated by the paucity of detail. Her daughter had returned to the land of the living but was unreachable. There was nothing to seize or hold on to. Once again, her frustration rose to choke her.

Fidelina was watching her closely. '*Era una chica muy linda.*' She was a very nice girl.

Dee smiled sadly.

Pedro looked at his watch and said something to Stephen. Dee stood up in anticipation of their departure, taking a last look at the meticulously swept courtyard, the mismatched chairs, the wisteria growing over a rusted metal frame, Fidelina planted solidly in the middle of her domain. Corrie had stood here, she thought. She came looking for help and this good woman helped her. She stepped towards Fidelina and was seized in a fierce embrace. After a few moments, Fidelina broke away, motioned for the three of them to wait and hurried back inside her house. She returned with a jar of dark-coloured marmalade for Stephen and a little card for Dee. Soft and grimy with handling, the card bore an image of the Virgin Mary. It was the Virgin of Luján, the patroness of Argentina, the one credited with miraculous healings and restorations. Dee had seen it all over Buenos Aires – the familiar triangular blue robe with gold embroidery, the jewelled crown, the little hands clasped in prayer at her breast, the halo of stars, the crescent moon at her feet. There was a little bump in the card, a bulge of gold thread in the centre of the Virgin's robe.

'It's a piece of fabric from the robe of the statue that was carried in last year's pilgrimage to Luján,' Stephen explained. 'Fidelina hopes the Virgin's prayers will help you.'

Dee shook her head vigorously and tried to pass it back. 'I can't accept this. It's obviously something very precious to her and I don't believe in this stuff. It's wasted on me.'

Fidelina frowned and pushed Dee's hand away.

'Then accept it as a symbol of her good wishes for you. She has nothing else to give,' Stephen murmured.

Dee wished she had her purse with her so she could empty it into Fidelina's generous hands but perhaps it was better to have nothing to exchange. Perhaps she needed to get over the compulsion to avoid vulnerability by keeping the scales of obligation weighted in her favour.

She embraced Fidelina again.

'*Gracias, Fidelina. Muchísimas gracias.*'

Fidelina waved them off at the gate and they made their way back through the labyrinthine alleyways, past the *cartoneros*' mounds, the dealers' fenced-off property and down the main street with its makeshift kiosks advertising *gaseosa* or *cigarillos* on handwritten cardboard signs. When they got back to the parish house Pedro wrote an address and telephone number on a piece of paper and handed it to Dee.

'The contact details of the Sisters at Barrio Moreno,' Stephen told her. 'He hopes they can help you.'

Dee stared at the paper. 'He's sure this is the place Felipe would have referred her?'

'He thinks it is the most likely possibility.'

It felt like a very tenuous one to Dee. Nevertheless, she folded the paper carefully and put it in the handbag that Pedro had returned to her.

'*Gracias, Padre.*'

'Pedro,' he corrected her again, clasping her outstretched hand in both of his. 'I pray for you.'

She was grateful for the confident and kindly grasp of his hands around hers, grateful for his offer of prayers. If there was a God, she was sure this was the sort of man He would listen to.

If there was not, it was still consoling to know that someone would hope on her behalf in a disciplined kind of way, although she didn't know why this should be so. She was suddenly leaden with weariness.

She and Stephen did not speak as they trudged back to the tram stop. When the tram arrived, she took a seat by the window and leant her head against the grimy glass. She had found evidence that her daughter had lived for at least two years in Buenos Aires, but that same evidence suggested that she might not have survived much longer than that. Or did it? She couldn't think clearly. She couldn't credit that Corrie had cut off her family without a word. Why? Why would she do that? She understood the appeal of charming strangers. Sister Mary Frances had spoken very wisely when she observed all those years ago that there was no accounting for the movement of the human heart. Dee did not condemn her daughter for being attracted to beauty and romantic rebellion, but how had she allowed herself to get so deeply involved with such a shady character? And why had she not contacted Dee when things started to go wrong? That was the cruellest indictment of all. In her darkest moments Corrie had still spurned her family. What kind of a mother must I have been? Dee felt a stab of pain at the question. Was it because of the fights we had about Liam? Did I frighten her so much that she didn't dare tell me about this Niko? But how could her fear of me have outweighed her fear of him? And then she forced herself to confront what had, of course, occurred to her almost immediately. Was she pregnant? Is that why she felt that she couldn't come home?

Dee despised herself then. She despised herself for the nagging voice of accusation and petty condemnation that she must have set up in Corrie's head.

'What are you thinking?' Stephen swayed alongside her in the uncomfortable moulded seating of the tram.

'That I let my daughter down very badly.'

'I thought that's what you were thinking.' But he did not attempt to fill the ensuing silence with arguments to the contrary.

'You're supposed to say "No you didn't".'

'Would you believe me if I did?'

'No.'

They sat in silence again for some minutes.

'What are *you* thinking?' she asked.

'I'm still reeling from the irony that my boyfriend may have been killed on the assumption that he was straight.'

'Fidelina said that was just a pretext.'

'Which doesn't make it any less ironic . . .'

The tram pulled into Plaza de los Virreyes and Stephen led the way along the platform and down the steps to the *subte*. It was peak hour and the station was crowded. They squeezed onto an already packed train, jammed too close to others for comfortable conversation.

When they emerged from the *subte* at Plaza de Mayo, a wind had whipped up and there was a smell of rain in the air.

'Buy you a drink?'

'Only if you let me buy you one as well.'

They pushed through the glass doors of the Gran Vía and headed straight for the bar.

'Let me run something by you,' Stephen volunteered as their gin and tonics softened the edges of the jagged day. 'It's not unlikely that Corrie was trying to console herself over her father's death by finding another strong male to look after her. And that she might have wanted to keep that to herself. Build another world where she felt safe, a world removed from all the pain and grief back in Australia. Especially if she felt you might be in any way disapproving. Which any mother worth her salt would have been.'

Dee felt the restoration of a certain dignity in being compared favourably with other responsible mothers. Or perhaps it was just the gin.

'Thanks. I needed to hear that.'

'You've never been tempted yourself?'

'To what?'

'To start afresh. Reinvent yourself. Get away from the accumulated weight of all your mistakes.'

'Only every other day.'

'There you go.'

Dee looked at him thoughtfully. 'How do you know all this stuff?'

His smile was rueful. 'I've been running away all my life, in one way or another. I'm a world expert. Felipe was the first person I met who made me want to stay exactly where I was. If he could love me, I began to suspect that there might be something worth loving and then it became more fun working out what that something was than trying to be someone and somewhere else.'

But this reflection made Dee sad again. 'So, we're back where we began. If I had loved Corrie enough she wouldn't have had to go looking for love somewhere else.'

Stephen snorted at that, emboldened by the gin. 'My mother loved me to death but there comes a point in life where that's just not enough anymore. Who told you that you had to be the be-all and end-all for everybody?'

'Your mob.'

'Pardon?'

'The Church. The Moral Majority. Freud. The margarine commercials. We mothers are your sainted icons and your greatest whipping boys.'

'Sorry – I'm not sure where to start tackling that mélange of ridiculous assumptions, but firstly, I take great umbrage at being lumped in with the Moral Majority. Secondly, I don't think we had the same margarine commercials in the UK, but I'm assuming it's some sort of media stereotype of suburban motherhood and thirdly, how did Freud sneak in there?'

'The whole Fort-Da thing. Mummy here. Mummy gone. If Mummy leaves for five minutes to take a pee the child is profoundly traumatised and Mummy is culpable.'

Dee rummaged in her handbag for the holy card that Fidelina had given her.

'This. This is what I'm talking about. This image of sainted womanhood was held up to me all my life by the Church. How can we possibly live up to this? How can we be gentle and calm and ethereal and passively enduring *all the fucking time*?!'

The barman glanced over at them curiously.

Stephen took the card from her and studied it affectionately. 'Maybe that's it,' he mused, as though talking to himself. 'You think you have to *be* the Virgin Mary. Fidelina would never presume such a thing. She just loves the Virgin because she believes the Virgin loves her.'

'Lucky her,' Dee remarked, not without bitterness, taking the card back from him and tossing it angrily into the bottom of her bag. 'And by the way, all this emphasis on virginity also gets up my nose.'

'I can see it's going to be a long evening.'

But Dee was not really interested in pursuing the argument. It was an old one and the cherished idols persisted in spite of all her best attempts at intellectual deconstruction. Or came creeping back in even more insidious guises. She directed her gaze at the bowl of nuts on the table.

'Stephen, do you think Corrie managed to get away from this Niko character?'

'Unless she was threatening his business interests I can't see that he had any incentive to hurt her, especially if he hadn't done so in the past. If she really wanted to leave him, I think she would have managed it.'

'What do you mean – "if she really wanted to leave him"?'

'It's not always so easy to walk away from someone we've been in love with.'

'I think Corrie had more sense than to stay with someone like Niko.'

'Maybe. But she met this man at a very vulnerable time in her life. Don't be too surprised if she ended up making some foolish decisions. We've all done that.'

Dee stabbed at the ice cubes in her glass with her drinking straw. 'Yes,' she replied dully. 'We have.'

Chapter Nine

After a number of aborted forays down dirt roads and unmarked streets, Alicia pulled up outside a property surrounded by a three-metre-high wall. An intercom was mounted beside a metal gate.

'*¿Listas?*' she asked Dee. Are you ready?

Alicia had kept up a one-sided conversation in Spanish for the duration of the ninety-minute trip from the city. It reminded Dee of the way she herself might soothe a distressed toddler or skittish animal with a determined flow of gentle noise. Alicia was, as always, effortlessly chic in jeans, a tailored jacket and a long scarf of midnight blue wound loosely round her neck. Dee had dressed demurely with the Sisters in mind: slacks and a twin set, sensible shoes.

'*Sí. Vamos.*'

At the gate, Alicia buzzed the intercom and announced their presence. Dee pulled together the shreds of her diffident hope. The gate was opened by a small woman in a blue apron with toffee-coloured streaks through her dark hair. Her gap-toothed smile advertised her lowly economic status. Alicia made the introductions and the woman announced her own name as Viviana. She carefully locked the gate before directing them down a pathway shaded by tall trees to the front doors of a Spanish colonial house. To the left of the pathway was a children's play area furnished with brightly coloured equipment and a wooden cubby house. The interior face of the high wall bore children's paintings of flowers and rainbows, birds and jungle animals.

Viviana waved them into a spacious entrance hall. Five women and a clutch of small children were seated around a large table just beyond the doorway. Two of the women were heavily pregnant. They were sharing *mate*. The children had plastic cups of milk. They looked at Alicia and Dee curiously. Alicia greeted them warmly and ready smiles blossomed on the women's faces. They invited Alicia and Dee to join them. One woman, much older than the others, rose and approached Dee. She was white-haired with faded blue eyes in a face that would have once been considered beautiful for its high cheekbones and proud chin. She was still striking, but her skin was deeply lined and drained of youthful colour.

'I'm Catalina. And I imagine you must be Deirdra. What a wonderful name.'

She spoke perfect English with the singsong lilt of the Irish. Dee laughed with relief.

'You're Irish!'

The woman smiled. 'No, but apparently I have the accent.'

'You've never been to Ireland?'

'I'd never been outside Argentina until a few years ago when the order sent me to a conference in Bolivia.'

'Where does the accent come from?'

'My grandparents were from Ireland and I spoke English with them when I was a little girl.'

For a second Dee forgot her nervousness and trepidation. She laughed in wonder at the incongruity of this quintessentially Irish Catholic nun who had grown out of the soil of Spanish–Italian Buenos Aires. She could be any one of half a dozen nuns who had taught Dee in Australia in the 1970s.

'Thank you for seeing us Sister Catalina.'

The nun waved away her gratitude. 'Would you like a cup of tea?'

Dee smiled again. Tea. Not coffee. 'Yes, thank you.'

She turned to Alicia, who indicated her preference for sharing *mate* with the other women.

Catalina led Dee down a corridor that ran at right angles to the main entrance hall and turned into a large kitchen, with several industrial-sized steel ovens and deep sinks. She lit one of the blackened gas rings and shifted a kettle over the flame.

'I think the water's still hot from the *mate* but we'll need to bring it up to the boil for tea.' Then she located white ceramic mugs and teabags and leant against the bench next to the stovetop, her hands lightly clasped in front of her bony hips.

'So, Deirdra. How can we help you?'

'I'm not sure how much Alicia told you over the phone.'

The kettle started to blow steam. Catalina filled one mug and passed it to Dee. 'I'll let you do your own teabag.' Then she filled the second cup.

She waved Dee over to one of the laminate-topped tables in the adjacent dining area.

'I believe you've been looking for your daughter,' she said. Her tone was light and matter-of-fact. Her impassive eyes were like rolled river stones, buffeted by the currents of all the lives that had flowed over and around hers. Dee shrugged and let out a long sigh, cupped her hands around her mug of tea, and began to cry.

Perhaps it was the sound of Catalina's voice setting up echoes from a time of childhood dependence. Or it might have been the woman's implacability, the feeling Dee got that she was acquainted with all kinds of suffering. Or perhaps Dee had just come to the end of her tether. Since the day before, when she had heard Fidelina's story, she had felt as though she had been holding herself in a kind of mental padded cell, observing a range of conflicting emotions while remaining essentially removed from them. There was the terrible frustration of knowing about Corrie's secret life in Buenos Aires but still not knowing the final outcome. Was Dee pulling together the last few pieces of a murder mystery or following a trail of deliverance? There was the persistent bewilderment over her daughter's cavalier abandonment of her family, and an anger that could in no way be indulged as long as a potential tsunami of grief was gathering mass in some yet to be revealed finale. Was everything over or just beginning? In the presence of Catalina, for some reason, the door of Dee's padded cell swung open and she stepped out into raw pain.

'That's the way,' Catalina said kindly. 'You have a good cry.'

Dee lowered her head and abandoned herself to noisy sobbing.

Women came and went in the kitchen. Dee was conscious of the sound of their footsteps, a tremble of hesitancy in the air, muted conversations with Catalina. A box of tissues materialised from somewhere.

As the storm of wretchedness abated Dee became aware of the blood pounding behind her eyes and in her swollen nasal membranes. Her lap was full of sodden tissues and her heart was full of weary resignation.

'Can I get you another cup of tea, Deirdra?' Catalina asked at last. 'That one will have gone cold.'

Dee nodded.

'Have you got a picture of your daughter that I could look at?' Catalina asked when she returned with another steaming cup.

Dee proffered the usual photograph.

Catalina reached into her apron pocket for her glasses and put them on. 'Oh,' she murmured softly, smiling. 'It's Corrie.'

Dee froze with a tissue halfway to her nose. She stopped breathing, blinked her puffy eyes, once, slowly.

Catalina met Dee's incredulous gaze with renewed interest. She passed the photo back to her. 'Corrie was with us for about six months. She left us last year, just after Easter.'

Tears welled again and spilled down Dee's cheeks, but this time they were tears of relief. 'She's alive?'

Catalina smiled. 'Last time I saw her she was very much alive.'

'Oh, thank God. Thank God. Thank you, God.' Dee directed her gaze to the heavens. 'Thank you. Thank you, Sister Catalina.' She got up from her chair and threw her arms around the old woman. 'Where is she now? Where can I find her?'

Catalina frowned slightly. 'Well, I'm not entirely sure, but I have the forwarding address she gave us when she left.'

It was a beginning. A place to start. And now that Dee knew she was no longer tracking a spectre she was confident that there would be evidence, a trail. There would be ways and means to achieve the end she had barely dared hope for. She sat down and took a few gulps of her tea.

'Can you tell me how she was? Can you tell me what happened to her?'

Catalina regarded Dee thoughtfully for several seconds before speaking. 'Corrie had got herself into a difficult situation.'

'They told me at Villa Soldati that she got involved with a drug dealer.'

'Yes. He was a drug dealer. Among other things. Corrie had known about the dealing for some time. She met him when she visited Iguazu. He was shoring up his relationships with certain border officials. This is not necessarily something culpable in the eyes of the young. It can even look glamorous. A good-looking young man with such power and influence and so much money to throw around. Corrie thought for a long time that he was just providing party drugs to the North Americans. She said to me, "Sorry, Sister, I know that might seem irresponsible to you, but if rich people want to shove cocaine up their noses, why shouldn't poor people make some money out of it?"'

Dee could see the logic of that position but there was a youthful naïveté in the assumption that evil could be so easily contained.

'Did he harm her in any way?'

Catalina shook her head slowly. 'Not in the way so many of the women who come to us are harmed. I've seen such terrible violence over the years.' Her face clouded. 'A woman came in the other day and I invited her to sit down but she couldn't. She'd been so badly violated in the back passage by her husband. I didn't know men did that to women . . .'

Dee didn't know what to say. She felt sorry that the elderly nun had been exposed to something like that and heartsick for the woman who had had to explain the cause of her pain so explicitly. She grimaced in sympathy with the nun's bewilderment. Catalina shook her head to rid herself of the distressing image and continued.

'I don't really know, but it sounded like there was real feeling between Corrie and this man. She was with him for two years and, on the whole, he seems to have treated her well. There were other women towards the end, but she had discovered more disturbing things about him by then: the terrible damage caused by the *paco* trade that was the other side of his business. The unsavoury thugs who reported to him. The casual violence directed at anyone who got in their way. The night she came to us she was in a terrible state. A very good man had been killed in front of her—'

'Felipe?'

'You know of him?'

'I know a close friend of his.'

'Such a beautiful man. He referred many women to us over the years. Very quiet and lovely. So much integrity. He took great risks to help people in need. I was not surprised when I heard what had happened to him, but I was very sad.'

'And he was killed in front of Corrie?'

'They attacked him one night. After that letter was put in the paper exposing what the dealers were doing and calling on the government to intervene. It was the night she went to him to get our address. They crept out of the dark. They said they were going to kill her "boyfriend" and they were going to kill her, too. She screamed for help but, of course, nobody came. She tried to find assistance for Felipe, but everyone's doors were locked against her. She ran away in fear for her own life. Somehow she got back to the city. After wandering the streets all night she caught a train out to us in the morning. When she arrived here she was catatonic and in a state of collapse. It took us over a week to get the whole story out of her.'

'Did you call the police?'

'Corrie was terrified of going to the police. For a number of reasons. She felt implicated in the crime because of her association with Niko. She was fearful for her own life and she believed that the police were in Niko's pocket. I didn't think it was our place to encourage her to put herself in any more danger. She was distraught enough as it was. Besides, we know how these things go. Everyone knows who killed Felipe, but no one saw anything. No one ever sees anything.'

'But a man was killed! A man who was working for the Church – for a local charity.'

'Corrie didn't want any attention drawn to her whereabouts. We have to respect the confidentiality of our clients.'

And now Dee came to an even more pressing question. She fixed her eyes on Catalina's. 'And why did you never try to get in touch with us? Her family? Or at least with the Australian Embassy? That would seem to me like a logical thing to do.'

Catalina continued to regard her steadily. She may not have intended her expressionless face or disciplined posture as censure, but Dee found it easy to slip into this assumption and it fuelled her stirrings of resentment.

'Why didn't you call us?'

Catalina took off her glasses, wiped them with the hem of her apron and put them down carefully on the table. She turned her pale, naked eyes on Dee.

'It took us some time to get to the bottom of Corrie's story. Obviously we kept asking if there was someone we could contact. She was disoriented and didn't seem to understand what we were asking. Then, later, she became very fearful and agitated every time we raised the matter. And she led us to believe that she was a resident in this country.'

'I suppose she was by that stage. At least in her own head. Having apparently decided to shake the dust of her previous life from her sandals.' Bitterness spilled into Dee's voice. Two years ago Corrie's circumstances had come to the attention of the Sisters. Dee and her sons might have been saved two years of anguish if they had bothered to speak up.

'But you must have been under some obligation to tell the police what you knew about Felipe's murder?' she pressed.

Catalina continued firmly. 'We are a refuge. Our first priority is the wellbeing of the women who come to us. We cannot take on the entire justice system. Much as we might like to. It is not easy to build trust with women who have been systematically abused over a lifetime—'

'That wasn't Corrie's experience.'

'Perhaps not, but we cannot ever – ever – betray that trust by putting a woman at risk again. Corrie was adamant that she could not go to the police and she was adamant that there was no one we could contact on her behalf.'

Viviana came into the kitchen bearing a tray of used plastic cups. She was followed by a small girl with long plaits who sucked her thumb and stared at Dee with fierce, black eyes. Dee stared back dully. The child edged around her and climbed into Catalina's lap. Viviana exchanged a smile with Catalina, ran water in the sink and began to wash the cups.

The girl continued to stare at Dee from the safety of Catalina's lap, her thumb still jammed in her mouth, her dark head reclining on Catalina's chest.

'You know,' Catalina said at last, taking the girl's hand in her own and stroking the plump fingers gently. 'It can be very difficult for young people to come to terms with the mistakes they've made. Having met you, I can understand Corrie's reluctance to be more open with us.'

'Oh? And why is that?' Dee braced herself for the blow that would, of course, be framed as something delivered *for her own good.*

Catalina smiled at her with simple kindness. 'You seem like such a good and sensible woman to me. I imagine your daughter would have felt terribly ashamed about the situation she had got herself into.'

*

'*¿Qué querés hacer?*' What do you want to do?

Alicia had put the keys in the ignition but had not started the car. She rested one elbow on the steering wheel and turned to look at Dee. Dee stared down at a piece of yellowed notepaper bearing Catalina's careful old-fashioned copperplate: Corrie's last known address.

'I don't know.'

The gate in the wall swung open and Viviana ushered two children, boys of about seven years of age, out onto the street. They were wearing white cotton coats over their track pants and T-shirts and had school packs strapped to their backs. Viviana took their hands and led them off down the road. One boy looked back over his shoulder and pointed. His companion also strained backwards to look at the women in the car, but Viviana urged them both forward.

The sky was clear and blue. The windows of the car had magnified the warmth of the sun. Alicia turned the key a notch in the ignition and lowered her window, allowing a soft breeze to waft in. She nodded at the piece of paper.

'San Miguel. Is no far. *Veinte minutos.*'

Dee was thinking about Catalina's reading of Corrie's self-imposed exile. *I imagine your daughter would have felt terribly ashamed.* Is it 'shame' that leaves a mother and two brothers in wretched limbo for so long? Or something altogether more self-righteous? Something closer to blame? But what did it matter? The main thing was to establish that her daughter was all right. Catalina's suggestion that Corrie was ashamed of the hurt she had caused was plausible and tempted Dee with images of reconciliation, but there was no way it was going to be that simple. Corrie had made a decision not to include her family in the process of putting her life back together. It was entirely possible, therefore, that Dee turning up unannounced on her doorstep would be highly traumatic for her. It needed to be handled carefully. On the other hand, she may have moved on long ago from the address Catalina had given Dee. In which case, all this agonising would be entirely irrelevant.

'*¿Qué querés hacer?*' Alicia's voice had an edge of impatience to it.

The long drive back to the city suddenly felt unbearable. Dee had to know. She had to know one way or the other.

'Would you do it for me?'

'*¿Qué querés que haga?*'

'We will go to the house, but I will stay in the car. Would you ask if Corrie is there? And if she is, maybe say that the Sisters have asked you to drop in to see if she is OK, but don't tell her that I am here.'

Alicia considered the request with a slight frown.

Dee added, by way of explanation, '*No quiero asustarla.*' I don't want to frighten her.

Alicia nodded. '*Entiendo. Sí.* I think is better.'

'Thank you.'

Alicia squeezed Dee's hand and arranged her face in a look of tight-lipped comradely determination.

'*Vamos*, let's go.' Dee was suddenly impatient to get it over and done with.

They did not speak much during the ensuing journey. Once they got into San Miguel, it was not easy to find the address that Catalina had given them. Many of the streets were unmarked and Alicia had to stop several times to ask directions. The street, when they eventually located it, was almost impassable, so deep were the potholes around which Alicia was obliged to carefully steer. They idled in front of a house that was not as dilapidated as Dee imagined it might have been. It had a high fence, a straggling avocado tree and a little patch of lawn out the front. The rendered walls were pink and there were the usual black bars at the windows. A mongrel dog barked at them through the gate.

Alicia drove another two hundred metres up the road, engaged the handbrake and switched off the engine. Dee clutched at her friend's hand. She was too nervous to speak. Alicia smiled reassuringly then slid out of her seat, slammed the door and walked back down the road in the direction of the house. Releasing the seatbelt, Dee hunched forward in her seat in nervous anticipation. She did not dare look behind her lest she jinx what was about to happen next. The minutes crept by. She waited and she prayed.

Please God, please God, please God, please God . . .

She kept her head bowed and her eyes firmly shut. Her breathing was shallow and harsh. Every extra minute was agony, but every extra minute was also a good omen. It meant Alicia was talking to someone. Just at the point at which she began to feel light-headed from hyperventilation she heard the car door click and swing open. She jerked her head up sharply. The look on Alicia's face told her instantly that she was not about to hear the news that she had been hoping for.

Alicia touched Dee's hand. '*Yo lo siento, Deirdra. Corrie ya no vive allí.*'

I'm so sorry. Corrie doesn't live there anymore.

Chapter Ten

They drove back to San Miguel and found a restaurant where they could sit and talk. Alicia ordered a small pizza that she insisted was for sharing. She had deferred explanations until they had found the restaurant, saying she could not drive and speak English and be hungry at the same time, although Dee suspected it was also because she was nervous about lingering too long in the barrio and didn't want to communicate this anxiety. Nevertheless, Alicia fell on the pizza with gusto when it arrived and Dee realised that it was way past lunchtime. She had been so caught up in her own agenda that she had lost track of time.

'Sorry, Alicia. I didn't realise it was this late.'

Alicia waved away her apology and pushed the plate towards Dee. The pizza was heavy with melting slabs of pale mozzarella. Dee wasn't sure that she could manage so much cheese, but took a slice anyway, to keep Alicia company.

'What did they say at the house? Who was there?'

Alicia nodded her awareness of the urgency of the question, swallowed what was in her mouth and wiped her lips with a paper napkin.

'A family. Mother. Five children. *Han vivido en la casa para un año.*'

'They've lived there for one year?'

'*Sí, pero . . .*' Alicia paused to gather her scattered fragments of English '. . . the mother, she remember Corrie.'

Another link. Another witness to the fact of her daughter's existence. Dee leant forward across the table to drink in the information.

'She say they talk a little. Corrie is happy. She work in a restaurant and she have . . . *¿novio?*'

'A boyfriend?' Dee's stomach tightened. 'Not Niko?'

Alicia hastened to reassure her. 'No. *Se llama Santiago.* Very nice boy. Corrie is happy . . . *porque iba a vivir con él.*'

'She was moving in with him?'

'*Sí.*'

Dee sat back in her chair and considered this. On one level it was a much more comforting image than the thought of Corrie living in a run-down house in the middle of a dodgy neighbourhood by herself. But then, who was this boy? And what did 'nice' mean? 'Nice' compared to the thieving, violent, substance-abusing barrio norm? Or 'nice' as in clean, polite, employed, and responsible? And where had they gone?'

'Did they leave a forwarding address?'

Alicia shook her head. '*No específicamente, pero . . .*'

'But?'

'*La mujer piensa que Santiago tenía un apartamento en la ciudad.*'

'An apartment in the city? With this boy?'

'She ask Corrie where but she no say. I think, maybe *tenía miedo de Niko.*'

Yes, Dee thought, it would make sense that Corrie was still reluctant to pass on information about her whereabouts to strangers in case it got back to Niko. An apartment in the city? That meant money. That meant something pretty close to a life that Dee would regard as normal. That meant her search for her daughter was narrowed down to two hundred square kilometres and three million people. But it also meant that there was a positive reason to keep looking. Or perhaps, conversely, it meant that she could finally stop. Dee had always told the gods, she had told anyone who asked, that she just needed to know her daughter was OK. Like the good mother before Solomon, she had bargained away her maternal rights in the hope that her child's life might be spared. But was that enough? Could she really leave it at that?

She didn't know what to feel anymore. And she didn't know what to do. If Dee went to the police she would be exposing Corrie to an investigation she had declared herself unable to face. Dee may even be exposing her to danger. She would almost certainly be jeopardising whatever potential was left for a relationship with her daughter. But if she didn't go to the police, what hope did she have of finding Corrie on her own? Especially given the fact that she obviously didn't want to be found. But why not? Maybe after Felipe's death, her daughter had gone into hiding out of fear and shame, but before that? What was behind her initial impulse to vanish? What had triggered the desire to cut herself off completely from her past and all those she loved? What had driven her to such a terrible act of cruelty?

'*Cansada?*' Alicia touched her arm. Dee stared at her friend wearily. If only there was someone who could tell her what to do. Or wrap her in a blanket and tell her not to worry, that they would take care of everything. She was tired of being responsible. She was tired of having to make so many difficult decisions on her own. She thought of Ben and Luke. What would she tell them? What would they expect her to do? She smiled weakly at Alicia.

'Yes. Exhausted. I need time to digest all this. Time to think,' she added, in response to Alicia's slight frown of incomprehension.

'*Sí. Entiendo, pero, Dee, Corrie está vivo.*' Alicia scanned Dee's face and squeezed one of her hands for emphasis. 'Corrie is alive!'

'Yes.' Dee forced herself to focus on that single essential fact and returned Alicia's smile. 'Yes, she's alive.'

Despite Dee's conviction that she needed time alone, Alicia was even firmer in her determination that some kind of celebration was in order.

'*Un pequeño*,' she insisted. Just a little one. And when Dee studied her friend's beaming face, she remembered that the fear and grief of the last four years had not only been hers. So she deferred her Anglo need to privately order and sort and file away her chaotic thoughts and emotions to the Latin imperative for a party and let Alicia ring Stephen and Marco and Paola and Juan Pablo. Dee made a feeble offer to assist when they arrived back at Alicia's home, but Alicia showed her to the guest bedroom and ordered her to rest while she made the necessary preparations. This was not a feat Dee imagined that her overwrought brain was going to allow her to accomplish, but as soon as she lay down sleep crashed on top of her and knocked her into complete oblivion.

When she awoke it was dark. She couldn't remember where she was, but it didn't matter. She knew that she was somewhere safe. For the first time in four years she hadn't woken to fear and dread. She had woken to hope. She became aware of the rise and fall of voices in another part of the house and remembered Alicia's party. Reaching out in the dark, she located the bedside lamp, fumbled for the switch and then squeezed her eyes shut against the sudden, bruising light. The mirror hanging on the opposite wall reflected back the image of a pale, black-eyed, slack-jawed woman.

'I have escaped from the attic,' she thought and smiled before shuffling on sleep-numbed feet to the mirror to clean up her smudged mascara with a forefinger dipped in spit and claw back her hair into some semblance of order.

The first person who noticed her in the kitchen doorway was Stephen. He came forward to hug her. He had been sitting at the table with Juan Pablo, Marco and Paola, who had glasses of wine in front of them. Alicia was frying schnitzels on the stove.

'We wondered if you were going to join us.'

'I can't believe I slept so long. What time is it?'

'Nearly nine.'

As Dee approached the table the others got up to kiss her. She was grateful they had decided to leave their partners at home. What Alicia had called a 'party' was really her attempt to gather those who particularly needed to know the latest developments.

Marco looked as though a weight had been lifted from his shoulders. Paola, who had already been married by the time Corrie came to stay with the Torreses, looked similarly relieved and happy. Dee felt a wave of sadness at the extent to which Corrie's disappearance had impacted on this generous family.

She sat down in a chair next to Marco. Juan Pablo fetched an extra glass and poured her a wine. 'We are so happy to hear your news, Dee.'

Part of her wanted to blurt out her apologies to the family, but she thought perhaps it was the wrong tone for the gathering. Alicia had wanted it to be a celebration.

'Thank you, Juan Pablo. It still feels surreal. But yes, it is very good news.'

'We are relieved,' Paola smiled at her.

'Yes, very relieved,' Marco added, 'but . . .' He trailed off under the gaze of the rest of the table.

'It's all right, Marco,' Dee sighed. 'You may as well say it. It's the elephant in the room. Why did she not get in touch with any of us? I don't know. Obviously she would have known that we wouldn't approve of her boyfriend. Sister Catalina at Moreno thinks perhaps she was ashamed. I don't know, Marco. You're Corrie's age. Does that seem plausible to you?'

Marco frowned. 'Maybe.'

'I think maybe she had a little breakdown,' Paola opined. 'She was still so sad about her dad when she came here. She could not have been in her normal mind to do such a thing and yes, I think Sister Catalina is probably right. Afterwards, when she realised what she had done, she couldn't face us.'

'But,' Juan Pablo added firmly, 'it seems she is OK now.'

'Well, a year ago she was trying to pull her life back together. We don't know what has happened in the last twelve months.'

'Will you go to the police?' Marco asked, anxiety lingering on his face.

Dee shook her head. 'I don't know. I don't think so. Not right away. The situation is delicate. She was afraid of the police, afraid that news of her whereabouts would somehow trickle back to this Niko, afraid of being implicated in Felipe's murder. Those fears might be unfounded, but I don't want to be the one bringing the police to her door.'

Alicia placed a salad in the middle of the table and Juan Pablo got up to fetch a bowl of creamed potatoes from the oven.

'Anyway, it's very good news.' Stephen echoed Juan Pablo's original statement.

Paola fetched the platter of schnitzels and sat down. She raised her glass. '*¡Salud!*'

But when the clink of glasses died away it was replaced by the heavy silence of unanswered questions.

*

When she got back to her hotel just before one, Dee went straight to bed but lay awake for hours, chewing over the details of the day. It was difficult to sustain elation about Corrie's resurrection when she could not see her or touch her. Especially when it seemed to bring with it a strange kind of personal indictment. Underneath the relief the dark questions stirred and stirred again.

At four am she gave up all hope of sleep, pulled on track pants and a polo shirt and took herself down to the lobby. The receptionist on duty glanced up as she walked past him to the computer booth.

When she logged on to her email account there was, however, little of immediate interest. Her email inbox had become no better than the letterbox in her front yard back in Australia – stuffed with bills and unsolicited advertising material, another conduit to remind her of all the petty desires she could be cultivating while simultaneously demanding payment for those to which she had already succumbed. Her heart leapt when she scrolled down and saw Liz's name, but it was only one of those forwarded jokes, an intricate animation of a complicated machine juggling a hundred tiny balls and purporting to depict the mental state of the average woman. Dee studied the animation, hypnotised by the progress of the balls through tubes and into chambers, launched by various levers, triggers and counter-weights. One thing leading to another by inexorable logic. Clean. Predictable. Controllable. Action and consequence. Counter-consequence. Things that made sense. Things that could be anticipated. Or avoided by scrupulous attention to detail. Such order appealed to Dee but she knew that it wasn't enough. The human spirit yearned for something that transcended its own capacity for prediction and control. Was that what Corrie had gone chasing? Risk? Adventure? Something urgent and alive in contrast to the terrible finality of her father's death? Maybe that was what had underpinned Corrie's attraction to Niko. Dee knew how the experience of being desired swept you out of banality and up to the plane of the gods. It glutted your heart with hope and set your blood singing, tantalised and satiated in equal measures, endowed you with a wondrous sense of your own significance even as it blinded you to the significance of everything else in your life. Dee understood these things only too well but could not necessarily forgive them. Succumbing to such impulses was a weakness that caused all the little balls to fall down and the machine to jam and the mechanics of ordinary life to fail . . .

She refocused her attention on her mail, scrolling rapidly through the column of spam looking for any news from Luke or Ben, but there was none. She wondered if she should inform them about recent developments, but decided that it was definitely not the sort of news that should be delivered by email. She imagined what they might be doing at this moment. Dinnertime in Australia. They'd either be arguing about whose turn it was to cook or heading down to the local pub for a 'countery'. Perhaps Luke was enjoying a cheap meal in Chinatown with Belinda, while Ben flicked through one of Dee's Jamie Oliver recipe books at home. Suddenly she longed to be with him, helping him work out what they had in the pantry that could substitute for the more fandangled ingredients, chopping up things, teasing him about his cluelessness. She toyed with the idea of ringing him but she noticed herself tensing as she tried to work out what she would say. How could she explain things in a way that wouldn't trigger a complexity of feeling that she couldn't temper for him at the moment? Perhaps it would be best if she waited until she was feeling less confused and could speak more confidently about what was going on. She needed to stay strong for what was left of her family. That much she had always known.

Dee kept scrolling until she got to the last message. It was from Julio Ruiz.

Your photograph is ready. Please tell me when you would like to collect it.

Why did her heart jump just a little at the prospect? It was a distraction, she told herself, a way of taking her mind off other things, a chance to discuss what she had discovered with an interested but objective third party. Some respite from all her miserable self-examination.

Dear Julio . . .

She knew that 'hi' was the preferred form of address in emails these days, but she stuck to 'dear' out of a snobby allegiance to old forms and, in this instance, because it allowed her a kind of ambivalent intimacy.

Thank you for your email. I will collect the photograph tomorrow if that is convenient. You said that you might have some time to show me the town. That would be nice. I look forward to seeing you soon.

Was it too suggestive? Nothing she couldn't wriggle out of later, she decided, and hit the 'Send' button.

Back in her room she ran the shower and stood for a long time under the stream of hot water, slack and heavy with fatigue. Words and images circulated in her head like tape loops. Corrie, the last time she had seen her at the airport, restless and jumpy and pulling away . . . Corrie with her face averted in Julio's photograph, wearing the jacket that Ross had bought for her . . . Ruiz's silver-ringed gypsy hands . . . *She was also a gringa* . . . the mother and daughter on the ferry wrapped in silent affection . . . Fidelina's courtyard, the Virgin of Luján . . . Catalina rubbing at her glasses, *I imagine your daughter would have felt terribly ashamed* . . . The run-down house in the over-grown yard just outside San Miguel . . . *I could have shown you around* . . . The strange stirring of responsiveness aroused in her by the invitation. She had always been too grateful for being desired. *Perhaps she doesn't want to be found* . . . And too shattered by rejection.

Eventually, reluctantly, she turned off the water. She dried herself and lay on the bed, naked, contemplating the silver streaks across her belly. She did not mind those old battle scars. Proof that she had once contained the babies who had grown into such large presences in her life. Once, she thought, I was spacious enough to contain you. She touched the loose, pale flesh. She did not feel spacious anymore. She felt as though she had withered around a large, hard stone, like an old prune. But her flesh still breathed a longing to be touched, to take the teasing imprint of teeth, the inquisitive tracing of a blind tongue. She thought of Julio's mass of white curls against his brown skin, the long curve of his dark eyebrows, his strong, lean hands. She thought of the last time anyone had really wanted her and closed her eyes against the pain of the memory. And then she began to wonder, sadly, if she would ever be wanted again. And if she actually deserved such good fortune.

Chapter Eleven

Dee arrived at Colonia late the following afternoon. Julio came to the door in black jeans and a red T-shirt emblazoned with the image of Che Guevara. He appeared slightly taken aback to see her.

'Didn't you receive my email?' she asked.

'I was busy. I haven't checked. But please, come in.'

There were no signs of pleasurable anticipation in his face. There was no sexual tension detectable at all in his polite but distracted manner. Dee followed him into the cluttered lounge room. He ran one hand through his unruly white hair, gestured vaguely at the couch.

'Do you have time to wait? I'm in the middle of some developing.'

'That's fine. You go ahead.'

'Five minutes, maybe ten.'

'No problem.'

He smiled perfunctorily and hurried back to his darkroom.

Left alone, Dee felt predictably foolish. He was more attractive in the flesh than she had remembered. But he showed no evidence of a similar attraction to her. He probably had a score of women, she decided. His flirtation was, no doubt, simply reflexive. But it was also likely that her own half-formed expectations were completely transparent to him. Men had a nose for it. Especially the men here. They were convinced you were panting after them if you accidentally glanced at them on the bus. Any undercurrent of actual desire might as well be a pulsating neon sign hanging over a woman's head. She therefore resolved to be as charming as possible while being equally determined to field any such presumptions.

It took half an hour for him to finish what he was doing and when he finally appeared he did not apologise for the delay. He did not even seem to be aware of it. But there was a change in his manner. He was more relaxed, more attentive.

Dee continued to flick through one of the photographic journals she had picked up from the pile on the coffee table, feigning casual absorption.

'Can I offer you a drink?' He waved a half-empty whisky bottle at her.

'I'm fine.'

'You won't mind if I celebrate my good day's work?' He poured himself a generous measure and lifted the glass in her direction.

'*Salud*. Tell me, were the priests at Villa Soldati any help to you?'

Dee closed the magazine, opened her mouth to say something and then closed it again. 'Actually, I might have a whisky.'

He fetched another glass and poured her a similar measure to his own. She took a large mouthful and winced a little against the searing heat of its passage.

'Yes, as it happens. Well, not so much the priests, but a local woman called Fidelina.'

He smiled with delighted recognition. 'Fidelina! I remember her! Good woman. Very good woman.'

'She remembered my daughter.'

'So it *was* her – the girl in my photograph? That was your daughter?'

He was more excited than Dee had imagined he would be, but she found herself reluctant to elaborate further. It felt like a betrayal to disclose too many details about Corrie's situation to someone who had no vested interest in her fate.

'Fidelina said that Corrie had been looking for emergency shelter and the priests told me that if she had asked Felipe – the man in your photograph – he would have directed her to the Sisters at Barrio Moreno.'

She took another mouthful of the whisky. When she lowered the glass, Julio reached over with the bottle and topped it up.

'Anyway, to cut a long story short, we – my friend and I—'

'You have a friend here in Argentina?'

She smiled at his interest in this detail. 'Yes, Alicia. Corrie lived with Alicia and her family before she went missing. Anyway, Alicia and I visited the Sisters and they also remembered her.'

'This is amazing.' He smiled and shook his head in mock disbelief.

'They gave me a forwarding address, but she isn't there anymore. The current tenants thought she had moved to an apartment in the city.'

'But they didn't have an address?'

'No. So now, well, I'm not sure what to do now.'

'*¡Increíble!*'

'But I guess I am in your debt. Because of you I know my daughter is alive.' Dee struggled to make her face look dignified and calm, but she suspected it was only communicating wretchedness.

'*De nada*. It's nothing. I am pleased for you.' He looked at her thoughtfully. 'You don't seem very happy.'

She shrugged, look away. 'It's all a bit difficult to take in. Especially as I still haven't actually *found* her. And probably won't anytime soon.' She drained the remaining whisky in her glass. 'It seems fairly obvious that she wants nothing to do with me. But that is my business, not your problem.' She gave him a sad, whisky-mellow smile. 'You have helped to resolve my greatest fear, the fear that she was dead. For that I am more grateful than I can say.'

Julio acknowledged her thanks with a slow nod, lit up a cigarette and blew a long stream of smoke at the ceiling.

'The most important thing is that you know she is OK,' he observed. 'As to the rest, there is little you can do but wait. Your daughter is young. For young people everything is very dramatic. Everything is about them. But things change. I didn't speak to my own father for ten years.'

'Why was that?'

'He was a fucking bastard.'

'That doesn't make me feel any better.'

'No,' he continued, deadpan and unconcerned. 'The whisky is for that.' He reached over and poured her another glass.

'What happened? Between you and your father.'

'He wanted me to be a lawyer like him. I wanted to go to art school. He told me I could live somewhere else if that was my intention. So I did. And we didn't speak for ten years.'

'Did you ever reconcile with him?'

'I graduated, got a position at the college. That made me more respectable in his eyes. But I still thought he could go fuck his idea of respectability. My poor mother kept running between the two of us. He was a fucking bastard and so was I. Two fucking bastards.' He grinned at Dee, stubbed out his cigarette by way of punctuation, then sat back with his arms over the back of the chair.

'What happened in the end?'

'I can't remember. Nothing extraordinary. I would come home to visit my mother. One day he stopped leaving the room. And then one day he asked when I was going to get a haircut.'

'I notice you've continued to resist him on that score.'

'It was a badge of honour in the seventies.'

'That was thirty years ago.'

'¡Hasta la victoria siempre!'

'At least you lived in the same city as your family. I don't even know where my daughter is.'

'What was she into?'

Dee found the question slightly intrusive. She pushed aside what was left of her whisky. 'What do you mean?'

'What was she into? What did she like doing? What sort of ambitions did she have for her life?'

'Oh. Theatre. Acting. She was studying Drama at university in Australia.'

'The reason I ask is that it might give you some clues about where to start looking.'

Dee stared at him.

'Amateur theatre groups. Film festivals—'

'There must be hundreds of those. I could spend a lifetime looking and still never find her.'

'Not necessarily. Once you get to know the scene there are many overlapping networks. She may have gravitated back to the university drama scene. That might be a place to start. If she is still interested in charity work—' Dee decided not to correct this assumption. '— she might be assisting with arts projects in the barrios. A lot of young people are involved with those. Anyway, you'll find that many artists and students live in Recoleta. It's near the university and there are a lot of cultural activities in the area. Perhaps you could start by making some inquiries around there.'

'At the artists' markets maybe?'

'Not a bad place to start. I could also give you a list of some of the people I know at the university and in the local area. They could suggest other names.'

Dee considered this information. In some ways it felt like going back to square one. On the other hand the search would not be as blind or feel as futile as the first time round. It would be a huge task to undertake on her own. Could she involve the police without telling them about Niko? They would surely get quicker results than she could. But would the police put any resources into looking for an adult foreigner who had merely cut off ties with her family to pursue a more independent life?

'I guess I could try. I'd be grateful for your list of contacts.'

'Sure. Anyway, it's an interesting part of the city to hang out. Either way, your time would not be wasted.' He shrugged. 'Well. Would you like to see your picture?'

Dee had forgotten about the picture. 'Yes,' she said quickly. 'Of course.'

He led her through to his studio where the enlarged photograph was displayed on an easel. Dee was immediately glad of her rash decision to purchase a copy of the print. It was black and white: one girl, unfocused in the foreground, two shirtless boys, light spilling through the open door behind them, lean bodies, graceful hands. There was delight in the wide smile of one of the boys, tenderness in the eyes of the other. Dee could tell that Julio was pleased by her sudden stillness.

'Oh, it's beautiful.'

'I will wrap it for you. Please don't roll it. And you owe me another hundred.'

'Yes, of course.' Dee smiled at the bluntness of the transaction and went to fetch her purse. When he brought her the package she handed him the money and he pocketed it casually.

'Can I take you somewhere for dinner?' She blurted it out quickly before she had time for self-censure. 'As a gesture of my gratitude.'

He considered the proposal with less overt eagerness than Dee might have hoped for. 'Sure. Why not? There's a good *parrilla* in the old town. They sometimes have a tango show.'

'I thought tango was an Argentinean thing?'

'We like to think so, but the Uruguayans claim it as their own.'

'Really? I suppose the tango is worth arguing over. We feud over pavlova with our nearest neighbour.'

'*¿Cómo?*'

'It's a dessert – a soft meringue with kiwifruit and cream.'

'Kiwi?'

'Yes. That fact doesn't do much for the Australian cause.'

Julio picked up a jacket from the back of a chair. 'If you're interested we can look at the old fortifications on the way.'

'I'd like that.'

The light was fading outside and the temperature had cooled considerably, but the air was clear and refreshing compared to the gritty atmosphere of Buenos Aires. Dee fell into step beside

Julio. They did not speak for a while, tuning into the washy intimations of the river and their own footfalls on the cobblestones. Julio steered her towards the shoreline and pointed out a grassy mound of tumbled rocks – all that was left of the old Portuguese fortress. Further along there were simple stone cottages and more elaborate structures with turreted roofs, arched windows and white-rendered façades.

A low wall bordered the river on the western side of the town and they followed it around to a pier beside the local yacht club. The river slapped against the pylons and boats bobbed on the dark water. They gazed out over the river in comradely silence.

'Do you have children, Julio?'

'I have managed to elude that fate.'

'You never wanted any?'

'I liked my freedom too much. And I wanted my time for art. I didn't want to be like my father, chained to his work, his status, the need to provide a certain lifestyle for his family.'

'You were wise to know what you wanted and what you didn't want at such a young age.'

'We are one of the first generations to have such choices, eh? Is it a good thing? I don't know.'

'Do you regret your choices?'

'I don't know what the alternative feels like. I look at my brothers and sisters, my nieces and nephews, and I am not jealous. I am not jealous when I see what you are going through.'

Dee was not offended by the remark. She would not be jealous of herself either. And yet . . . there was nothing in her that could wish Corrie's life undone. Nor Ben's, nor Luke's. It was a cliché. It was what all parents said: *I wouldn't be without them.* Children disrupt the designs you have for yourself, but at the same time as they are breaking your heart and breaking your spirit, shattering your pride and undermining your self-esteem, they are also breaking open your world and changing the way you look at everything.

'*Bueno*. The restaurant is this way. You can't see the river but the food is better.'

The *parrilla* was a dimly lit, homely place with a charcoal barbecue, well-stocked bar and small tables with checked cloths and candle stubs in coloured glasses. It was already filling quickly with a noisy crowd. Before long the patrons were spilling over into the outdoor tables and places were being set at the bar.

Julio was good company. He enjoyed talking about Latin American history, about writers and artists that he liked, about philosophy and politics, and Dee was happy to be lectured about things that were of interest to her. It was nice not to have to work too hard to keep the conversation going.

At ten o'clock, a guitarist and a *bandoneón* player set up in a corner of the restaurant where a small patch of wooden floor had been left clear for the tango show. A woman in a low-backed dress of blue crepe split to the thigh, wearing impossibly high-heeled shoes, stood to one side of the musicians, adjusting her shoulder-straps and smoothing her skirt before being spun out onto the floor by her older, light-footed partner, a man in pin-striped trousers, waistcoat, fedora and Cuban heels. The erotic drama of the dance was captivating: invitation and evasion, feint and counter-feint, haughty disdain crossed with yearning intimacy. Stylised moments of defiance cut across moments of studied mimicry. Outbreaks of passion alternated with simmering restraint. It was as evocative of a knife-fight as it was of seduction. No other dance, thought Dee, is as candid about the unacknowledged power struggles of our most intimate relationships.

When the show finished Julio asked if Dee was ready to leave. She paid the bill and they walked back to his house to pick up the picture.

'Where are you staying?' he asked as he put the package in her arms.

She felt embarrassed. 'I haven't made a booking. I'm sure there will be a room somewhere.'

'You could stay here.' His face was non-committal.

It was what she had hoped he would ask, but suddenly she was overtaken by a familiar wave of panic. This was the bit she hadn't got around to explaining to Stephen when he had asked about her current love life. It wasn't that desire was dead. And while opportunities were scant, they hadn't been entirely absent. It was just that, at the crucial moment, when such opportunities were about to assume a more palpable reality, she lost all her nerve. She couldn't believe that the consequences of succumbing to such desires would be anything other than dire and she didn't have enough emotional resources left to take the chance. She smiled nervously at Julio. He smiled back, raised his eyebrows suggestively.

'Thanks. I'll be right.'

His smile vanished and then he shrugged. 'Suit yourself.'

When he opened the front door for her, she hesitated. 'You were going to suggest some people I could contact.'

The reminder seemed to spark his interest again. 'Of course. One moment.' He collected a paper and pen and scribbled down a few names and numbers, then stood close to her as he explained.

'This is one of the drama lecturers from the university. She will be able to tell you about the amateur groups and local companies. This is my friend, Sergio. He runs a local artists' cooperative at Recoleta and has very good English. I have written the address for you. Candelaria has some connections with NGOs who coordinate various barrio projects, but you could also ask your friends from the Church about those.'

'Thank you. I really appreciate your help.'

She looked up at him with genuine gratitude. His face was close to hers and his black eyes were very still. She could have moved away but she didn't and when he bent to kiss her it was only what she had been hoping for. He smelt of cologne but tasted of ash. She allowed herself a moment of sweet oblivion and then she pulled away and fled.

Dee hurried back towards the new part of town. On her way to Julio's studio that afternoon she had taken note of a small hotel on the street that led up from the ferry terminal. She hoped it wasn't too late to secure a room. She tapped at the front door of the Hotel Rivera and a sleepy receptionist let her in and assigned her a small upstairs room overlooking a central courtyard. The room was clean and simply furnished. Dee placed the packaged photograph carefully against a wall, lay down on top of the white coverlet and closed her eyes.

Her heart was still racing. She felt both relieved and disappointed by her own timidity. Not because she had rejected the offer of a one-night stand – she needed a more elaborate narrative around sex than pure physical gratification – but because she had started to become very interested in Julio and wished she could have dealt with the situation in a more lighthearted and amusing way. Coquetry, however, was not something at which she was particularly skilled. She had never imagined herself beautiful enough to wield any great power over men and was convinced that middle age had stripped her of the few physical assets that might once have counted in her favour.

Which explained, paradoxically, the terrible mistake she had made six years ago.

When she and David had bumped into each other in the book tent at Writer's Week during the Adelaide Festival, he had seen her not as the faded, middle-aged frump she assumed she had become, but as the feisty, slightly superior girl he remembered from his university days – the one with the compellingly intimate gaze and disconcertingly candid opinions about everything from Chaucer to Kerouac. That was what he remembered about her, that was how he treated her and that was what she slipped into being again in his company. He gave her back a version of herself that she'd assumed was irrecoverable and it was completely intoxicating.

The fact that he'd done so much better than she – graduated from Law and been made a partner with a prestigious local firm, bought a home in a well-to-do suburb, enrolled his two children in the most expensive private school in town – didn't temper the deference with which he still treated her and his essential delight in catching up again. He claimed to have carried a torch for her in their younger days. She'd had no inkling that he'd fancied her, but was thrilled to think that she had evoked such clandestine longing.

Dee had not been looking for romance and she was sure she hadn't flirted with David or deliberately led him on. But she hadn't needed to. They fell into an easy, familiar pattern that felt more like camaraderie than anything else. Although perhaps she wasn't being entirely honest about that because she never told Ross about their encounter at Writer's Week. Nor did she see any reason to mention their subsequent rendezvous. No point in creating false cause for jealousy and resentment, she'd reasoned at the time. No point in making a potential problem out of what was merely a pleasant nostalgic indulgence. Except that over time the relationship slipped out of the boundaries of the past and began to inhabit the present. *How was your day? What are you up to tomorrow? How did that case go, David? You're looking so tired. I bought you a little something to cheer you up . . .* The solicitousness of two people pretending not to be in love. And then one day he bent down and gave her a lingering kiss goodbye and they couldn't pretend anymore.

Had she been 'in love'? Wasn't she just narcissistically revelling in the idea of being desired again? Or using David to recapture the youthful entitlements she now believed had been snatched from her precipitously by her first pregnancy? Perhaps she was hoping that his status and success might compensate for all her own disappointments and unachieved ambitions or, at the very least, that his attentions would distract her from the dreary encroachment of middle age.

She could analyse it right back to its basest motivations, but she could not will away the pathetic symptoms of infatuation. She fretted, waiting for his phone calls – was elated whenever she heard from him, devastated if more than a week went by without contact. He was the first thing she thought about on waking, the last thing as she drifted into sleep at night. She got lost in frequent reveries at work and at home, returning again and again to recollections of murmured endearments and gestures of tenderness. She lived for the rare occasions when they could both slip away from work or make plausible excuses to their respective partners in order to spend a few precious hours together. And then they were like two children at Christmas, lit up and lifted out of ordinariness by the enchantment of each other.

If they'd actually got around to having sex, perhaps the whole thing would have fizzled out a lot quicker than it did. As it was, their ardour was fed by a great deal of kissing and touching and an agonising suspension of consummation that felt a little less like infidelity, even though they were old enough to know better. Thus did they assuage their consciences even as they willed their imaginations towards more powerful betrayals.

In the end, external factors intervened to break the spell. Dee applied for the Deputy Principal's position and, to her surprise, was appointed. Suddenly she had more pressing demands on her time and more significant challenges to engage with. Marco came to stay and her family life began to swirl with new energies. She and Ross started to reconnect.

The night Ross died, Dee had taken David out to dinner to announce her intention to stop seeing him. But she had switched her phone to silent and lingered far too long over the bittersweet farewell. By the time she walked away from the restaurant full of sighing self-pity and a perverted sense of her own courage and virtue, Ross was dead. Ross was dead and her betrayal was complete. She had forfeited the last hours she could have spent with him. She had forfeited them in the worst possible way and there was nothing she could do to redeem herself.

David continued to call and send text messages for about six months afterwards, but mostly she didn't answer him. There was no solace to be found in the reminders of her capacity for wretched duplicity. She didn't believe she had a right to solace anyway.

Chapter Twelve

Dee checked the address on the piece of paper that Julio had given her and walked past several more shopfronts until she was standing before the Recoleta artists' cooperative. The exterior was painted red and bore graffiti-styled murals arranged around the usual slogans. An extended complaint against the city council over their rental arrangement had been taped in the bottom right-hand corner of the window. Inside the open door she could see various counters displaying the work of the *artesanos* – leather and silver, carvings and jewellery. Dee wondered if Sergio, the coordinator, was likely to be around on a Saturday.

She moved slowly past the counters, picking up pieces as though looking to buy. There were ornate *mate* gourds and *bombillas* – the silver straws through which the tea was drunk – bags, belts and bracelets. The pieces were different to the usual tourist offerings. The work was sharp-edged and strident, rough-textured, asymmetrical, ironically ugly. It wasn't really Dee's taste.

A young artisan with a long face and hooked nose sat behind a trestle table at the rear of the shop, stamping pieces of soft leather with a hand-held tool. He looked up at Dee and waved the stamp at the various displays.

'All products by local artists. All original pieces.'

'Yes, I see.' She made a show of looking around. 'Is Sergio in today?'

The youth consulted a Dali-esque glass clock, melting down the wall. 'Sometimes he comes in on Saturday afternoon. Maybe try after one.'

It was only eleven thirty.

'Do you know any of the theatre groups involved with the collective?' Dee asked the boy on a whim. What did she have to lose?

He frowned over some problem he had encountered in his leather design. 'Sure. Which group are you interested in?'

Dee frowned herself, wondering how best to proceed. 'I don't really know. Are there any groups with foreign actors?'

'Do you want to join?' He smirked at her.

She mimicked the smirk back at him. 'Yes. Why not?' Then let the expression fall away. 'Actually, I'm looking for some-one – a young actor from Australia who I heard was working over here.'

Dee took the photograph of Corrie from her handbag and passed it to him. She wondered if Julio's name would carry some weight. 'Julio Ruiz said you were a reputable network. He thought she might have been in touch with you.'

Was it just her overactive imagination that made her think the leatherworker was dwelling on the photograph a little too intently? When he handed it back his eyes were carefully blank.

'Nobody I know.'

'But you don't know all the local groups?'

'Of course not.'

'Would Sergio know more people?'

He shrugged. 'If you like you can leave the photo with me and I will ask him.'

'I'll come back,' Dee said firmly, replacing the photograph in the side pocket of her handbag.

As she left the shop she noticed flyers advertising films and local theatre productions on the front counter. She took one of every kind. Even though she didn't look behind her she could feel the leatherworker's eyes boring into her back.

Or could she? Outside in the street she was not so sure. She glanced back through the window and his head was bent over his craft again, in the same absorbed pose. She would come back. She would ask Sergio. She sorted through the flyers in her hand, noticed that there was a poster-sized reproduction of one of them in the window, advertising a play called *Sueños Azules*, and that it was showing that evening at a small cabaret theatre in Palermo. She supposed that was as good a place as any to start familiarising herself with the local scene. If she took Stephen they might be able to strike up a conversation with cast members at the end of the performance, ask if anyone knew of a young Australian woman frequenting or assisting with local productions. Dee took out her phone and sent off a quick text message, asking if Stephen was free that evening.

In the meantime, she decided to visit the Japanese Garden at Palermo. It was a longish walk but it would fill in time while she waited for Sergio to make an appearance. The exercise would do her good.

The *Jardín Japonés* was an oasis of restraint and order to the north of Recoleta. It was structured around an ornamental lake and incorporated compact shrubs, stone sculptures and miniature waterfalls. Dee sat down on a bench overlooking the lake. Family groups picnicked on the lawns, tourists took pictures on the oriental bridges, and lovers strolled hand in hand along the pathways. The sun shimmered on the green water of the lake. A light breeze picked up strands of Dee's hair and swept them across her face. She closed her eyes and let her awareness drift with the pulsating smudges of red-and-gold light behind her eyelids.

When she opened her eyes again there was a young couple on the bridge at the foot of the grassy knoll where she was sitting. Their voices drifted up and it seemed to her that there was something familiar about the timbre of the female voice. The woman had her back to Dee, leaning over the water, but Dee noted slight build, pale skin and black hair. She noted the eclectic layers of colourful fabrics, the armful of silver bangles. It was a familiar style.

'Corrie?' she called out her daughter's name, but not too loudly.

Dee knew that the chances of this random stranger being Corrie were too remote to even entertain, but she couldn't tear her eyes away.

The young man pulled his partner by the hand and led her over the bridge. Dee rose to her feet and hurried after them.

The couple were circling the lake and Dee kept behind them, stopping whenever they stopped, pretending to be absorbed in things adjacent to whatever it was they were absorbed in, but finally she could stand it no longer. She caught up with them and touched the girl's arm.

'*Discúlpeme.*'

The girl turned and looked at her. 'Sorry. We don't speak Spanish.' It was the Australian accent that had fooled her. Dee smiled apologetically at the girl who was not her daughter and walked quickly back the way she had come.

It would be like this from now on, she guessed, the constant scanning of crowds, the compulsion to follow, to verify and to rule out. It felt like a return to purgatory and she didn't know if she could bear it. She hurried out of the garden and in the direction from which she had come. When she arrived back at the artist's collective, the young leatherworker was packing away his tools and materials. An older man, with thick, grey hair and a flourishing silver moustache, was sorting through some accounts.

'Sergio?'

Both men looked up at the same time.

'Yes?' The older man replied.

'Julio Ruiz gave me your name. He said you know a lot of the theatre groups around here.'

'Yes, I know most. How can I help you?'

'I'm looking for someone. It's a long shot. I don't know if she's involved with any of your projects here, but I don't have much else to go on.'

She held out the dog-eared photograph. He took it from her and examined it closely.

'Joaquín!' He called out to the leatherworker, who was on his way out the front door, and fired off a question. The younger man responded briefly with a shrug and a shake of his head, then continued out the door. Sergio frowned.

'There are a couple of young women who have recently volunteered to assist with one of our children's projects, but Joaquín says they are students from the United States. I will ask around for you. If this woman is involved with the scene someone will know her. Who is she?'

'My daughter. I haven't seen her for four years. She's been living in Buenos Aires but we – we lost contact.'

'Ah.' Sergio's eyes were sympathetic. 'I guess you just want to know if she's OK?'

'Yes.' Dee didn't trust herself to say more. She was always undone by unexpected kindness.

'I have a son who has been travelling for several years. Sometimes we don't hear from him for months. It's hard on his mother. She gets so worried. Let me make some inquiries for you. Can I make a copy of this picture?'

Dee nodded. Sergio took the photograph over to a computer workstation, scanned it, and then brought it back to her.

'Here's my phone number.' Dee scribbled her number on a piece of notepaper. 'Please ring if you find out anything. Her name's Corrie.'

'Corrie? Sure. I'll be in touch.'

'Thanks. Thanks so much.'

Dee paused at the front counter. Picking up another flyer for *Sueños Azules*, she waved it in Sergio's direction. 'I was thinking of going to see this tonight.'

'You should get there early. It's opening night. There'll be a crowd.'

*

Sergio was right. There was a queue at the theatre door when Dee arrived an hour before show time. Stephen had not answered her message so she had come alone. It had seemed like a good idea at the time – quitting the hotel room and exercising her restlessness on a tangible project – but she had forgotten how loneliness could coil itself around you, slowly and slyly, when you were the only one in a large crowd with no one else to talk to. She shuffled forward in the queue, eavesdropping on conversations, trying to see if she could decipher meaning from the slangy, heavily accented Spanish of the young *porteño* crowd. She was conscious of her foreign appearance, although she didn't really understand why her foreignness was so noticeable in such a cosmopolitan city. Perhaps there were stylistic markers to which she was oblivious, or some wariness or hesitancy in her bearing that gave her away. And she was conscious of her age. This was brought home by the deference of the young people around her, their polite smiles, their careful attempts not to jostle or crowd her. It always surprised her, this deference, caused her a pang of worry about whether or not she had been behaving in a manner commensurate with her age. Or had she unwittingly revealed the tragically vacant space where her mature sense of self was supposed to reside? She wasn't quite sure how to act like a middle-aged person, but then, she'd never been quite sure about how to act as a young person, either. Dee found herself half hoping that the performance would be sold out so that she would have an excuse to flee, but when she got to the box office there were still a number of single seats available, scattered throughout the auditorium. She chose one in the back row, partly so she could observe the other patrons as they took their seats, and partly because she feared it might be one of those avant-garde performances where the cast tried to drag the people in the front rows up on stage.

    Programme in hand, she slipped past the crowd in the foyer who were enjoying champagne and *cerveza* before the show. The theatre was a high-ceilinged, gutted space, painted black, with scaffolding and tiers of fold-down plastic chairs erected on two sides of a diamond-shaped stage. Loose webs of knotted rope were strung from the roof. Gleaming orbs were strewn at random throughout the webbing and the stage was awash with blue light. A large backlit screen rippled and shimmered with projected images of water. The soothing wash and abatement of waves formed a backdrop of continuous sound.

According to the programme, the work was narrated by a dead man. With a start of familiarity Dee recognised an allusion: *Phlebas the Phoenician*, T.S. Eliot's drowned merchant. She had spent an entire term analysing *The Waste Land* at university, awestruck by the literary cross-referencing and mythical cadences of the work. It was not long afterwards that Eliot was dismissed as passé by the new generation of academic elites so Dee was surprised to find his work resurfacing here. She wondered how the players would interpret Eliot's spiritual ambivalence. And then she wondered again how such an archetypal English modernist came to feature in an Argentinean post-modern play. She scanned the programme for references to the scriptwriter, but the play seemed to be one of those improvised ensemble collaborations. There were no writing credits.

As it turned out, the production was something of a pastiche of references to famous seafarers. Odysseus got a mention. As did Cristóbal Colón and the indigenous inhabitants of Tierra del Fuego who, Dee learned, travelled by canoe around the islands of the archipelago, warmed only by a layer of seal grease and the fires lit in the central well of their boats. The fire motif created a nice contrast to the water theme that had predominated up until that point. Dee couldn't understand a lot of the dialogue, but the soundscape and shifting visual textures, the stagecraft and the multimedia projections were pleasantly engaging.

There was no interval. At the end of the performance she remained in her seat, scanning the audience members as they left the theatre. She thought she saw Sergio rising from one of the seats at the front. And in the other bank of seating, towards the middle, surely that was the young leatherworker, Joaquín?

'*¿Permiso?*' A line of four people waited for her to shift her legs to one side so they could squeeze past.

By the time they had shuffled through, the man she had thought was Joaquín was no longer where he had been. Dee sought him out in the crowd ebbing towards the exit doors. Was that him? And the couple with him? She stood quickly. The girl was shrugging herself into a brown bomber jacket. Dee grabbed her bag and hurried down the steps of the scaffolding, but got caught in the jam of people. When she tried to push past she was blocked on one side by the bank of seats, on the other by the edge of the stage. She stood on tiptoe trying to spot the group, but they had already disappeared through the doors and into the foyer. Two burly men in front of her remained stationary, allowing other patrons who were descending from the seats above to go before them.

Dee began to push her way through in a high panic, no longer caring what anyone thought. The bottleneck at the doors hampered her for another tense minute. When she finally cleared the doorway, she stood for a moment, staring wildly about, trying to spot the girl in the jacket. There was no elevated vantage point from which she could take in the whole foyer so she pushed her way aggressively towards the exit where she planned to stand vigil and watch people as they spilled out onto the street. Dee walked up and down the pavement trying to survey everyone before they dissipated into the night. Even so, her eyes couldn't be everywhere at once. As the crowd waned her task became easier but her heart heavier. She stepped back inside the foyer and glanced around. Had Joaquín and the girl stayed to chat? There were several groups standing around but no one she recognised.

Were they perhaps mingling with the cast? Was there a stage door? She didn't know how or who to ask. She dashed out the front again to see if there were any side roads or laneways that might lead to a private exit. Nothing that she could see. The few remaining patrons in the foyer started to make arrangements to catch up for drinks elsewhere. They left slowly until there was only a dark-skinned man in a worn shirt bearing the badge of a security company, locking the doors behind them.

'*Discúlpeme*. Do you speak English?' Dee begged.

The security guard took in her wild-eyed appearance and shook his head kindly.

'The cast?' She didn't know the word in Spanish. '*¿Los actores?*'

He looked at her in puzzlement.

'*¿Dónde están los actores?*'

He shrugged and shook his head again. She didn't know if he was responding to her question about the players' whereabouts, indicating that he didn't understand or just politely trying to get rid of her so he could close up on time and go home. If only Stephen had been here. She felt a momentary flash of anger at his absence. What was so important that he hadn't even returned her phone messages?

Dee stepped aside to let the security guard lock the last door and gazed forlornly into the empty foyer until, finally, the lights were switched off.

*

'Where were you?' She found herself bleating into the phone when she finally got hold of Stephen on Monday morning.

'I'm sorry. I've had a few issues of my own to deal with lately.'

She felt immediately chastened by his curtness of tone. 'What's been happening?'

'Long story. I'll tell you when I see you.'

'Are you OK?'

There was a slight pause before he answered. 'I'm fine.'

'Can I do anything?' The opportunity to be of service to someone else relieved her, momentarily, of the weight of her own self-pity.

'No. No. Some prayers maybe.'

'Are you at the university today?'

'Not until Thursday.'

She didn't know whether to interpret the lack of warmth in his voice as active irritation with her or floating irritation with the world in general.

'Could I take you out for lunch?' she asked in the meekest tone she could muster. 'I'd like to hear how you're getting on. If you want to talk about it. Or if you don't I could just blather on about myself as usual.'

When he answered she could hear the smile in his voice. 'I'm sure we could both do with a good blather. Lunch on Thursday sounds good. Same place as last time?'

'That works for me. Nice and cheap.'

He laughed then. 'Wait until you see the wine I'm going to order.'

'I knew there'd be a catch.'

When she ended the call she sighed deeply and stared across the table in the hotel restaurant where she was finishing off her breakfast. She had spent all of Sunday brooding on her experience at the theatre. She had even taken herself off to Mass in a nearby cathedral, looking for guidance from the Almighty, but, as usual, none had been forthcoming.

She kept trying to believe in a personal God, knew all the apologetics about prayer – God wasn't Father Christmas; prayer was supposed to be a process of opening oneself to the will of a transcendent power; of aligning one's will with the will of Love Eternal. But she didn't *feel* terribly loved. Wasn't she supposed to *feel* something slightly more consoling than this aching emptiness? *I only believe because I'm too frightened not to*, she had confessed once to a sympathetic priest. 'I'm sure God has compassion on you for that,' the kindly old gentleman had counselled, as though Dee needed reassurance for her lack of belief instead of a remedy for the fear that was slowly eating her alive.

The fear was always there. Sometimes it was overt, manifested in a heart that thumped like a faulty piston in her chest, which caught and stopped and hiccupped painfully into life again, which made it difficult to breathe and impossible to see things clearly as panic rose up in nauseating waves and left her whimpering in a curled-up ball on her bed. But most of the time the fear just lurked in the background, undermining hopeful anticipation, tempering all joy, adding an invisible weight to her day and a restless anxiety to her nights.

It had gathered force and momentum in the last few days and she just wanted it to go away. She didn't know if the girl she had seen in the theatre was Corrie. She felt a strange kind of certainty about it. But then, she had felt that same certainty about the girl she had followed in the Japanese Garden, even though she had not admitted it to herself at the time. And was that really Joaquín she had seen or was her mind playing tricks with her again? Was it worth trying to chase him up? In the unlikely event that he actually *did* know something, she suspected that he would be no more forthcoming than the first time she had spoken to him. She felt dull dismay at the prospect of hopping back on the roller-coaster of exultant hope and devastating disappointment. Just thinking about it caused her heart to surge painfully and erratically. She had survived on sheer willpower for a very long time, but her body was beginning to crack under the strain. Maybe the knowledge that Corrie was alive and well had to be enough for now. That was, after all, no small gift, following years of much darker imaginings. On a whim, she picked up her phone and dialled Luke's number. She was expecting it to go straight to voicemail so was surprised when he answered.

'Hey Mum! How's it going?'

There was one of those disconcerting echoes on the line.

She gave the automatic response. 'Good. Good, love. How are you getting on?'

'Flat out. Exams start next week.'

Perhaps it was not the most opportune time to be distracting him with unsettling news about his sister. 'Are you all prepared?'

'Yeah, more or less.'

'Less? Or more?'

'I'll pass.'

'Fifty and a half per cent?'

'That's all I need.'

'Ever thought of aiming a little higher?'

'So, Mum, what's been happening with you?'

She decided not to challenge his evasion. 'I've been following up a few bits and pieces,' she replied cautiously.

'Any luck?'

'A couple of things look promising . . .'

'That's good.' She could hear a guarded note in Luke's voice. Neither he nor Ben felt comfortable discussing Corrie's disappearance. Such conversations seemed to provoke them to brace a little against further flare-ups of their mother's pain and sadness.

'I'll let you know how it all pans out.'

'OK. Great. Look, I'm sorry to rush off on you, Mum, but I'm running late for work. Take it easy, OK?'

'Do some study.'

'Yeah, yeah. See ya, Mum.'

'Give my love to Ben—'

But he was already gone. She stared at the photo of the boys she used as wallpaper on her phone. They were both grinning into the camera. The latest news about Corrie was going to cause them a great deal of emotional upheaval. Dee decided to leave them in peaceful ignorance until she had followed the current trail to its end. She would break the news to them in its entirety when she was back in Australia.

*

By Thursday the changeable spring weather had turned cold and blustery again. When Dee arrived at the restaurant at Puerto Madero, following a brisk walk along the canal, Stephen was already waiting for her. He smiled a greeting as she wriggled out of her jacket and unwound her scarf.

'How are you?' he asked.

'All the better for seeing you.' She sat down and turned the wine bottle that was already open on the table to look at the label. 'Will I need to take out a second mortgage?'

'Believe me, it will be worth it.'

Dee laughed her approval of his indulgence, poured herself a glass and leant across the table. 'So tell me what's been happening. I've been worried about you.'

He swirled the wine in his glass and took a sip. 'Oh, just the ongoing saga. I received a note from my bishop the other day. I've been called back to London for a chat.'

'Sounds ominous.'

'They're keen to resolve my status. They want some decisions.'

'What are your options?'

'There are strong pressures afoot for public recanting. If I put up my hand to being a defective heterosexual and submit to re-education camp—'

'Re-education camp?'

'They like to think of it as "counselling and spiritual direction". If I agree to those terms they might give me some closely monitored role of limited influence to be going on with.'

'And would you accept that?'

'Probably not.'

'So then what happens?'

'I suppose they could throw me out. It depends on how hardline they want to be.'

'Would that be so terrible?'

Stephen's face registered his distress at the question just as the waiter returned to ask if they were ready to place their food order. Dee made a quick choice for spaghetti marinara and Stephen ordered a risotto.

'I'm sorry,' she added as soon as the waiter left. 'I didn't mean to sound flippant. But there's a great big world out there that could benefit from your skills. The Church doesn't have a monopoly on good works, you know.'

'I've never assumed it had. But I've devoted my whole life to the Church. It goes beyond what I want or need. I told you before, it's a calling.'

'And you don't think you can live out that calling in any other way?'

'Well, that's up to God, isn't it?'

Dee dropped her eyes, not wishing to communicate her essential scepticism. 'I don't understand.'

'No. And it's impossible to explain.'

They sat in silence for a while.

'I could let go,' he said at last, matter-of-factly. 'Being an ongoing irritant is not a role I relish, but slinking away quietly would feel like a betrayal of everything I am, everything I believe in. What is the most loving response? For the Church, for the people I serve here, for myself? They are the key questions. And I'd have to say that I don't know the answers. I can only continue to pray about it for the grace to let go or the courage to stay, whatever is required.'

'Not so dissimilar from the decision I need to make, I guess.'

'How so?'

'I'm torn like you. Do I let go? Or do I keep searching? I'm erring towards the former because I just don't have that much fight left in me.'

'You too, eh?'

'I've – I've not been well this last week. I feel like the endless running on adrenaline's beginning to take its toll. The spirit is willing but the flesh ain't coping too well, I'm afraid. I keep seeing Corrie everywhere, like I did in the early days, and it's really draining. I've spent a lot of time thinking about my options. I'm heartily sick of hotels and I want to go back to my boys. Corrie's alive, and she knows where I am if she needs to get in touch. I don't know whether or not I should inform the embassy. They'd be obliged to tell the police and I still feel worried about the repercussions of that for Corrie. I don't want to tempt the fates. I've found out that she's alive. Maybe I just need to be content with that for now.'

The waiter delivered their meals.

'You don't know what the future might hold,' Stephen mused. 'Maybe Corrie just needs a little more time before she can face her family again.'

'That's what I'm hoping. It's just—' Dee closed her eyes and sighed wearily. 'It feels like such a monumental waste of time. Time we could be sharing together. Time we'll never get back again. And all because of – what? I don't understand. I don't think I'll ever understand.'

She picked up her fork and stabbed at her spaghetti.

*

On the way back to her hotel Dee walked past the Plaza in front of the presidential palace. *Las Madres*, the mothers of those who had disappeared under the military junta, were making the preparations for their regular Thursday protest. They had set up trestle tables and laid out T-shirts, postcards, badges and key rings for sale. Tourists stood about awkwardly, taking the odd apologetic photograph. Dee slowed her pace and then stopped at the edge of the plaza to watch.

At three thirty a handful of elderly women dressed in square-cut overcoats and sturdy shoes, wearing white triangular headscarves, shuffled into a line near the Pirámide de Mayo – the monument to the city's freedom. A long blue-and-white banner was unfurled carefully, passed from hand to hand and held at waist height. Some of the women gripped canes as well as their portion of the banner. Some leant on the supporting arms of younger relatives. Then the line of old women, poorly dressed, colourless and unremarkable, with serious intent but without exaggerated solemnity, started to make one of several slow circuits of the monument.

They fussed a little to get their banner straight, turned to converse intermittently with each other as they hobbled forwards, picking their way carefully around the cracks in the paving to avoid stumbling, ignoring the crowd that had gathered to watch. A North American woman standing next to Dee among the scattering of spectators touched the elbow of her partner, a man in an anorak with an oversized Nikon camera.

'Do you wanna walk with them, honey?'

'Sure.'

After the first circuit a number of people slipped into step behind the mothers and their local supporters. There was no sign of welcome, or affront, from the women. They seemed removed from the reactions of the spectators. There was no rage, no triumphalism, no hypnotic chanting. No appeal to heroics. The flags that their supporters carried aloft read, '*Asociación Madres de Plaza de Mayo, Ni un paso atrás.*' No going back. Dee puzzled over what was written on their banner: 'Distribute the wealth immediately.' Their original cause had been subsumed. The loss of their children and grandchildren had been officially acknowledged. The forensic scientists were doing what they could with the remains that were recoverable. Early amnesties against the murderers had been overturned and new convictions were being upheld. But the world had, largely, moved on. The generals were now anachronistic detail; the children they killed, fodder for Wikipedia.

On the third circuit of the monument Dee fell into line behind the women. Not because she felt any particular desire to do so – part of her was embarrassed by their sad shuffle, their stubborn witness to the detritus of a historical debacle. Nevertheless, she felt a strong sense of identification with them. Her face soon ached with tears she didn't believe she had any right to shed. It was a preposterous presumption. She was not one of them. She was not one of the brave and battered survivors of that dirty, dirty war. But if she was not one of them who was it exactly that she thought she was? And in what community of yearning did her own loss belong?

At the end of the third circuit the walk dribbled to a kind of questioning conclusion. Enough for today? Some of the spectators clapped tentatively. A couple of young supporters rolled up the banner, the women embraced each other goodbye. A few wandered off in pairs across the square while others folded away the T-shirts and packed the postcards and key rings back into their cardboard boxes.

Dee's phone began to ring. She glanced at the display before answering. It was Stephen.

'Dee? I've just had a call from Pedro. Sister Catalina's been in touch with him. A former client's come back to barrio Moreno and she's got some news about Corrie.'

Chapter Thirteen

Dee paid the taxi driver at the gates of the Barrio Moreno shelter and buzzed the intercom.

'*Hola. Soy Dee Sutherland. Quisiera ver a la Hermana, Catalina.*'

It wasn't long before Viviana came hurrying down the path to open the gate for her.

'*¡Hola, Viviana!*' The excitement in Dee's voice made Viviana's face light up in response and she greeted Dee with the kiss usually reserved for compatriots. It felt like a good omen, this small, symbolic act of solidarity.

Viviana took Dee to Catalina's office, a small room next to the kitchen. Catalina was seated behind her desk, frowning at an antiquated computer screen. She smiled when she saw Dee in the hallway.

'Hello, Deirdra. I can't for the life of me work out this infernal machine.'

'What are you trying to do?'

'One of the North American Sisters rang last night. She said she'd sent some photos of her last visit, but I can't get into my email account.'

Dee went around to the other side of the desk and sat down at the computer. 'Does this connect automatically to the internet when you turn it on?'

Catalina looked blank.

'Is it a dial-up connection?'

'I'm not sure.'

'What sort of email account do you have?'

Again, Catalina looked blank.

'What's your email address?'

'Catalina Ortiz at hotmail dot com.'

'That's easy then. We just have to get onto the internet. Do you remember your password?'

Dee located the appropriate icon and triggered the electronic blips and wash of static that signalled dial-up. It took several attempts to connect but eventually she succeeded, found the hotmail homepage and got Catalina to type in her password. The old nun clapped her hands happily as the first photograph slowly revealed itself. A group of elderly women in colourful, knitted pullovers and cardigans smiled at the camera. They stood before a backdrop of garden foliage and climbing roses. Catalina pointed out each woman by name and told Dee which countries they came from. Dee opened a second photo showing a liturgical setting of coloured silks, candles and indigenous pottery. The same group of women was seated in a large circle around the setting. The third and last photograph showed the women dancing in a light-filled, whitewashed room, with all the chairs now pushed back against the walls. Dee couldn't help smiling at the joyous theatricality of their poses and Catalina laughed as she explained how they'd all danced until late in the evening to celebrate the Feast of Our Lady of Mercy. Dee couldn't remember the last time she had felt free enough to dance in public.

'Oh, it's lovely to see those pictures!' Catalina exclaimed. 'Thank you, Deirdra!'

'A pleasure. That's probably the extent of my computer skills though.'

'It's a miracle, isn't it? What they can do these days?'

Yes, Dee thought, and how quickly we lose consciousness of the miracle and get irritated when it doesn't appear on cue.

'But you've come to hear about Corrie. Let's see if we can find Angelica.'

Catalina led Dee out to the back garden and knocked on one of the doors in a self-contained structure opposite the main house.

'We built these flats a few years ago with a donation from the mayor's wife,' Catalina explained.

'Is that how you keep the place running? On donations?'

'The North American Sisters help out, but the building and repairs are funded by local benefactors. We always seem to get what we need. And if we don't, perhaps we weren't meant to have it.'

God can't lose that wager, Dee thought wryly.

The door was opened by a short, dark-skinned woman juggling twin baby girls in pink jumpsuits. A boy of about seven or eight, with a freshly laundered white school coat buttoned over his jeans, jostled to get in front of his mother.

Catalina introduced the family group to Dee: Angelica, her son, Emilio, and the twins, Rosario and Gabriela.

'Emilio is making great progress at school,' Catalina told Dee, translating the remark into Spanish for Emilio's benefit. 'He is one of the best readers in his class.'

Emilio tugged at Catalina's apron, asked her something in Spanish and raced off to the main house.

Angelica, while keeping up a stream of conversation with Catalina, beckoned with her head, indicating that Dee and Catalina should follow her inside.

The space was partitioned into three rooms. There was a single bedroom, a small area that contained a television, a pram, two upright chairs, and a tiny bathroom. Angelica insisted that Catalina and Dee take the two chairs. Dee held out her arms to relieve Angelica of one of the babies and Angelica shifted the other to her left hip.

'I have twins,' Dee told Angelica '*Tengo gemelos.*'

Angelica quizzed Catalina to make sure that she had understood correctly then laughed in surprise and directed a flow of Spanish at Dee. Dee didn't understand a word, but she persisted with the conversation, regardless.

'Luke and Ben. They're nineteen. *Diecinueve.*' She nuzzled the child in her arms. '*¿Es Rosario?*'

'*¡No!*' Angelica laughed again. '*¡Es Gabriela!*'

The baby stared into Dee's face for a few seconds. Her dark eyes widened and her little mouth shaped itself into a drooly grin. She began to pant excitedly and wave her small arms in the air. Dee hugged her close in gratitude for the affectionate welcome. The child smelled sweet and warm and clean. Dee held her cheek against Gabriela's velvety softness and looked up at Angelica with a sideways gaze.

'You know my daughter, Corrie? *¿Conoces a mi hija?*'

'*¡Sí!*' Angelica replied in the deep, upward inflected delivery that implied, 'Of course – what a silly question!'

Dee found herself laughing incredulously in reply. Laughing at the ridiculous simplicity of the response. After all these years.

'When did you see her? How is she?'

Angelica waved away the flow of English she did not understand and turned to Catalina who translated for her.

'Angelica and Corrie met here,' Catalina said. 'Angelica was pregnant. She found out that she was expecting twins just before Corrie left. They have kept in touch. Angelica went back to her husband, but it didn't work out for her. Corrie has been helping her with the babies. She saw her a few weeks ago. Corrie gave her something for Emilio.'

Angelica went into the bedroom and started to rummage around in a large plastic carry-bag next to the bed. She returned with a crumpled flyer and handed it to Catalina. Catalina smiled slowly as she read it, then passed it to Dee.

Dee looked down at the flyer. It was instantly familiar. She searched in her handbag and produced its twin from the bundle she had picked up from the artists' collective at Recoleta.

'You already have one?!' Catalina was both surprised and perplexed.

'On someone else's advice, I've been acquainting myself with local theatre groups. Just on the off-chance.'

Angelica pointed to the flyer and continued her narrative in Spanish.

'Ah,' said Catalina, nodding, and then turned to Dee. 'Corrie has started a Saturday-morning drama group with some of the local children. She told Angelica that she wanted to make a contribution to the community in honour of Felipe's work. Their first performance is next weekend in San Miguel, at the plaza. She thought Emilio might like to go, but Angelica doesn't want to take him into San Miguel in case they bump into her husband.'

Dee continued to study the flyer closely, trying to digest the information. She shook her head slowly in a kind of reverie.

How bizarrely simple it all seemed once the last piece of the puzzle clicked into place. And yet still she held the burgeoning hope cautiously at bay. Gabriela, however, she held close, rocking her back and forth and chanting softly in her ear, 'Ga-bri-e-la, Ga-bri-e-la...' The little girl reached up a chubby hand and touched Dee's lips as if to grasp the sound of her own name from the stranger's mouth.

*

On Saturday morning, Dee left the Hotel Gran Vía early and hurried to the railway station, pushing through the crowds at Retiro to reach the terminal for the San Martín line. She had told Stephen and Alicia about the Saturday-morning performance and they had both offered to go with her, but Dee knew it was something that she needed to do on her own. She couldn't run the risk of overwhelming Corrie with a posse of rescuers. Alicia had told her there was a train that would take her straight to San Miguel from the city and had assured her that the plaza was within walking distance of the station.

When she had located the correct terminal, Dee joined the queue to purchase a ticket. A large, heavy-limbed girl of about fifteen, shoeless and unkempt, perched cross-legged on the ledge beside the ticket-seller's window. She breastfed a baby held in the crook of one arm. Her free hand was casually cupped and extended to receive the twenty centavos change from the standard 1.8 peso ticket. Most commuters obliged her and Dee did likewise.

The train was already waiting on platform one. Dee took a seat by the window. Peak hour was over and the passengers were mostly down-at-heel: broad-faced and broad-bodied with clothes that were clean but ill-matched and dull-coloured from many years of washing. They squeezed close together in the small seats. Dee moved to accommodate a large woman who shuffled over and unselfconsciously pressed herself up against Dee. She smelt of soap and sweets.

The train pulled slowly out of the station. Alicia had told her that the journey would take about an hour and had named the stations she should look out for as she approached San Miguel.

Spruikers boarded the train at almost every stop, attempting to offload packets of stickers, greeting cards, teaspoons, notebooks and pens. They stood near the doors, declaiming the virtues of their products in dejected monotones, then picked their way carefully up and down the aisles, proffering the items to individual commuters. Dee bought one of everything.

At one point a girl of about ten jumped onto the train with nothing to sell. She stood near the doors, shouting at the top of her voice in a well-rehearsed drone: 'My name is María. I am twelve years old. My mother is dead. I must look after my six brothers and sisters. We have no food. I am very hungry. Please I ask you to give me a little money to feed my brothers and sisters. I ask God to bless you.'

All Dee had left was a ten-peso note. She reached past the woman next to her with the note between her fingers. The girl gave her a startled look before snatching it and scurrying off into the next carriage. Dee's neighbour turned and regarded her curiously for a few seconds, but Dee looked away and stared out of the window. She was feeling increasingly sick with nerves.

It was quite possible that she would arrive at the Plaza San Miguel only to find, once again, that fate had intervened to obstruct her efforts. She would be told that the production had been cancelled or postponed, or it would turn out that Corrie was not in attendance. Dee was not unprepared for such scenarios. It was the other possibility, however – that she might finally be brought face-to-face with her daughter – that was really playing havoc with her nerves. Over the last few days she had tried to anticipate how the scene might play out, had tried to imagine herself in her daughter's shoes, but she could not make the required leap. Of course Corrie would be shocked, that was a given, and it was up to Dee to manage that shock somehow, to dissipate the threat that she herself posed, to soothe and reassure her daughter, through what would be an inevitable moment of dismay at being discovered. But then what? This is where Dee drew a complete blank. There were no templates in her experience for helping her to predict what might happen next. She had seen parent–child reunions broadcast on the evening news from time to time, but these invariably centred on small children who had wandered off into the bush for several days or on families separated by wars or forced emigrations and the scenes were all tears and relief and fierce embraces.

The other story that played in her head was the parable of the Prodigal Son, the wayward boy falling into his father's loving arms, but that was a story of a son choosing to return home, and Dee was painfully conscious that her own daughter had made no such choice. Corrie would be caught unawares, and that could lead to a tide of strong emotions. Dee knew how much she, herself, hated being taken by surprise, even by pleasant things like parties and friends dropping by unexpectedly. She had always been deeply unsettled when deprived of the opportunity to prepare her responses in advance. Perhaps she should have pursued a more oblique method of making contact with Corrie – gone back to Sergio, solicited him to make inquiries on her behalf or to set up a meeting, but she had been too frightened of losing the trail again. And if she were honest, she supposed she had not really wanted to give Corrie a chance to elude her. Attending the public performance gave Dee a unique opportunity. If Corrie was there, Dee had the option of simply observing her from a distance. She would be able to make her own assessment about how her daughter was going. She would be able to gauge for herself the wisdom of making her presence known, and the best way of doing this. And it was even possible, Dee thought, that if she handled things properly, Corrie might actually be relieved that she hadn't been forewarned. Dee's unexpected appearance might give Corrie licence to surrender to a reunion she had secretly longed for but been too scared to initiate. Was that too much to hope for?

No, Dee decided firmly, it was not too much to hope for. It was where all the evidence pointed. Her daughter had left home four years ago, grieving and confused. She had got swept up in something that had later terrified and shamed her. She had allowed a chasm so great to open up between her new life and her old one that she was incapable of bridging it herself. She needed someone else to do it for her.

Dee took new heart from this line of thought, but her breath continued to come in ragged puffs and she found it difficult to suppress the compulsive rhythmic twitching in her left leg.

When the train finally pulled into San Miguel station, most of the passengers alighted with Dee. The platform was crowded with people heading towards the railway crossing on the main road. Dee followed them. Beyond the station, the pavement vendors and loitering youths had a dark, street-sharp look that made Dee feel unsafe. She crossed the strap of her bag over her chest and wove tentatively through the crowd looking for someone trustworthy to ask for directions.

A woman selling fruit pointed her towards Plaza San Miguel, gesturing at a leafy area several blocks down on the other side of the road.

Dee approached the Plaza cautiously. She had brought a wide-brimmed sunhat and a large pair of dark glasses, props that were, she could argue, practical necessities for an outdoor event, but which also served to obscure her identity. The plaza was located on the corner of two main roads and covered a very large area. Market stalls were arranged around the perimeter, which was also fringed by trees, but beyond the stalls and the trees, there was an open, paved area where a makeshift stage had been erected. It was hard evidence that the event Dee had come to observe was actually going to proceed. Her heart began to pound even more fiercely in her chest.

She hovered by the stalls for some time, irritating the vendors by picking up random trinkets, putting them down, picking them up again, always keeping one eye on the stage, waiting for a crowd to gather so that she could slip in among them unnoticed. According to the flyer, the performance was due to start in half an hour, but Dee knew that nothing ever started on time in Argentina. In the meantime she observed, from a distance, a group of young men, hauling equipment from a ute parked close to the stage area. They unloaded a large supply of plywood props, musical instruments, several battered black amplifiers, cardboard boxes and bulging plastic bags. One of the men straightened up and looked in her direction for a moment and Dee recognised Joaquín, the leather artist. The one who had denied all knowledge of knowing Corrie.

A white van was inching its way across the plaza on the same pedestrian pathway the ute had obviously taken. It pulled up and a girl in a short summer dress hopped down from the driver's seat. A dozen children accompanied by a group of mothers emerged from the sliding door on the other side of the van.

They gathered under a nearby tree and, under instruction from another young woman wearing a red-and-gold skirt and black singlet top, the mothers began to assist the children to wriggle into the costumes they had brought with them. The woman in the red skirt collected an empty crate and a flat wooden box from the back of the ute. She opened the lid of the box, placed it on the ground and sat down on the crate. As the children finished dressing, they lined up in front of her to get their faces painted. There were boys in loincloths and T-shirts carrying spears, a tall girl in shiny white silk with a sparkling tiara on her head, another in blue with white clouds pinned to her dress, carrying a doll swaddled in rags. Dee watched curiously as the young woman carefully painted tiger stripes and whiskers on the face of a stocky boy dressed in orange and black. As she paused with the brush in her hand and turned the boy's face gently to one side with a touch of her fingers on his chin, it slowly dawned on Dee that she was looking at her daughter. Dee closed her eyes against a wave of dizziness and blinked several times to refocus her gaze.

Corrie's arms were more wiry and muscular than Dee remembered, and her usually pale skin carried a slightly burnished tinge. She had allowed her hair to return to its original black. It fell loosely below her shoulders and was held off her face with a headband in the same fabric as her skirt. The girl with the tiara hovered next to her and when Corrie turned to address the child Dee could see her whole face clearly, lit with an encouraging smile, before she turned away again to resume work on the boy's tiger face.

Dee took a shuddering breath, but then her breath wouldn't stop coming in rapid, laboured gasps. Her throat was very dry and she couldn't swallow the claggy spit in her mouth. Nor could she tear her eyes away as Corrie carefully painted stars and clouds and warrior designs on the faces of the children. Eventually, when they were all done, Corrie closed the lid of her paintbox and ushered the children towards the stage.

While her daughter herded the performers into position, Dee moved forward on unsteady legs to join the crowd of mothers and the other spectators. A group of guitarists and children with hand-held percussion instruments and wooden flutes occupied one side of the stage. One of the guitar players handed Corrie a microphone. She tapped it several times to no avail until it occurred to one of the other musicians to turn up the volume control on the amplifier.

'*Uno, dos, uno* – ¡*Hola!*'

The microphone kicked into life and Corrie began to address the crowd. While it was a novelty for Dee to hear a foreign language emerging from her daughter's lips, the vocal cadence was, at the same time, painfully familiar. At one point Corrie gestured towards the mothers and they responded with an outbreak of smiles and clapping. The joyful expression that crept across Corrie's face awoke in Dee powerful memories of Ross, Luke and Ben and even of herself. Her daughter's face was full of the unmistakable tracings of familial history, of genes and unconsciously acquired expressions. They broadcast an intimacy of connection that Corrie shared with no other person in that crowd except Dee.

'*Bueno,*' Corrie said finally. '*Esta es la historia Guaraní del árbol del mate.*' This is the Gaurani story of the *mate* tree.

She signalled to the musicians and after several false starts they gathered volume and rhythmic fluency, warming slowly into the first folk tune. Corrie then passed the microphone to two teenagers, a boy and a girl, who had taken up positions on either side of her in order to narrate from crumpled scripts clutched in their nervous hands.

Dee could only pay cursory attention to the story. Her eyes kept straying back to Corrie, standing at the side of the stage, prompting the action forward whenever it faltered. The girl in white, the narrators explained, was Yasi, the moon-woman. She stood with outstretched arms as two miniature warriors with wooden spears approached. One warrior hearkened in a stagy manner to a noise that sounded like the whoop of an owl. The moon-woman pointed to a stylised cardboard cut-out of a bush and the warriors crept forward, reacting with exaggerated surprise to the discovery of a swaddled doll. They carried the baby back to a group of girls who gathered around the child with exclamations of delight.

Corrie prompted the musicians to begin the next piece as the stage was reset. The following scene opened on a young warrior boy, asleep on a woven mat outside his hut. Yasi, the moon-woman, beckoned. He awoke and tried to follow her, but she eluded him, finally jumping from the edge of the stage.

A second time, Yasi beckoned him while he slept. Again he followed her but was stalked and pounced upon by the tiger. A carefully mimed, slow-motion conflict ensued which eventually saw the hapless tiger felled to the sound of several loud drumbeats.

As the warrior bathed his wounds, Yasi appeared with the girl in blue, the cloud-woman. This time they allowed the warrior to take their hands and the three enacted a dance that simulated the soaring and swooping movements of flight. But, the narrators explained, the warrior pined for his home and his people, so Yasi returned him to the earth. She placed her hands above his head and the cloud-woman raised the *mate* tree from the floor of the stage to conceal the warrior from the sight of the audience. The band reprised the original folk tune and the other players formed a circle around the tree and mimed the familiar *mate*-drinking ritual. Corrie took the stage and organised the children to hold hands and take their bow to enthusiastic applause from the audience.

Dee retreated to the back of the crowd as the children jumped from the stage and ran to their mothers. Corrie turned laughingly to the musicians. The girl in the summer dress and the boys who had unpacked the ute, including Joaquín, strolled over to join in the conversation.

Dee didn't know what to do next. She was reluctant to intrude on Corrie's moment of triumph, but she knew that her presence was going to become more noticeable as the rest of the onlookers began to drift away. She withdrew even further, back towards the market stalls, but was too frightened to take her eyes from the crew in case some of them decided to make an abrupt departure with Corrie in tow. Joaquín retrieved a polystyrene drink cooler from the back of the ute, along with a column of paper cups and began to distribute cordial to the children. When they had finished their drinks, Corrie ushered them back on stage to collect the discarded props. After everything had been dismantled and put away, the group of organisers stopped to confer.

As the children and their mothers climbed back into the van, Dee stepped forward hesitantly. It seemed, however, that the girl in the summer dress was going to drive the van, accompanied by Joaquín. Several of the guitar players packed up their instruments, waved their goodbyes to the group, and walked off in the direction of the railway station. Corrie was left behind with two men who were tying down the load in the ute with thick ropes. At one point her eyes drifted in Dee's direction, as though she could feel the intensity of her mother's gaze, but she did not register any recognition. Instead she turned and put her arms around one of the men who was checking the knots and the tautness of the ropes. He turned to face her and kissed her before resuming his task.

And then Dee realised, with a sudden wash of panic, that they were about to drive away. Before she could think any further she found herself running across the plaza towards them.

'Corrie! Corrie!' The sound of her voice was panicked. It wasn't the tone she had been hoping to adopt. And this last-minute act of desperate waylaying was not the dignified approach she'd hoped for.

Even though Corrie was facing away from her, Dee could tell by the unnaturally frozen set of her shoulders that she had triggered an intense reaction in her daughter. The two men had turned more quickly and were regarding her quizzically. It seemed to cost Corrie an immense effort of will to turn and face Dee, but as she did so, Dee could see that she had already recognised her voice and had known exactly who it was she was about to be confronted by.

Dee took a step towards her. 'Corrie. Love. I can't believe I've finally found you.'

She took another step forward and raised her arms as though to catch her daughter in an embrace, but stopped abruptly when Corrie drew herself back as far as she could against the side of the ute.

'What do you want?'

Dee was momentarily confused. Did Corrie not recognise her? What was going on?

'Corrie, it's me. It's Mum.'

Corrie's tone, when she answered was hard and cold. 'I know who it is.'

Dee lowered her arms slowly in the manner of one not wanting to frighten a cornered animal, but she continued to scan her daughter's face hungrily, drinking in the familiar features, looking for some sign of answering joy. Corrie turned her head away, her eyes narrowed, her mouth set hard.

'Corrie, we've been out of our minds with worry. We thought you were dead.'

'Well, as you can see, I'm not.' Corrie spoke between clenched teeth, directing her comments at the ground.

'Corrie, please. I know what happened. There's no need to be ashamed—'

Corrie's head jerked up, her cheeks flushed, her eyes wide, her lips white with fury. 'Ashamed? Why should *I* be ashamed? *You're* the one who should be ashamed!' She was spluttering and spitting with rage.

Dee tried to reach out a hand to touch her daughter, but Corrie flung her arm above her head, turning her face away and holding her hand, palm outwards, in front of her eyes.

'Corrie, I'm sorry. Whatever it is you think I've done, I'm sorry. But I've been looking for you for four years. I never gave up hope. All I wanted to do was find you and look after you.'

'Look after me? What suddenly made you want to start looking after me? You've never wanted to look after me. You never wanted me and you never cared about me. You only ever cared about the boys.'

Dee was having problems following the logic of the argument. All she could imagine was that Corrie was in a state of high shock.

'Corrie! Calm down. You're not making any sense.'

'Where were you?' Corrie screamed at her. 'Where were you? You were never there. Where were you the night Dad died? Hey? Where were you? Don't bother to answer. I know where you were. I saw the messages on your phone!'

Dee was registering her daughter's fury but only half hearing the words. All her energies were directed towards trying to break through the barrage of emotion and reassure Corrie that everything was going to be OK. She turned and appealed to the two men for support.

'I'm her mother. *Yo soy su madre.*'

'Mother? Some mother! I don't have a mother. I never did.'

The two men were gazing wide-eyed and wary from one to the other of them. Corrie sobbed something at them in Spanish and scrambled into the front seat of the car. Dee could hear her urging them to follow her. The man Corrie had embraced earlier moved quickly to the other side of the vehicle and took his seat behind the wheel. The other man shrugged apologetically at Dee, slid in beside Corrie and slammed the passenger door behind him. The engine coughed into life and Dee watched helplessly as the ute headed out of the Plaza, turned onto the street and roared away down the main road.

She was left standing alone staring after the retreating vehicle. Her emotional comprehension had shrunk to a focus on one key fact. Corrie had stood before her, flesh and blood, corporeal. Alive. While her daughter's shouting had alarmed her, she had been prepared for some measure of distress, and had not fully registered the details of the hostility directed towards her. There was something almost welcome in the familiarity of her daughter's fury. It lent weight to the most essential fact of the matter: *Corrie was alive.*

She became aware that people were staring at her. A portly, middle-aged man drawing on a cigarette watched her closely from the shade of a nearby tree. She smiled at him. The smile was real. My daughter was dead and now she's alive. But she knew how foolish that would sound if she said it aloud. Perhaps it would also be best not to continue to draw attention to herself by standing alone in the middle of the plaza. She made her way over to an unoccupied bench and lowered herself carefully and deliberately into a sitting position. It was not that she was frightened of collapsing. On the contrary, she was charged with a strange, slow-moving energy, which both sharpened her perceptions of her surroundings and seemed to hold her at a remove from them. Corrie was alive. And Dee had seen her with her own eyes. But what was it Corrie had been shouting at her? Before Dee's brain could recall the words, her body experienced their significance as a sudden cascade of icy water pouring down her gullet, pooling in the pit of her stomach and trickling slowly into her bowels. *I saw the text messages.* Dee knew those words were laden with some alarming import, but just for a moment, she couldn't think why. It was so long ago. Text messages? David. Oh, God.

And then, with the obtuseness of someone inebriated, she began to painstakingly retrieve and piece together the other fragments of Corrie's tirade: *You're the one who should be ashamed . . . Where were you the night Dad died? . . . You never cared about me . . . I don't have a mother. I never did.*

Dee frowned over the recollection. Is that what Corrie had shouted at her? Or had she misconstrued the words? Disparate associations and scraps of distant memory began to slowly coalesce in Dee's beleaguered brain. Text messages. All those text messages from David that she thought she had been so careful to delete. *You're the one who should be ashamed.* Oh, yes. And she had been. Ashamed of the duplicity. And the cowardice. The creeping around. The schoolgirl naughtiness of it all. *Where were you the night Dad died?* Dee whispered the words aloud to herself: 'I was trying to make things right.' It was an irony but it wasn't an excuse. She knew that. She had known it ever since that fateful night. She had just hoped that her poor timing would never be exposed to anyone else. But it had been.

Was it such a terrible thing? The only person she had ever confessed it to was Liz, late one night over too many brandies. And that's what Liz had asked in her typical matter-of-fact, don't-sweat-the-small-stuff style. *Was* it such a terrible thing? According to Liz, her relationship with David had been somewhat old-fashioned and quaint, compared to what went on in other arenas like the Public Service, where Liz's sister-in-law worked. 'They're all doing each other on a rotation,' Liz had quipped to Dee. 'And by that I don't mean sitting in parked cars, holding hands and staring into each other's eyes.' But, Dee had long ago decided, it *did* become a terrible thing when you were exchanging passionate goodbye kisses with your lover while the life was draining out of your husband on the kitchen floor and your daughter was the one left to deal with it. It *was* a terrible thing, when, although the general consensus was that there was nothing Dee could have done, even if she had been there, no one actually knew that for certain. There was always a shadow of doubt. If she had been there, she might have picked up the early warning signs. Ross was notorious for shrugging off physical symptoms until they were completely debilitating. Dee had maintained the CPR training that was compulsory for teachers. Corrie didn't know CPR and even though it had only taken the ambulance ten minutes to arrive, Dee's training might have made a difference. Her absence might have deprived Ross of the last chance he had. She knew that and Corrie had known that. And then, obviously, somewhere along the line, Corrie had discovered the real reason for her absence. *I saw the text messages.*

David had continued to send solicitous messages after Ross died, and, at a respectful distance of some months, had made allusions to the intensity of the time they had shared together, assuring her of his continued affection and regard. Corrie must have discovered one of those messages the day Dee had left her phone at home, put two and two together and come up with five. Five? No. Corrie had come up with the correct answer. Dee had long ago given up trying to hide behind the fallacy that if one kept one's underwear on, infidelity could be deemed not to have occurred. She was, of the old-fashioned school of morality that equated desire with deed, modern enough to award a few points for not proceeding to the latter, but only a few. And sophisticated enough to deduct them again because *not* proceeding to the deed had actually inflamed and prolonged the ardour and that was surely even *more* culpable.

You never cared about me. That was Corrie's other accusation. Dee knew that that particular accusation was completely false, but, for the last four years, she had been agonising over whether or not her actions had conveyed something different to her daughter. And it appeared that they had. *I don't have a mother. I never did.*

Dee had never stopped caring about her daughter, not from the moment Corrie had been placed in her arms as a newborn, but somewhere along the line, as she had attempted to juggle so many other competing demands, she had begun to rationalise her emotional resources. She had stopped being attentive to kindness. Kindness had assumed the status, in her utilitarian imagination, of the sort of commodity that, when resources were low, could be dispensed with. Had she actually made this economic calculation? She couldn't remember. She just knew that, at some point, she had ceased to make the effort. She had hoped, in retrospect, that no one had noticed. That the practical acts of service, which she had never neglected, had somehow compensated. That had been her wager, but it seemed to be a wager she had lost. Corrie had just stated the case unequivocally. Her labour and her diligence had not compensated. She, Dee, had failed in the most important task that she had ever undertaken, in the most serious responsibility with which she had ever been charged. *I don't have a mother. I never did.* She turned the phrases over calmly in her mind, calculating the potential pain but not yet feeling it. So, she thought. Now I know.

She got up from the bench with the same deliberate care with which she had sat down, passed under the dappled shade of the trees, skirted the trinket stalls and waited at the edge of the busy road. She felt vaguely somnambulant and she knew people were staring at her, but for once it didn't bother her. Cars hurtled past. She thought she detected a break in the traffic. Although she knew there was something wrong with her perception of this information she hastened to take advantage of the opportunity to cross. Stepping out onto the road, she felt the rush of air before she heard the cacophonous horn and was hauled back to the kerb by a wrenching grip on her upper arm. The car, coming from her left, not from the right where she had been instinctively looking, grazed the fabric of her shirt as it blared past without any attempt to swerve or avoid her. The driver and passengers hung out of the windows gesticulating and shouting as she stood there in a daze staring after them.

'*¿Señora? ¿Está bien?*'

The man she had seen smoking in the plaza shook her arm and scanned her face with heavy-browed eyes.

She studied him curiously. 'I'm fine, thank you. Fine.' She smiled to reassure him. He let go of her arm cautiously and asked her where she was going. She frowned, realising that she didn't know.

'The Sisters,' she announced eventually. '*Las Hermanas de la Misericordia.*' She began to walk away, but the man caught her arm again.

'*Señora.*' He pointed to himself, mimed a steering wheel, and indicated a car parked by the side of the road.

She smiled again. In the absence of any other plan, it was a convenient solution. She seemed to have lost the energy to be afraid.

'*Bueno.*'

She followed him to the car and got in while he held open the passenger door for her.

He asked her the Sisters' address. She knew she had it written down somewhere. Without any particular sense of urgency, she began to slowly remove every scrap of paper from her wallet, smooth each one out and read it carefully before filing it away again. In the meantime, her self-appointed rescuer took out a mobile phone from his jacket pocket, punched in numbers and started haranguing someone on the other end of the line. Eventually he appeared satisfied with the results of his conversation. He put the phone away, turned the key in the ignition and yelled at her over the sound of the engine. She didn't understand the words, but gathered it was an assurance that he now knew where he was going. Nevertheless, Dee continued to sift with exaggerated conscientiousness through her papers and receipts. When the car pulled up twenty minutes later in a busy commercial street, she assumed the driver was visiting one of the local shops and remained in her seat, staring out of the window, but he came around to her side of the car, opened the door for her and pointed at a nearby building. Dee frowned and shook her head. He pointed again at a sign affixed to the front door. She got out of the car to read it. It was the Sisters' local office. Of course. The address of the shelter was unlikely to be publicly listed anywhere. This would do. Someone inside would assist her.

'*Gracias. Muchísimas gracias.*' She withdrew her purse from her bag and surveyed its emptiness. She had given the last of her local currency to the girl on the train. There were emergency American dollars in a pouch under her T-shirt. She reached inside the shirt and extracted a fifty-dollar note. She offered it to her rescuer and he took it with a dignified nod. She watched as he returned to his car, completed an awkward U-turn in the busy street and drove away, glancing at her in his rear-vision mirror as he sped past. Then she mounted the steps and knocked at the front door of the Sisters' office. No one answered. She knocked again. And then she remembered that it was Saturday.

Dee sat down on the top step. She didn't know what she was going to do next and she didn't really care. The step was warm and sunlight spilled across her face. She closed her eyes against the speckled brilliance and leant her head on the doorframe. She sat there for a long time. Eventually she heard footsteps slow and stop in front of her. She opened her eyes and saw a well-dressed, middle-aged woman carrying a loaf of bread staring down at her.

'I'm looking for Sister Catalina,' Dee explained.

The woman held up a finger, signalling her to wait. She handed Dee the loaf of bread and reached a hand heavy with gold rings into the Gucci bag on her shoulder to retrieve a mobile phone. After dialling a number, she reacted excitedly to whoever answered it and spoke rapidly for several minutes. When she hung up she retrieved the loaf of bread from Dee, fixed her with a firm gaze, spoke to her at length in Spanish, then flashed her a reassuring smile, trotted on her four-inch stilettos to the residence next door and buzzed herself inside.

Fifteen minutes later, a taxi pulled up alongside Dee and Sister Catalina clambered out.

'Dee!' she exclaimed, her voice full of concern. 'What are you doing here, darling?'

The final endearment set up a trembling in Dee that she could not control. She could not control it and she could not speak. Catalina called out to the taxi driver who hurried to her side. Between them they managed to lift Dee from the steps, hoist an arm over each of their shoulders, guide her stumbling feet to the car and lower her gently into the back seat.

Chapter Fourteen

Dee awoke in the small guest bedroom of Catalina's house. Sunlight streamed through a window that overlooked a wooden desk at the foot of the single bed. A small bookcase containing an array of Spanish titles occupied the wall opposite, next to a narrow wardrobe and a chest of drawers. Dee could smell unfamiliar laundry soap in the bedsheets and hear foreign birdcalls from the trees outside her window. She was thirsty and needed to go to the toilet. Pushing aside the faded cotton eiderdown, she sat up, swung her feet onto the bare floorboards and waited for a wave of dizziness to pass.

Dee glanced around the room, looking for her handbag. She found it on the table at the end of the bed. Her mobile phone read nine am. She pulled on the jeans she had dropped on the floor the night before and opened the bedroom door. The house was very quiet. She knocked tentatively on the closed bathroom door and when no one responded she entered. After she had used the toilet she headed towards the kitchen at the end of the hallway.

She had spent hours in that kitchen yesterday, all through the late afternoon and early evening. Catalina shared the house with two other Sisters: Florencia, a woman in her mid-fifties, and Laura, who looked to be about thirty. Dee remembered thinking that the three women were the right ages to be grandmother, mother and daughter. Laura with her graceful figure, long black hair and indigenous features had made the strongest impression on Dee, perhaps because of her youth and beauty, but she had no English and therefore they had not spoken. Catalina and Florencia had sat at the kitchen table with Dee, making her cups of tea, chatting with her about things of no consequence, keeping up a soothing patter of conversation while she obsessively folded and refolded a paper serviette into different shapes.

'You've had a big shock,' Catalina had said to her. 'Tomorrow will also be difficult, and probably the next day, but after that, I promise you, you will start to feel better.'

These were the only words Dee remembered clearly from the flow of reassurances. She didn't necessarily believe that she would feel better after three days, but the observation gave her licence to feel bad in the short term, and that was what she seemed to need most urgently.

Towards midnight, Florencia had made up the bed in the spare room and left her a towel and a nightgown, showing her the bathroom and offering her use of the shower, but Dee had just stripped off her jeans and fallen into bed in a kind of stupor, seeking oblivion but plagued by an avalanche of emotion every time she started to drift off, the two compulsions competing throughout the long, nightmarish night.

Dee found Catalina sitting at the kitchen table, reading the newspaper. For the first time, Dee took in the view of the garden from the large windows at the end of the room. She could see fruit trees and flowering shrubs, vegetable patches and a small area of cultivated lawn with an outdoor table and chairs.

'Good morning, Deirdra.'

'Hello, Catalina.'

'How are you feeling today?'

Battered. Bruised. The shock had worn off and with it, its anaesthetic properties. Every thought her mind alighted upon seemed to pulse with unendurable pain.

'OK.'

'I've left out the bread. There's some jam, or marmalade if you prefer. One of the North American Sisters left us some nice tea. In the tin.'

Dee willed herself to be interested. She picked up the square tin on the breakfast counter and examined it. 'Earl Grey?'

'Florencia likes it.'

'Yes. I like it, too.'

The persistence of ordinary things. She put the kettle on to boil.

'I seem always to be collapsing on you,' she said, rinsing out the teapot with hot water at the sink, her back to Catalina. 'I don't know what's wrong with me. I'm not normally like this.'

Catalina turned a page of her newspaper. 'We all need a safe place to fall apart every now and again. Why should you be different?'

Dee shrugged. She had never really liked being lumped in with everyone else. Had always prided herself on being above the common herd in her capacity to cope. But it didn't seem to matter much anymore. She didn't have a lot of pride left. The ballast of her life had blown away leaving her with a disorienting, but not entirely unpleasant, sense of weightlessness. She spooned tea into the warmed pot, filled it with boiled water, then carried it to the table with an empty cup and saucer.

Catalina watched her pour out the tea and add a teaspoon of sugar to it.

'I've talked with Florencia and Laura and you're welcome to stay here for as long as you need. We don't think you should be by yourself.'

Dee recalled the bleak impersonality of her hotel room, the frightening anonymity of the sprawling city. 'Thank you, Catalina. I really appreciate that.'

'Florencia will lend you some clothes. She and Laura have been at the refuge this morning, but they'll be back in a minute. We're going to ten-o'clock Mass in the local parish.'

Catalina didn't ask Dee to come with them, but the invitation hung silently in the air. Dee sipped her tea and stared out at the garden.

A horn sounded outside.

'Well. You know where everything is.' Catalina pushed back her chair and picked up a woven bag with a stout shoulder strap that was lying on the table next to her.

'We'll be back around twelve. Laura's going to make a tortilla for lunch.'

'Can I do anything?'

The old nun smiled at her and patted her shoulder. 'We'll put you to work later, but today you should rest a little.'

Dee heard her unlatch the front door then pull it closed behind her. A car door banged shut in the street and an engine revved, eased into gear and receded into the distance.

She glanced down at the newspaper on the table. It was full of news of the recent elections. The page Catalina had been looking at featured a photograph of the annual sixty-kilometre youth pilgrimage from Buenos Aires to the cathedral in Luján. It showed a dense crowd of scruffy teenagers with backpacks and water bottles trudging behind the familiar triangular-robed, star-crowned statue of the *Virgen de Luján*. The paper claimed that over a million people were in the crowd by the time it reached the cathedral. Apparently some people walked to give thanks for prayers that had been granted, others to earn the Virgin's favour. Dee recalled the little artefact Fidelina had given her. The intended miracle had been achieved, only she'd never been warned that miracles could be so painful.

Dee decided to take her cup of tea out to the outdoor table. From this vantage point she surveyed the garden again, noting a flourishing fig tree in one corner and thick plantings of other trees and tall shrubs along the fence line. A washing line was strung across an unshaded patch of lawn and two rectangular plots had been dug for salad greens and herbs. Dee noticed that there were shoots of spring weeds proliferating among the edible plants.

She crouched down next to the edge of the vegetable bed and began to pull out a few of the larger offenders. The smell of grass and earth rose up to meet her, nostalgic scents that always reminded her of childhood, of time spent lying on the ground, observing ants and beetles, oblivious to the acquisition of rashes and bites and clothing stains. She pushed the leaves of the little self-seeded mignonette lettuces to one side and gently tugged at the tender grass shoots pushing up among their roots. It was satisfying work, clearing the patches of dark earth around the bright clumps of lettuce and spinach, endive and radicchio. She worked her way slowly and methodically around the bed, leaving little piles of wilting weed in her trail. If only it were as easy to root out the mistakes and failings of life, she thought;

if only one could identify the problematic flourishings before their roots started to tangle with other things that really mattered and became impossible to dislodge. She worked on as the sun climbed high in the sky and sweat started to drip from her face. When the Sisters returned from church she was halfway through the second patch.

Florencia clapped her hands over the cleared beds. 'Laura will be so happy! She's been avoiding that job for weeks.'

'I like weeding,' Dee sat back on her heels. 'It probably reflects my neurotic need for order.'

'We give thanks for your neurosis,' Catalina commented dryly. 'Would you pick us some leaves for our lunch today?'

It was a simple meal: tortilla with potato and spinach from the garden, some salad leaves and the bread left over from breakfast. Because it was Sunday and they had a guest, Catalina poured each of them a glass of wine. The Sisters ate slowly. Laura's culinary skills were noted and complimented. Dee got up quickly at the end of the meal to do the dishes, determined not to be a burden, to earn the hospitality that had been granted her. Catalina watched her thoughtfully but did not say anything. When the dishes were finished, Florencia announced the afternoon siesta and they all retired to their bedrooms. Curtains were drawn and silence descended on the house.

Dee lay awake on her bed listening to the birds and the occasional swell of children's voices in the street outside. Though nauseous with exhaustion, she knew she would not sleep and found herself envying the gentle rhythm of the Sisters' life. She had observed something similar among older women in her own country, witnessed it in rural settings, where working days were longer but the pace of life slower, where the rituals of simple meals and cups of tea and time to rest were part of everyone's regular routine. Dee's life, by comparison, was a wearying blur of relentless endeavour in the quest for some elusive and undefined expression of perfection, a manic careering across many fronts to stave off multiple possibilities of humiliating failure. She couldn't remember exactly how she had acquired these damaging habits. Perhaps the compulsion for constant activity dated from the time of her mother's death.

That had been such a strange and surreal time in Dee's life. She had blurry memories of being encouraged to pursue her usual routine of school attendance, sport and homework, while her mother struggled through her last weeks in the front bedroom at home. Aunty Beryl had come over from Melbourne to help them out. She had taken over Dee's bed and Dee had been relegated to a camp stretcher in the same room. With her father also occupying a stretcher in his study, in order to snatch enough sleep to get him through his working day at the university, an incongruous atmosphere of holiday camp had settled over the entire household.

At four o'clock one morning, Aunty Beryl shook Dee awake to stand vigil with her father and brother as her mother took her last laboured breaths. When it was finally over Paul had begun to cry. Dee had wanted to dredge up tears but none would come. Her senses registered the scene but her mind seemed to be drifting elsewhere. There was some measure of relief that the axe had finally fallen and a guilty hope that perhaps now the comforting patterns of ordinary life could resume.

Afterwards she had thrown herself into her studies, seizing on the activity as a distraction. It was necessary to get on with things. She couldn't allow herself to dwell. She was frightened that if she started to dwell she would never be able to stop.

Over time, however, memories of her mother began to float to the surface of their own accord, odd fragments and images: her mother in the kitchen in the early hours of the evening, peeling vegetables over the sink or turning chops under the grill with a fork, on her knees scrubbing the kitchen linoleum or wiping scuff marks from the walls, sitting at her sewing machine, pushing folds of fabric under the frenetic pecking of the needle, hosing water over the garden beds in the summer twilight, baking trays of biscuits and slices for the church fête. Lying on her bed with the blinds drawn in the late afternoons, her forehead furrowed in pain and a tissue pressed to her nose . . . Dee was acutely aware of her mother's body in these images but she could never see her face. And the only sound that she could conjure to accompany them was the sound of sighing. Her mother had battled to maintain her normal activities in the last two years of her life, but the shock of the diagnosis and the chemotherapy had extracted a heavy toll. The mother who had presided over Dee's childhood, the one who could be relied upon to have the answer to every problem, who took an active and eager interest in all Dee's childish projects, and whose unconditional affection was a safe haven from the unjust and unreasonable behaviour emanating from the world at large, had been replaced by someone who was frightened, frequently in pain and whose emotional energies had been turned inwards to navigate an epic journey that Dee couldn't even begin to imagine. Dee had felt abandoned long before her mother died and afterwards she had despised herself for her selfishness and her inability to offer her mother more understanding and support. Diligence and hard work had become a form of atonement, a way of proving herself worthy and beyond further reproach.

Her relationship with Ross had offered her some respite, but subsequent circumstances had triggered her compulsion to take on the self-sacrificial role again. For so many years afterwards she had flip-flopped between the roles of victim and saviour, regarding everyone around her as contributors to her suffering or objects for rescue and repair. Even though she had tried to temper this attitude, she was profoundly conscious of the number of times her interactions with Ross and the children had been characterised by irritability and resentment. If Corrie had therefore believed that she had never been wanted, that Dee had emotionally neglected her, on what grounds could Dee plead her innocence? She rolled onto her side on the narrow bed and drew her knees up protectively. *I tried*, a small voice within her protested. *I tried my best but sometimes I was just too tired to keep trying anymore . . .*

An hour or so later Dee heard the Sisters moving around the house again. Emerging from her room, she discovered a scene that would not have been out of place in a 1950s musical. Laura was carting sheets, towels and pillowslips from the laundry to the washing line and pegging them out to billow in the afternoon breeze. Catalina was ironing in the living room while singing along to a CD of modern hymns and Florencia was remaking the beds with fresh linen. Recently washed underwear was hung neatly over a drying rack in the hallway.

'Did you sleep, Deirdra?' Catalina called out to her.

'Yes,' she lied.

She joined Florencia in Laura's bedroom, glancing briefly around at the girlish pictures and trinkets, as she helped tuck in the corners of the bed sheets.

'It's nice how you do the housework together,' Dee commented. 'I've always hated having to do it by myself.'

'Oh, yes,' Florencia smiled. 'There are some advantages to religious life.'

'Did you ever think about having a family?' Dee asked, genuinely curious.

'When I was young I had a few boyfriends but nothing serious. In my thirties I desperately wanted a baby. That was hard for me. I still love babies, but now I'm quite happy to hand them back.'

'It must take a lot of self-discipline to choose religious life,' Dee mused. 'I think I liked boys too much.'

Florencia shrugged. 'Every life has its challenges. Sometimes I am tempted to feel sorry for myself because I won't have the joy of children and grandchildren in my old age, but—' she looked at Dee kindly, 'I haven't had all the pain and worry, either. I have the other Sisters and, as you see, we do our best to look after each other.'

'Better than some families do.'

Florencia laughed. 'Don't be too jealous of us. We are not always so lovely to each other!'

When the housework was finished, the women paused again for cups of tea and ham and cheese sandwiches. Florencia excused herself to check emails in her room. Laura curled up on the sofa in the lounge room to watch television and Catalina invited Dee to sit with her in the kitchen where she intended to do some knitting.

'What are you making?' Dee asked, as they settled in the easy chairs at the far end of the room, overlooking the garden.

'It's a sleeveless pullover for Emilio,' she replied, holding it up. 'Red is his favourite colour.'

'Red was Corrie's favourite colour.' There was a kind of relief in mentioning her daughter's name and not falling apart.

'Well, now,' Catalina mused. 'I wonder how Corrie is getting on today.'

'Yes.'

'It must have been quite a shock for her, too.'

Dee watched Catalina's needles weaving to and fro. 'Not entirely. There was a boy from Recoleta who knew I was looking for her. She wouldn't have expected to see me yesterday, but she would have known I was in Buenos Aires. Catalina—'

The day before Dee had only alluded vaguely to the reasons for Corrie's rejection, but she now felt an urgent need to confess. The words, however, jammed in her throat.

Catalina looked at her curiously, but seeing that she was struggling, removed the spotlight of her attention back to her knitting.

'I told you Corrie was angry with me yesterday,' Dee said eventually, 'that she accused me of not wanting her, of favouring my sons, of – of not supporting her very well when her father died.'

'Yes, I remember.'

Dee chewed at a fingernail. 'She also accused me of something else.' She glanced up at Catalina who raised her eyebrows inquiringly while keeping her eyes on the slip of the stitches over her needle.

'Corrie was the only one with her father when he died. That was something that was very difficult for her. She was only seventeen and she was very close to him. I – I had a friend, an old friend, who I had been seeing and I was having dinner with him that night. Corrie found out about it afterwards. It seems that over time she has come to see that as an unforgivable betrayal. Of both herself and her father. That's the main reason that she doesn't want to see me anymore.'

'Ah.'

Dee looked at the old nun expectantly. She was bracing herself for an awkward question about her 'old friend', but Catalina was counting stitches.

When she had finished counting, she asked instead, 'And do you think that's fair?'

Dee thought about the question for a long time. 'I don't know what fair means anymore,' she said at last. 'I think about what I did – falling in love with someone else when I was already married, and that seems manifestly unfair on my part – but I never went to bed with him. I know that's no excuse,' she hastened to add, 'but the night Ross died I was in the process of breaking it off. I was trying to do the right thing. So it seems to me very unfair that I should be punished for that. Although I guess, from Corrie's point of view, if I'd never started anything in the first place, I wouldn't have been absent that night, trying to finish it.

'As far as her other accusations go, well, I have never, ever, wished her out of my life. I turned myself inside out trying to be the best mother I could be. I admit that I probably got a lot of things wrong. I probably succumbed to that old-fashioned sin that no one talks about anymore – well I guess they *do* talk about it, but they call it Obsessive Compulsive Disorder now – that old sin of over-scrupulousness, trying too hard to be perfect – but I never, *never* didn't want her. And if I was different with the boys it was because I'd learned a few things by the time they came along and we had a little more money and Ross was staying home with the children. He never did any housework or anything like that, but it took a bit of the pressure off, knowing he was there. It wasn't my choice to be at work all day, but Ross didn't have any qualifications and I had the capacity to earn more money. It broke my heart never being able to help out at school with reading or canteen or sports days, like the other mothers, but you have to earn a living don't you? Truth was, I felt damned if I did and damned if I didn't. Whichever way I turned I was letting someone down. When I took the promotional position a few years before Ross died, part of the motivation was thinking about all the things that I'd be able to buy for the kids, the things they'd missed out on over the years – nice clothes and theatre tickets and holidays and travel . . .' Dee's voice faltered, contemplating the last irony.

'And why do you think you found such comfort with that old friend of yours?' Catalina asked, straightening out the garment on her lap, comparing the length of one side of the V-neck to the other.

Dee gazed out of the window at dusk falling over the garden. 'I liked myself when I was with him,' she said eventually. 'It was so nice to be loved for who I was not for all the things I was obliged to do.'

'Who told you that you had to *do* things to earn love?'

Dee shook her head. 'I don't know.'

Catalina, satisfied that both sides of the V-neck matched up, rolled up the pullover, prodded the ball of wool onto the end of the needles and put the knitting into a tapestry bag at the side of her chair. She joined Dee in gazing out at the garden in the last of the fading light.

'What was it you said people call over-scrupulousness now?'

'OCD – Obsessive Compulsive Disorder. I don't know if that's really what anyone else calls it. It's just what I think.'

'But it's the same thing isn't it? That voice that keeps telling you you're not worthy until you do something else and something else and then keep doing it and keep doing it and no matter how many times you do it, no matter how hard you try you can't relieve the fear that something terrible is going to happen because you're just not good enough?'

Dee was intrigued by the old woman's insight.

'Do you know what they used to call the devil back in the old days?' Catalina continued. 'An old superior of mine once told me. In the ancient texts the devil is known as The Accuser. You know that voice in your head that breaks down your will to do good by accusing you of all kinds of evil? Well, I believe that's the devil. We have to work very hard to resist that voice sometimes. Tell me, when you look at that daughter of yours, what do you see? What is there to be proud of?'

That was the easiest question of all to answer and Dee's response tumbled out quickly.

'She's strong. She's brave. She's created a new life for herself in a foreign country. She's committed herself to helping other people. She's gentle and kind with those children and proud of what they've been able to accomplish. She seems to have won the affection and loyalty of their families. And she can stand up for herself. Whether I like it or not, I guess she's not afraid to speak her mind.'

'Well, then.' Catalina cocked her head at Dee and smiled. 'You must have done something right.'

*

The next morning, Florencia invited Dee to choose some fresh clothes from the simple collection of blouses, skirts and trousers that she owned. There was a black skirt bordered with colourful Peruvian embroidery that Dee liked and a white peasant blouse.

Florencia smiled when she put them on. 'You look like a young girl!'

'Not quite.' Dee turned to assess the sideways view of herself in the mirror on Florencia's dressing table, conscious of her matronly bosom, grateful for the skirt's elasticised waist. In the meantime, Florencia located a pair of sandals in Laura's room and the ensemble was complete.

'More importantly,' Dee joked, 'do I look like a Sister of Mercy?'

'¡Sí! You are one of us now!' Catalina laughed from the doorway.

The Sisters didn't own a car and relied on the services of a local driver who collected them every morning. When they arrived at the refuge that day there was a flurry of activity underway in the kitchen. A large woman with yellow-blonde hair and arms like a wrestler was instructing a group of residents on the art of pastry making.

'It is Father Luciano's tenth anniversary of ordination next weekend,' Catalina explained. 'So we need to make two hundred empanadas.' She settled herself at one of the tables while Dee moved to the edge of the circle of women in the hope of picking up a few tips. They made a space for her. Angelica gestured at Dee's skirt and blouse and nodded her approval. Dee made a mock curtsy and the women laughed.

The pastry ingredients were simple enough, but the recipe involved an inordinate amount of rolling, buttering, folding and resting the dough for long periods of time in the refrigerator while the *mate* was passed around. The women seemed oblivious to Dee's limited grasp of their language and chatted away to her in Spanish, content with her smiling attention and willingness to join in the group laughter. She felt like a small child again in her ignorance and her dependence on their patience, grateful for their readiness to include her in their circle, despite her incapacity to offer anything besides an appreciation of their camaraderie.

When they had buttered and folded and put their rectangles of pastry in the refrigerator for the last time, the women removed their aprons. Angelica returned to the double pram, parked close by, that contained her sleeping twins. Emilio wandered in with a book and, catching sight of Catalina, ran over to show it to her. She explained to him that she needed to talk with his mother but with a nod of her head indicated that Dee might read the book with him. He looked at her sceptically. Catalina insisted that Dee needed his help to learn Spanish.

'*¡Sí!*' Dee chimed in. '*Por favor, Emilio.*'

She took his hand and led him out into the garden. They sat down together in the shade of a large tree by the playground equipment. Two other children who were playing on the swings paused to watch them. Emilio opened the book and began reading, sounding out the words with exaggerated care as he stabbed each one with a chubby brown finger.

'*¿Puedo probar?*'

Emilio looked up at Dee and held his finger under the first word for her to begin.

'*Este. Es. El. Cocodrilo.*' She stumbled over the last word. He repeated it for her.

'*Cocodrilo.*'

'Crocodillo?'

'*No!! Co-co-drrree-lo!*'

'*Cocodrilo! Cocodrilo!*' The children on the swings shouted at her.

'Ah. *Cocodrilo! En Ingles:* Cro-co-dile.'

Emilio repeated the word, exaggerating her Australian diphthong. 'Cro-co-dy-ill.'

She laughed. '*¡Excelente!*'

'*Tiene una sonrisa grande y llena de colmillos,*' Emilio continued.

'He has a big smile full of fangs,' she translated.

'Fay-ings?'

'Fangs!' She laughed at the broadness of her own accent reflected back to her by the child's acute imitation.

The other children left the swings and came to stand behind them, looking over their shoulders at the pages of the book.

Emilio continued the story in Spanish. When they got to the end the other children insisted that he begin again, while Dee translated the story into English so they could copy her. On the fifth read-through, Catalina appeared on the verandah to call them in for lunch.

Dee wandered in and sat down next to Angelica at the communal table.

'Emilio,' Dee began, then tapped the side of her head and made a thumbs-up sign. 'Very clever.'

'*¡Sí!*' Angelica agreed and began to elaborate in Spanish. Dee heard a reference to her husband in the flow of narrative and interrupted to ask about him.

'Bad man!' Angelica exclaimed in English. She unbuttoned the front of her blouse to show Dee long scars crisscrossing her chest, then held out her forearms, which were polka-dotted with cigarette burns. Dee placed her fingertips on the burn scars, looked at Angelica with a furrowed brow and shook her head slowly.

Angelica continued her explanation in rapid Spanish, but her tone was light and matter-of-fact. She re-buttoned her blouse and glanced over at the pram as one of the twins started to stir. Dee got up quickly to see if she could settle the baby, but

Rosario (or was it Gabriela?) was lying there with her eyes wide open so she scooped her up and brought her back to the table.

'Gabriela?' she asked Angelica.

'¡No! ¡Rosario!'

Angelica's delight in her children was infectious. She smiled proudly as she watched Dee entertaining Rosario with English rhymes and tickling games. Afterwards Dee gave Rosario her bottle while Angelica gave Gabriela hers. She sat with both babies while Angelica dressed Emilio in his white cotton coat and walked him around the corner for afternoon school.

'You haven't lost your touch then?' Catalina observed as Dee bounced Gabriela on one knee and pushed Rosario in the pram at the same time.

'Like Florencia, I'm very happy to hand them back these days. Angelica's amazing, though, isn't she? You can tell these kids have been well looked after.'

'Yes, but poor Emilio has had a lot to deal with. He's seen so much violence directed at his mother. Did you notice whenever we give him a biscuit or a treat he always takes two? He hides one away for Angelica. He thinks we don't see. He's very protective of her.'

Dee felt a sudden lump in her throat.

By the time Angelica had returned from the school run, Dee had managed to get both babies to sleep. Angelica sat down beside her on the steps at the front of the house as Dee continued to push the pram back and forth. She asked Dee about Corrie. Had she seen her?

Dee felt a predictable constriction in her chest. She knew she would have to get used to the question – find a way of fielding it with friends and family back in Adelaide. With Angelica, a stranger she would probably never see again, a woman well-acquainted with suffering and unlikely to judge, she would have liked to have been more forthcoming, but she came up against the language barrier and all she could share was the simple fact:

'*Mi hija,*' she said sadly, '*No quiere verme.*' My daughter doesn't want to see me.

Angelica looked at her incredulously then broke into a long outburst in Spanish. Catalina came out to join them and Angelica turned around and started questioning her. Eventually Angelica turned back to Dee, and Catalina translated her final remarks, smiling a little.

'Angelica says that she doesn't know what has got into Corrie and when she sees her she will give her a good talking to.'

Dee felt the lump rise in her throat again. She seemed to be constantly on the verge of crying lately. She threw her arms around Angelica, whose own eyes were brimming, and hugged her tightly.

*

Later that night alone in her bedroom in Catalina's house, Dee pulled a notebook from her bag and started to compose a letter. An hour later, after three pages of crossings-out, she looked at what she had written and wondered if it captured the truth she was trying to convey.

> *Dear Corrie,*
> *I understand that I have hurt you a great deal and why you do not wish to see me, but I wanted to let you know how sorry I am so I hope you will be prepared to read this letter.*
> *For four years I did not know what had happened to you and I feared the worst. I was afraid that I would never see*

you again. Those four years highlighted for me all the ways in which I had been absent to you in the past, all the ways in which I had failed you. I hope that one day you will be able to forgive me for not being as attentive to you as I should have been. That is time I will never get back again and I regret it deeply.

Since you were a little girl you have always been a very loving person and tried to make others happy. I always meant to tell you that I treasured that in you. I missed my chance. I missed the chance to share so many things with you.

Perhaps it's too late now, but I want you to believe that I have always loved you and wanted the best for you. That's partly why I worked so hard and wasn't around a lot. I suppose I hoped that the good relationship you had with Dad would compensate for my absence. Perhaps it was silly of me, but after a while I started to think that you would all be better off if I just left you alone to get on with the things you liked doing together. It was pride masquerading as humility, I suppose, but I knew that I wasn't as spontaneous or kind or as fun to be with as Dad. All I knew how to do was work so that's what I did. But I don't want to bore you with excuses.

I saw the play you put on with the children the other day and I couldn't help feeling very proud of what you have achieved here, of your courage and tenacity and your generosity in wanting to help others. It was wonderful hearing you speak Spanish and seeing how much your friends here love and respect you.

While of course I want to be a part of your life, I understand that the hurt I have caused probably runs too deep to allow that for a while. It is enough for me to know that you are happy and well. If you feel up to it, please get in touch *with Ben and Luke. I know they have missed you a great deal and would love to hear from you, but I don't want to put you under any pressure. You will know when the time is right. I just don't want them to miss out on the possibility of a relationship with the sister they love because I have failed you.*

Anyway, Corrie, hopefully you have read this far and I haven't made things worse.

Please be reassured that I won't be making any more unexpected appearances. I'm heading back home as soon as I can get a flight.

If you ever need anything, you know where I am. If you ever need money, please don't hesitate to ask. I will always be here.

I love you. I always have.

Mum

Corrie probably wouldn't read it, even if she ever received it, Dee thought as she folded the letter and put it to one side. She had considered asking Angelica to deliver it, but Angelica might not bump into Corrie again for months, if ever, and Dee suspected it would get lost in Angelica's transient and unpredictable life. She didn't trust Joaquín to pass it on, but she remembered Sergio's sincerity and concern for her. He would make sure it was safely delivered.

She began to undress, removing the clothes Florencia had lent her, hanging them carefully over the back of the chair. They reminded her of the sorts of clothes she had worn when she was a teenager. Such things had been in fashion for the 'alternative' set in the seventies – those who were slightly appalled by the prevailing discotheque phenomenon and continuing to cling to the remnants of sixties' idealism – but they were not clothes that she felt comfortable in anymore. Ben and Luke would have had a good laugh to see her in them. She wondered how they were getting on. And then she began to think about the life that awaited her back in Australia. In one way she was looking forward to returning to her familiar routine, but it was going to be awkward, facing all the questions and explanations.

The most difficult conversation of all, of course, would be the one with Luke and Ben. With other people she could fudge the details: *Corrie got herself involved with a bad crowd. There were some problems with the police. She was too afraid to seek help – worried about how we would react. You know how it is with young people . . .* She could imagine herself saying those things. If people pressed her further she would plead her daughter's right to confidentiality. She was not capable of telling lies – they had always stuck in her throat like thorns – but she was quite adept at omission. She did not want Corrie, or Ben and Luke for that matter, to be humiliated by public gossip and speculation.

With Liz she could be more frank. And with Luke and Ben? With Luke and Ben she would need to tell the truth, the whole truth and nothing but the truth. The thought of it made the residual sludge of anxiety in the pit of her stomach stir and bubble. But it was something that needed to be faced. And it needed to be faced soon.

Chapter Fifteen

On Thursday morning, Dee rang Qantas and asked about the availability of seats on flights leaving Buenos Aires for Australia.

'We have one on Sunday evening. Other than that, nothing until the following Sunday, unless you want to upgrade.'

It was sooner than she had anticipated leaving and her first instinct was to wait the extra week. She scanned her options: she didn't want to impose on the Sisters for much longer but spending another ten days in the lonely confines of her hotel room was an almost unbearable prospect. Four days would give her time to say goodbye to Stephen and Alicia without prolonging the agony. She was also increasingly conscious of the need to get home to Ben and Luke and let them know what was going on.

'I'll take that seat on Sunday.'

'OK. Just bear with me while I get some details from you . . .'

After she hung up the phone, Dee felt a new sense of forward momentum. The Sisters were at work in various locations around the barrio so she had the day to herself. The first thing she needed to do was some shopping.

The commercial district was a half hour's walk away but Dee was grateful for the exercise. She had been sitting around for far too long, she decided, as she strode off in the direction of the main road. It took a while to find the things she was looking for, but she enjoyed the process of hunting them down: new outfits for Gabriela and Rosario and books for Emilio, including a special Spanish–English illustrated dictionary, a leather-bound notebook and easy-to-grip pens for him to practise his writing. For Angelica, she purchased the biggest toiletry bag that she could find and stuffed it full of creams and cosmetics, nail varnishes, hair accessories and other pampering items from the local *farmacia*. For the Sisters, Earl Grey tea, chocolates, *alfajores* and red wine – the only luxuries that she had seen them enjoy – seeds for the garden and a hand-painted earthenware vase on sale in the same garden shop, a keepsake that she hoped would remind them of her.

Then she located the most prominent bank in town and checked the balance of her travelling account. She calculated what she would need to cover her hotel bill and her expenses over the next four days and withdrew the remainder. It was a considerable amount and she was a little nervous about carrying it in cash, but as she turned away from the teller, she concealed it discreetly inside her bra and directed an interior plea to the *Virgen de Luján* to look after her own. On her way out of town she passed an old woman by the side of the road selling flowers. They were a little the worse for wear, but Dee wanted to support the woman's enterprise and decided that the colourful poppies would set off the vase to good effect. She purchased three bunches.

When she got back to the Sisters' house, she helped herself to a packet of envelopes that she had seen next to the computer in Florencia's bedroom. She put the cash in one and the letter she had written to Corrie in another. She wrote a letter in halting Spanish to Angelica, thanking her for her help and support and wishing her, in the sincerest terms Dee knew, the very best of everything in the years ahead. She put that letter in an envelope, labelled it in large capitals with Angelica's name and taped it to one of the shopping bags that contained the gifts she had purchased for the family.

She filled the vase with water and the flowers, put it in the centre of the kitchen table and placed the other offerings for the Sisters around it. Finally she sat down at the table and wrote a note to Catalina. There were no words adequate to express her gratitude but she tried anyway. She asked Catalina to pass on the gifts to Angelica, to assure Florencia and Laura of her love and prayers and explained (relying on the protection of the English language against any potential break-in) the hiding place where she had secreted her cash donation for the Sisters' ongoing work. She put the note in another envelope and propped it against the base of the vase.

She hand-washed the clothes that she had borrowed from Florencia and hung them out on the washing line to dry, checked that the back door was locked behind her and that her handbag contained the letter to Corrie along with the few essential items that she had arrived with. She glanced at the clock on the kitchen wall. It was just after five. The Sisters would be home soon. Dee didn't want to be seen hovering around in expectation of acknowledgement or gratitude. She knew that the Sisters would understand. They were used to people passing in and out of their lives, and anyway, she would be in touch. She took one last affectionate survey of the sanctuary into which she had been welcomed five days earlier, stepped outside, pulled the front door shut behind her, tugged on the handle to check that the latch had caught, then set off in the direction of the town centre to find a taxi.

She arrived in the city just before seven. The reception staff at the Hotel Gran Vía seemed pleased to see her, no doubt grateful that she had not absconded without paying her bill. Back in her room she plugged in her mobile phone, which had run out of charge three days ago, and waited while a backlog of text messages was delivered. There were half a dozen from Stephen and Alicia and one from an unknown number. Irrational hope surged. Corrie?! Her fingers fumbled on the telephone buttons as she opened the message, but it was not from Corrie. It was from Sergio: *Please call me 4345 2002.*

Perhaps he had been in touch with Corrie. Perhaps he had further news. She quickly dialled the number.

'Sergio? It's Dee Sutherland.'

'*Hola*, how are you? I've been trying to ring but your phone's been switched off.'

'I'm sorry. I've been away and I didn't take my charger with me.'

'I made some inquiries and I think I might have some news for you. Joaquín was mistaken. One of the girls involved with the children's theatre project *is* Australian—'

'Yes, I know,' she interrupted, 'I went to see the performance.'

'So, you've seen your daughter already?'

Dee hesitated. She still felt profoundly upset every time she thought of that encounter. 'Yes.'

'OK. Good. That's what I wanted to tell you. The resemblance to the photograph you gave me was so strong. I was sure it was her. That's great news then.'

'Well, not entirely great.'

'No?'

Dee scraped around for the right words. 'I am very grateful for the trouble that you have taken, but I need to ask another favour of you.'

'Yes?' He sounded cautious.

'I went to see my daughter's performance but she didn't know I was going to be there so of course it was quite a shock when she saw me. It seemed to stir up a lot of difficult feelings for her.' She paused.

'Yes, I can imagine.' His voice was sympathetic and it gave Dee the courage to persist with her request.

'I didn't get the chance to say much to her. She was anxious to get away.'

'As you say, the shock.'

'And other things. I won't pretend there weren't other things, but I would like the opportunity to explain and she is refusing to see me again.'

'So, what is it exactly that you want me to do?' He was beginning to sound a little less accommodating.

She hastened to reassure him. 'Just a letter. I don't want you to persuade her to see me. I wouldn't ask you to do that. I've written her a letter. She'll probably tear it up. But there were things I needed to say, things I needed her to know. I was hoping that you might be good enough to deliver it for me. I don't know how else I can get it to her.'

The silence on the other end of the line seemed to last a very long time.

'Sure,' he said eventually. 'I can do that for you. I'll be in the city tomorrow so I can pick it up then. Where are you staying?'

She wanted to launch herself down the phone and kiss his feet with gratitude. 'The Hotel Gran Vía on Avenida de Mayo, but I can bring the letter to you.'

'I'm not totally sure of my movements tomorrow. Just leave the letter at reception and I'll collect it from there.'

His tone was practical, assured, and Dee sensed that she could rely on him.

'I'm not expecting it to change anything, but I needed to at least try.'

'I understand. That's OK. Happy to help out.'

'It's very good of you.'

'I might have to call in the favour one day when that vagabond son of mine ends up in Australia.'

'I hope you do.'

'Depend on it.'

She was smiling when she hung up the phone and turned to the texts from Stephen and Alicia. The tone of concern in their messages accumulated with each additional attempt they had made to find out how her meeting with Corrie had gone. Stephen answered her call on the second ring.

'Dee? Thank God! Where have you been?'

'Staying with the Sisters at Barrio Moreno. Sorry. My phone battery died. I didn't know that you'd been calling.'

'I thought that's where you might have ended up. How did you go with Corrie? Alicia and I didn't know whether no news was good news or . . .' He trailed off.

Dee gave an abbreviated version of Saturday's encounter, including the explanation of where she'd been the night Ross had died. She figured a priest who had been ostracised for having an affair with another man would probably have a fairly keen insight into the misery of her position.

'Oh dear,' he said. And then again, 'Oh dear.'

'Look, I can't pretend I wasn't devastated at the time, but I've had a few days to sort things through. I still feel pretty upset, but the main thing is Corrie's OK. That's all that matters.'

'Of course. Of course that's so. But – no, you're right. I'm sorry. I don't know what to say. I'm so pleased that you got to see her and she's fit and well, but it's tough that it didn't work out the way you'd hoped.'

'I know. And now I have to go home and face Luke and Ben.'

'Oh dear.'

'Yes.' She laughed shortly. 'Oh dear.'

'When are you planning to head home?'

'I managed to get a flight out on Sunday night.'

'So soon?! You don't think that's a little precipitous?'

'I need to go home. Waiting around will just drive me crazy. Someone from her theatre group has agreed to deliver a letter for me. I'm not holding out great hopes. I think Corrie's going to need a lot of time to come to terms with things. And she may never forgive me. But if she does, she knows where I am. It's up to her now. I've done everything that I can.'

'Hard decision, but it makes sense. You've obviously been doing a bit of thinking with the Sisters.'

'Yes. Yes, I have.'

'But we must see you before you go. Come to ten-o'clock Mass at San Cayetano on Sunday. Alicia will be there. What time's your flight?'

'Midnight. I can make ten-o'clock Mass.'

*

The traffic was light on the *autopista* on Sunday morning and Dee was early for Mass in Alicia's brother's parish, but there was already a large group of people at the front of the church rehearsing the day's hymns: belting out Latin rhythms on old acoustic guitars and bellowing in unison in low throaty keys. It was a contrast to the folk music Dee recalled in Australian Catholic churches in the 1970s, to the slowly strummed ballads in soprano registers and waltz time that reflected mournfully on gentle Jesus' long-suffering love for wayward humanity. The Latin dance rhythms seemed to evoke a deity of a more vigorous kind.

She picked up a photocopied sheet of hymn lyrics from a table at the back of the church and took a seat in one of the rear pews. 'Jesus Christ our brother', went the rousing chorus of the current hymn under rehearsal, 'you know the pain and the injustice suffered by the working people. Give us your strength in the struggle for work and for bread.' If it sounded more like a socialist manifesto than a hymn, perhaps it was because the words focused on people's agency rather than their neediness, Dee mused. There was dignity in the plea for strength and the acknowledgement of common endeavour, and it reminded Dee of the women at Barrio Moreno.

Putting the sheet to one side she watched the various preparations for Mass. Individuals and family groups began to settle in the pews, some kneeling with their rosaries, others joining in the singing practice. A woman trailing several squirming children paused to light a candle before a statue of the *Virgen de Luján* in a side alcove.

Dee remembered that she, too, used to go through the motions of kneeling and praying when she first entered a church – a habit left over from childhood. She would drop her head onto clasped hands, close her eyes in an effort of concentration, will herself to feel unearthly presences, to hear celestial voices. The expectation was very childish, really, and no doubt had its origin in the stories old Sister Brendan used to read from the *Lives of the Child Saints* when Dee was in primary school. The holiness of the protagonists was always confirmed by sacred visions and voices and Dee desperately wanted a share of their mystical experiences.

Looking around at the dark heads bowed in prayer, at the woman crossing herself before the rack of votive candles, Dee found herself, once again, envying the faith of others. Did they all experience some sort of ecstatic communion with the divine when the only thing she had been gifted with was eternal silence? A silence into which she had interpolated other voices. She play-acted God's voice in the censorious tones of her father, in the moral platitudes delivered by the priests from the pulpit, in the snide and clever backhanders she delivered to herself. But beyond the play-acting, beyond the voices from her past, voices that she had turned into strange, hard idols, there was only ever that blank wall of absolute silence.

Dee looked up and saw that Stephen had entered the church and was dressing the altar for Mass, laying out cloths and lighting candles, collecting items from the sacristy. He had not seen her. A priest dressed in full liturgical robes, who she guessed was Alicia's brother, Javier, was sharing a joke with the music group. He was an energetic, clean-shaven man, full of ready laughter. After borrowing one of the guitars and demonstrating a particular rhythm that he preferred for the song they had just finished playing, he moved over to the front pews and greeted a young family.

The church was not full when the service began. People were still drifting in and out, or hovering on the porch. There was a great wash of chatter and sociability, very different from the self-consciously reverent silence of Australian churches.

The conversations were muted but not entirely quelled as the music swelled from rehearsal into performance mode and the congregation hauled themselves to their feet to welcome the procession of priests and lay ministers down the central aisle. Stephen spotted Dee as he passed her pew. His face lit up with recognition and he waved. Her own face broke into a spontaneous grin and she waved back.

When it was time to deliver the readings, Alicia came from the front of the church to stand behind the lectern. She was an educated, professional woman like herself, Dee reflected, and yet Alicia's commitment to her faith had never wavered. Dee wondered what Alicia could see that she herself couldn't and whether or not part of Dee's essential problem was that she kept looking in all the wrong places.

After the second reading, Javier took his place at the lectern to proclaim the gospel of the day. It took Dee a few minutes to work out that it was the Parable of the Talents. It was not one of her favourite gospel stories, involving as it did an image of God as a vengeful overlord, rewarding the servants who had multiplied his wealth and punishing the timid, cautious one who had failed to do so. She strained to understand the interpretation of the story presented in Javier's homily, but was stymied once again by the language barrier.

While the offertory hymn was being sung a group of red-scrubbed children, solemn and big-eyed, trod cautiously down the aisle, bearing the wine and altar breads for consecration. Dee knew that the children's carefully combed hair and clean, pressed clothes were testament to hours of preparation by their mothers, who achieved these miraculous standards of cleanliness in makeshift houses with dirt floors and no running water. She wondered, not for the first time, how they found the will to persist. Javier bent down and spoke to each child as he took the gifts gently from their small hands and passed them to Stephen. Dee could see each child lighting up under his attentions.

At the end of the consecration the congregation were invited to exchange a sign of peace. '*Que la paz sea contigo*' the first hesitant murmurings swelled into a crescendo of animated greetings. Alicia walked down the aisle to find her friend. When she spotted Dee she held her gaze and then embraced her. '*Que la paz sea contigo,*' she said. Dee offered the reply in her own language: 'Peace be with you.'

When it came time to receive Holy Communion Dee hesitated over joining the queue to the altar, held back by her own ambivalence, but drawn by a desire to honour the beliefs of the community. As the line moved slowly forward – bent old women, the young mothers of the barrios dressed in their colourful castoffs and the local *borracho* trembling a little from his daily alcohol withdrawal – she was reminded of the shuffling progress of the Mothers of the Plaza de Mayo, of their dogged belief that love was more powerful than violence, of their determination to lay down their lives before they laid down their love or loyalty to their children. It was never glorious though, Dee thought, this triumph of love over all the glamorous and compelling things ranged against it; it always seemed to emerge a little shabby and a little broken and perhaps even a little foolish. It didn't ring out with the moral clarity and heroic presence one might expect. It just limped around a public square in an old overcoat and refused to go away.

As Dee approached the front of the line for Communion, she raised her crossed palms to receive the Host from Stephen. When he placed it in her outstretched hand he gripped her fingers briefly, willing her to understand the depth of his concern for her. When she returned to her place, Dee knelt alongside the other worshippers, bowed her head and, instead of trying to will herself to feel God's presence, simply gave herself over to gratitude.

Just before the final blessing, Javier invited the congregation to give voice to any special intentions they had. The prayers spilled out: for sick children and dying mothers, for those whose anniversaries were imminent. 'For Corrie,' Dee whispered under her breath, 'keep her safe.'

When Mass was finished, Dee waited for Alicia and Stephen out in the yard. She watched as trestle tables were set up and small cartons of juice and packaged *alfajores* were distributed to the children. Some boys kicked a soccer ball around in the dust while a few of the musicians sat down on old crates with their guitars and started to play Beatles' songs.

'Dee!' Alicia called out to her. She was assisting a young woman in a battered wheelchair down the church steps. Dee hastened to help her. Alicia introduced the woman as Dolores. When they had manoeuvred the wheelchair onto stable ground, Dolores wheeled herself into the shade of a bottlebrush tree and offered to prepare them *mate* with the thermos, gourd and *yerba* she carried in a wicker basket on her lap. Alicia studied Dee's face.

'¿Estás bien, Dee?'

'Yes, I'm OK. I'm fine.'

Dee caught sight of Stephen as he descended the church steps and headed towards her. Halfway across the yard he was hailed by a couple of teenage boys, one of whom struck a rock-star pose and began playing air-guitar. Stephen laughed as he turned back towards Dee.

'I think I've found the guitarist for our new rock group,' he said as he joined them. 'Remember Alejandro – the boy who got thrown out of home? That was him. The rock group won't solve all his problems, but it will give his week some structure and give us a way of keeping an eye on him. I'm so glad you could make it today, Dee. All packed and ready to go?'

'Sort of. You're heading off soon yourself, aren't you?'

'In a couple of weeks.'

Dee nodded in the direction of Alejandro's retreating figure. 'It must be very hard leaving all this behind.'

Stephen looked surprised. 'Oh, I'll be back. Regardless of how the dilemma about my own status plays out, I'll be back. That's a non-negotiable for me. This is where I belong.'

Dee smiled. 'I can see that.'

'How did you find Mass today? Not too much of an ordeal?'

'No, I liked it. But tell me, how did Javier make sense of that gospel?'

'The Parable of the Talents? That's a good one, isn't it?'

'I've never liked it. I don't understand why the careful servant who tries to protect his master's wealth gets it in the neck in the end.'

Stephen laughed. 'I think there's a bit of enlightenment in Luke's version of the same story. In that version, when the king is condemning the cautious servant, the servant engages in the usual grovelling: "I was afraid of you because you are a hard man etc. etc.," but the king replies, "I will judge you by your own words." Don't you think that's an interesting line? So much depends, doesn't it, on our imagination about who God is? That expectation of punishment and ill will can become something of a self-fulfilling prophecy.'

Dee pulled a wry face. 'Is it the poor servant's fault that he believes in that kind of a God?'

'No,' Stephen smiled, 'but he might enjoy life a little more if he could let go of that idea.'

'You think?'

'Well, it's an experiment I'm working on.'

Dee soaked up the sight of him, his slight figure and flyaway hair, the pale eyes behind round spectacles, the tentative smile that always hovered above his lips.

'Stephen. Whatever they decide – whatever *you* decide – I just want you to know that I think you're a wonderful priest. If God's anything like you, he might actually be worth believing in.'

He blushed in surprise. Before he could formulate an answer, Dee hugged him. 'Don't let those bastards in London convince you otherwise.'

She turned quickly to Alicia. 'Alicia, I don't know when I'll see you again.'

Alicia took hold of Dee's hands. '*Hemos pasado tantas cosas juntas.*' She looked to Stephen to translate.

He jumped in swiftly. 'We have been through many things together.'

Alicia continued, sentence by sentence, pausing for his translations. 'You have finally found your daughter . . . And for this reason, I'm very happy . . . I know that there is still much sadness in your heart . . . But I believe your daughter will return to you . . . I believe this very strongly . . . And I hope that you will also have the courage to believe.'

Alicia squeezed Dee's hands and searched her face for signs of acquiescence. Dee tried to arrange her features into the convinced expression she knew Alicia was looking for. She nodded earnestly.

'*Sí. Lo creo . . . Prometo.*' Yes. I believe. I promise.

Alicia let go of Dee's hands and hugged her close. '*Chau, amiga. Y suerte.*' Goodbye, friend, and good luck.

*

Dee sat in the lobby of the Hotel Gran Vía with her suitcase and the packaged photograph that she had bought from Julio. She waited until the public computer was free and then logged on to her email account.

There was a short message from her principal hoping that she was having a good break and flagging a few items of general interest for her information and reassurance. The Year 12s had finished with minimal mayhem and the senior teachers were confident that they were on track for good results. The graduation dinner and end-of-year Mass had been successes. A couple of the younger teachers were pregnant so that flagged the need to advertise some maternity-leave positions in the new year. An old retainer from the sixties had died. The school had won a significant amount of funding under the new Building the Education Revolution programme. Dee felt that strange head squeeze that occurred when she was being dragged out of one world of intense engagement into another. She had barely thought about her professional life during the last month, but she knew that once she returned it would start to consume a significant slab of her energy and attention again. The drama she was living now, what she had been through in Buenos Aires, would be pushed to one side. She would be called upon to direct her attention to the requirements of her colleagues, students and their families. And she would rise to the challenge. She always did.

It was a kind of salvation, being called out of introspective involvement with one's own concerns, but also a kind of hell. Ever since the children were small, when Dee had first faced the challenge of balancing family and professional life, she had felt torn and fragmented. She was accustomed to it now, but it had been more difficult when the children were little. Because small children cannot be forced into someone else's timetable. They cannot be loved at speed and they cannot be loved in compartments. But that was what the modern world seemed to demand.

Dee had a vivid memory of a time when Corrie had fallen ill at childcare and Dee had been summoned by the staff to collect her urgently. She had set reliefs for her classes, dashed to the centre, scooped up her limp and feverish daughter and taken her home. After dosing her with paracetamol and slipping her into a tepid bath, she had sat with her on the couch, stroking her hair and watching her eyelids droop until her lashes finally fluttered to rest on her plump, little cheeks. She remembered sifting her daughter's silken hair, tracing the curvature of bone that fitted so neatly beneath the palm of her hand, the suspension of time in that slow repeated caress, the absolute *rightness* of being totally present and focused on the needs of her sick child.

But it wasn't long before the worry about what she was going to do the following day caught up with her. Dee had been obliged to hoard her sick leave like a miser. It had to cover both herself and her daughter for the entire year in the face of all the weird and wonderful infections incubating at the childcare centre. She rarely took sick leave herself and weighed her daughter's illnesses with sharp-eyed calculation. Were the symptoms urgent enough to use up one of her precious paid days? It had been a relief to leave such calculations behind when Ross had become the full-time carer after the twins were born, but she had also grieved the loss of being the one who could be there for her children in those vulnerable moments of physical need, the moments that forged the strongest bonds of connection, the strongest memories of being deeply cared for. But there was no point rehashing the past. She had done what she had to do. She had fretted over those losses for too many years. At this point in history she was more inclined to be thankful for the fact that she had a job that distracted her from domestic woes, gave her an opportunity to succeed on a different front and provided the money she needed to support herself and to help her children make their own way in the world.

Dee continued to scroll down through the email spam, the forwarded jokes and sentimental PowerPoint slideshows from various friends, finding, towards the end of the list, a short personal note from Liz.

> *Hope no news is good news. How's the quest for my Latino toyboy going? Ploughing through week six of term here. Three weeks to go but who's counting? When are you back? I'm missing my drinking buddy. Reckon you can smuggle some more of those chocolate biscuit things through Customs for me? ;-)*

Dee made a mental note to pick up some duty-free *alfajores* at the airport but knew she only had a fifty-fifty chance of getting them into the country. For reasons Dee had never been able to ascertain, despite the milk content of the biscuits having been boiled for hours to turn it into caramel, these signature Argentinean sweet treats were regularly seized and binned by zealous Customs officers in Sydney. She suspected that they might be finding their way to the Customs tearoom.

She sent Liz a quick reply promising to do her best with the *alfajores* and to catch up with her the following week. She then checked her 'Sent' box to make sure the email had gone through. It had. It was sitting just beneath the email she had sent Julio Ruiz two weeks before. She opened the old email and read it again. It was strange to contemplate how much had happened since she'd written that note. She thought back to the second visit, the dinner they had enjoyed together, her abrupt and embarrassing departure. She'd enjoyed his company. She'd forgotten how much she enjoyed male company. There hadn't been much since Ross had died. She opened a new message and began typing.

Dear Julio,
I just wanted to thank you for a very nice dinner the other night, for all your hospitality in recent times and your kind assistance in helping me locate my daughter.

I have made contact with Corrie, and while it was good to see her, she was not as pleased to see me as I might have hoped. Like you and your father, I suspect it will take some time to rebuild our relationship. We may never find a way to share in each other's lives comfortably, but I continue to hope and I thank you for your part in restoring that hope.

Thank you also for the photograph, which I love and which will always remind me of you. If you are ever in Australia (!) don't hesitate to get in touch and I hope you don't mind if I call on you the next time I am in Buenos Aires, whenever that may be.
Best regards,
Dee Sutherland

Dee sent the email and sat at the computer for a few minutes wondering if there were any more loose ends to be tied up before she left the city. The problem of what to do about Richard Blaine, the Australian ambassador, had been on her mind, but no ready solutions had presented themselves so she had kept pushing the dilemma to one side. Dee didn't want to be hauled through another round of official inquiries and Catalina had told her that Corrie was downright terrified of the prospect. But Dee was conscious of the level of personal interest that Richard had taken in her case and it seemed wrong to leave him hanging in ignorance of the outcome. It wouldn't make a lot of practical difference to him, but Dee knew he would be glad to know Corrie had been found. In the end, she settled on a compromise. She logged off from her email account, collected some stationery from the reception desk and composed a careful letter.

Dear Richard,

I am writing to let you know that, through inquiries with various church-based charitable organisations here in BA, I was able, at last, to locate my daughter, Corrie. She is alive and well and as you can imagine I am much relieved to find her so. You said that you had closed off her file so I trust that I have not inconvenienced anyone by pursuing these inquiries on my own. It is a long story and I do feel that I owe you a more thorough explanation, but I do not have all the details to hand myself at this stage. Suffice to say there are major family issues involved and the situation is a little delicate. I hope it does not compromise you in any way to ask you to respect our privacy at this time while we sort through a few things.

I did, however, want to let you know, as you have been so personally supportive and I wanted to thank you again for everything you have done for me over the last four years. One day I would be glad to touch base and fill you in, in more detail, about what has transpired here over the last month.

Thanks, once again,

Dee Sutherland

Dee put the letter in an envelope, addressed it care of the Australian Embassy and left it at reception to be posted. By the time Richard received it, she would be back in Australia and, if required to do so, she would field the authorities on her own home ground. She then asked the concierge to call her a taxi to take her to the airport.

On the way out of the city, the driver took the route along Avenida del Libertador, heading for the *autopista*. He drove past the Cementario de Recoleta, the Museo de Bellas Artes and the Floralis Genérica – its giant aluminium petals open to the cloudless blue sky. Dee wound down her window, suddenly irritated by the panel of smudged glass that separated her from her last views of the city.

'You want the air conditioner?'

'No, thank you. Can we drive by the river?'

'Sure.'

The driver turned onto Avenida Rafael Obligado to give her one last view of the Río de la Plata. They picked up speed on the *autopista*, flashing past cheap hotels famous for quick afternoon trysts and the plethora of high-rise housing projects in various stages of completion. And so, finally, to Ezeiza airport. The cabbie hauled her case from the boot, pocketed the fare, pausing only briefly for her to wave away the change before climbing back into his car and pulling out quickly into the congested mass of traffic in front of the main terminal.

The check-in queues were slow moving. Dee became aware of Australian and New Zealand accents behind her. A large contingent of teenage girls, dressed in matching guernseys and armed with hockey sticks, leant on their cases, complaining of exhaustion. Their bleary-eyed teachers stared into the middle distance, no longer registering their charges' grumbling. Dee felt her teacherly instincts kick in but was glad to remind herself that the students were someone else's responsibility.

When she had finally deposited her baggage, received her seat allocation and paid her departure tax, she checked her watch. She still had an hour or so to kill. Now that the time had finally come to leave she found herself reluctant to step through Passport Control to the departure gate. Perhaps it was the prospect of the sixteen-hour flight ahead of her, or perhaps it was something else – some final glimmer of fading hope that she dared not even name. She turned away, resolving to defer the moment of departure for as long as possible.

The airport bookshop had a whole cabinet of English titles. She bought a copy of Borges' *Labyrinths*, took it to the café next door and ordered a coffee. She opened the book and began reading 'Emma Zunz', the story that had first caught her eye when flicking through it in the bookshop. She was so absorbed that she did not notice the passing of time. When she eventually glanced down at her watch, she realised that she had better start moving. Again, a strange reluctance stirred. She gathered her things together and made her way towards the double doors that led to the departure lounges. There was no turning back beyond that point. No turning back.

She began to realise that she was entertaining a strange little fantasy. Perhaps Sergio had delivered her letter and Corrie had contacted Alicia and Marco to find out when Dee was leaving. Perhaps she would materialise out of the crowd, call out urgently to halt Dee's departure, throw herself into her mother's arms. Dee scanned the clusters of people making their farewells. But this was not the movies. Corrie was not lurking in the wings. Life was not so neat. There were no prizes for Dee's attitude of disciplined restraint, or for the purity of her desire for Corrie's wellbeing.

There were no prizes for wanting or even for *not* wanting strenuously enough. All that was left to her was to make an act of faith in her own yearning, an act of faith in the love that she had for Corrie. However blind and blundering and poorly expressed it had been over the years, she needed to believe that it had not been futile or wasted. Is this the kind of prayer that counts for something, she wondered? It didn't matter. It issued more from her body than from her will and it was not one from which she could refrain.

She scanned the terminal one last time, slung her bag over her shoulder, checked for her boarding pass and pushed through the heavy doors.

After stopping briefly to buy a box of *alfajores* for Liz in one of the duty-free stores, Dee trudged down a series of long corridors looking for Gate 51. It was the last departure lounge in the vast terminal. She took a seat and became aware of an increase in the number of Australian accents. Her fellow countrymen expanded into the public space as they unconsciously noted their numerical ascendency. Conversations became louder, jokes about their experiences with the locals a little cheekier. When the flight was finally called – an hour later than scheduled – everyone stood up hastily to queue at the gate, only to be confronted with another arduous search of hand luggage. A small mutiny erupted amongst a group of men in T-shirts and board shorts who started singing, 'Why are we waiting?' in boozy voices but with grins friendly enough to deflect official censure.

It was close to two am by the time Dee finally flopped into her seat on the plane. Juggling the plastic-wrapped blanket, headphones, pillow, her jacket, passport, boarding pass and handbag, she squirmed about in her seat like a dog in a basket trying to get comfortable.

Finally settled, she retrieved her passport from the seat pocket in front of her in order to transfer it to the safety of her handbag and took out her mobile phone to switch it off. That's when she saw the message from Ben. She opened it. It was in screaming capitals.

MUM YOU HAVE TO RING ME CORRIE JUST LEFT A MESSAGE ON MY FACEBOOK PAGE!!!

Dee stared at the screen. Tears blurred her vision. Her hands shook and her thumbs kept hitting the wrong keys as she typed her reply.

On my way home now. Talk very soon. So much love, Mum

Acknowledgements

I am indebted to James Alison for the interpretation of Luke 19 presented in his text, *On Being Liked*, London, Darton, Longman and Todd, 2003, and to René Girard for highlighting the original signification of Satan as 'The Accuser', which I first encountered in *The Girard Reader*, edited by James G. Williams and published by Herder & Herder, New York, 2004.

I would like to express my heartfelt thanks to all those friends and relatives who have patiently borne with me as I laboured over this novel. I cannot name you all but I know that you will recognise in these pages fragments of conversation, ideas and experience, which, while re-crafted towards fictional ends, owe much to our shared explorations and endeavours.

Particular acknowledgement is owed to: Nicholas Jose, Anne Bartlett and Susan Hosking of the University of Adelaide for generous mentorship and ongoing encouragement; Sister Judith Redden, who invited me to accompany the St Aloysius College Mission group on three trips to Argentina and allowed

Acknowledgements

me extended leave to complete the manuscript; Craig Evans for introducing me to the wonderful city and people of Buenos Aires; and to María Bayá Casal, Pedro Bayá, Marita Corrazín, Josefina Gourdy, Sister Cristina Mira and Sister Marta Barry – their friendship, music, poetry and commitment to the poor have nourished my passion for their country and nourished my spirit. I would also like to thank Peter and Muriel Hussin for their gracious hospitality at the Australian Embassy in Buenos Aires and Robyn Clark and Paul Quigley who gave specialist advice in a number of areas.

Patricia Sykes, founder of Imprints Booksellers in Adelaide, gave positive feedback and constructive advice on early drafts. She sadly passed away in October 2010 but I know she would have been excited to see this project come to fruition. Her great kindness and the support she gave my family over many years is not forgotten.

Alex Nahlous of Pan Macmillan was an enthusiastic advocate for the manuscript and I thank her for her belief in the story. I received invaluable editing assistance from Ali Lavau and steady guidance through the publishing process from Emma Rafferty. Ana Ruben was a patient and engaging Spanish language advisor. I will be forever grateful to my parents, Mick and Maritta Hawkins, who nurtured a love of literature from my earliest days. Matthew Hawkins shared practical tips on narrative structure, most of which I ignored, and then had to rediscover the hard way several years later. Stewart Hawkins, and his partner, Ingrid Piper, managed to make a silk purse out of a sow's ear through their kind attention to publicity shots of the author.

Words fail me when I try to find a way to adequately thank my dear friend, Mary Price. She waded through numerous drafts and found endlessly creative ways to rebuild my shattered

Acknowledgements

confidence while sensitively alerting me to errors and lapses of good taste. This book would not exist without her dedicated personal support and intelligent literary critique.

My husband, Charli Holoubek, encouraged me from the beginning. Along with my children, Martin, Eloise and Damian, he endured my storms of exhilaration and despair with patience and good humour and allowed me the space to pursue my dream. These four, all gifted artists in their own right, have never stopped believing in me, and that has been the greatest inspiration of all.

Photograph by Stewart Hawkins